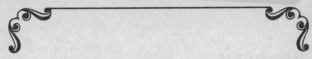

"Sweet Sibyl," he whispered. "I wonder what I'll do without you."

His fingers curved around the nape of her neck. Slowly, gently, he pulled her face toward his until their lips met. For a fleeting instant, there was an insistence in his touch, a barely suppressed power that thrilled and terrified her at the same time. Then he let go, his hand sliding from her neck to drop against the mattress. Sibyl stayed where she was, her lips pressed tenderly to his for several heartbeats before she realized he was asleep.

Shaky, her pulse hammering in her ears, she pulled back. She dragged the counterpane over him with trembling hands, then made her wobbly way out of the room. "Oh, my love," she sighed as she pulled the door shut behind her. "I don't know what you will do without me, either. . . ."

By Emma Jensen
Published by The Ballantine Publishing Group:

Books published by The Ballantine Publishing Group
are available at quantity discounts on bulk purchases
for premium, educational, fund-raising, and special
sales use. For details, please call 1-800-733-3000.

BEST LAID SCHEMES

Emma Jensen

FAWCETT CREST • NEW YORK

A Fawcett Crest Book
Published by The Ballantine Publishing Group
Copyright © 1998 by Emma Jensen

http://www.randomhouse.com

Library of Congress Catalog Card Number: 98-93036

ISBN 0-449-00234-9

Manufactured in the United States of America

First Edition: September 1998

10 9 8 7 6 5 4 3 2

For my father—the real Julius and a true gentleman

The best-laid schemes o' mice an' men
                    Gang aft a-gley,
An' lea'e us nought but grief an' pain,
                    For promis'd joy!
            —ROBERT BURNS, *To a Mouse*

The best laid schemes have a damnable way of
coming down to crash on a man's head when all
he expects is merely a logical, pleasant outcome.
                —TARQUIN, Sixth Earl of Hythe, to
                    anyone who would listen

1

THE EARL OF Hythe, who took a great deal of pride in the fact that he had never succumbed to the awkward and messy inconvenience of falling in love, was on the verge of salivating. Before him was a man's sweetest dream on creamy sheets, a treasure all but clamoring to become his.

He reverently reached out one perfectly manicured hand and stroked along the elegant spine. "Beautiful," he murmured. "Utterly exquisite."

Only heaven could have dictated such smooth, milk-pale expanses, such bold curves and delicate lines. And the colors, from the faintest blush of pink to glossy ebony, were of such perfection that any man's eye would be caught, his fingers itching to touch.

Damn his rule about impulse. This was something he could not possibly resist having.

"You are pleased with what you see, my lord?"

The earl smiled faintly at the eager catch in his companion's voice. "Perfectly." Satisfied, he drew a deep breath and stepped back. "We are agreed on the price?"

The book dealer mopped his shiny brow with a wilted handkerchief and gave his own shaky sigh. "Certainly, my lord. Thank you. I was most concerned the manuscript would not be up to your standards and I know you prefer to deliberate. When this came into my hands, however, I knew I must bring it to you immediately."

"Well done, Wilkins. I have long wished to add the Montefiore to my collection."

1

The dealer was correct in his concerns. The earl made spontaneous purchases only on very rare occasions, and very few books were up to his standards. Tarquin Theodor Fitzmorris Rome, the Sixth Earl of Hythe and possessor of enough lesser titles to fill their own printed peerage, demanded the best, the first, the unique in all he collected.

Books were his great passion. A Gutenberg Bible rested under glass in his Wiltshire estate's library, an Alciato's *Book of Emblems* from 1531 was the centerpiece of his library in Town, and he had only the week before obtained a priceless, handwritten copy of *The Canterbury Tales*, dated 1396.

Now he had the Montefiore.

Resisting the urge to trace the smooth pages and brilliant illuminations one more time, he turned away from the desk and gave the dealer a terse nod. "You said the owner was most eager to make the sale."

"Most eager, Lord Hythe. There are, I believe, several more medieval manuscripts available. I am certain any inquiries would be met with similar accord. The seller is not, should we say, in a position to haggle."

So, Sir Perceval Fraser was dead. Tarquin had suspected as much the moment Wilkins had unwrapped the Montefiore. The old coot would never have allowed the manuscript to leave his tight grip otherwise. And there was no question that this piece had come from Sir Perceval's collection. Of the four known to exist, the other three resided in the hallowed halls of Oxford, the university at Vienna, and the Vatican. The first two were carefully tended and studied by the great Classical scholars of Europe. The third was, to the best of anyone's knowledge, hidden away in disgrace, too valuable to destroy and too scandalous to display.

Wilkins had recognized a superior, extremely valuable manuscript but could not possibly have known just what he had found. Well versed as the man was, the Montefiore was an obscure book, known only to the most dedicated of scholars and bibliophiles. Fraser had certainly been aware of the book's value, which made Tarquin believe he had died suddenly, leaving no instructions for the disposition of his library. Had he done so, the manuscript would never have come so easily.

Such arrogance would have been just like Sir Perceval. No doubt he hadn't expected to die at all. Having defied everything and everyone in life, he would have expected to defy Death as well. And how very vexing it must have been for the crusty old coot to realize he couldn't take his collection with him.

Tarquin was surprised to feel a tug of sadness. He had never liked Fraser and the feeling had been returned wholeheartedly. There had been too many skirmishes over the past decade, sly battles over books, for anything but acrimony. But there had also been an equally potent mutual respect, albeit grudging, that only the most ardent of collectors could possibly understand.

The world of the bibliophile would be something less than what it had once been now that Sir Perceval was no longer in it.

Shaking off the uncustomarily sentimental turn of his mind, Tarquin considered how best to proceed. "I would be very interested," he said after a moment, "in hearing what else is being offered."

"I would be more than happy to make the inquiries, my lord."

Of course you would, Tarquin thought grimly. There was a tidy commission involved, not to mention his own patronage. "Proceed, then. I would request, however, that you do so on behalf of an anonymous collector. I would prefer not to have my name bandied about."

"I quite understand, my lord."

The dealer "quite understood" nothing, and Tarquin was not about to illuminate. Ordinarily, he was perfectly content to have his purchases known. This time, however, exposition would have to wait. He had no idea who had inherited Fraser's collection—and the debts that such a collection had clearly incurred. The man had never married and, to Tarquin's knowledge, had no family. Chances were that the entire estate had gone to the man's pack of mangy hounds.

Canine or of the same debatably human makeup as Sir Perceval, the heir might or might not know of the antipathy between the two collectors. If Fraser had mentioned his enemy, the Earl of Hythe, the words would probably have involved something along the lines of a promise to rise from the grave and wreak bloody havoc should even a single one of his books fall into the earl's possession.

One just had. Tarquin wasn't taking any chances on the others. Nor was he taking any chances on Wilkins. Striding around the massive desk, he removed a draft ledger from the top drawer. From the corner of his eye, he could see the dealer's hands opening and closing as he scrawled the amount and his signature. Antiquarian books was, at the moment, a somewhat unpredictable business.

Tarquin tore the draft neatly from the ledger and passed it across the desk. "You will contact me within the fortnight."

It was not a request. The dealer did not take it as one. Huffing in his tight waistcoat and mopping once again at his bald pate, he quickly pocketed the cheque and, mixing thanks and promises, took himself hastily off.

The mantel clock chimed just as Tarquin was opening the book. Sighing, he gently closed the embossed leather cover and, with his customary, proud glance around the mahogany-paneled, book-filled, and fastidiously dust-free library, headed toward the door. The Montefiore was not going anywhere, ever, and it was teatime. The earl's mother would be waiting in the salon and the earl was not a man to keep a lady waiting. Punctuality, he decreed, was every bit as necessary as neatness, honor, and a pressed newspaper at the breakfast table.

He glanced back once at the manuscript and smiled with satisfaction. There was nothing in life quite so satisfying as having made such a splendid purchase—and at such a reasonable expense. The earl was a very contented man. Perhaps he would even indulge in one of his Egyptian cigars after tea.

The Dowager Countess of Hythe was just approaching the salon as her son entered the hall. Tarquin had always thought—with an appallingly fanciful turn of mind, he admitted—that his mother resembled the fairies of his schoolroom books: diminutive, fair, and not quite of this earth. Age had added some lines to the lovely face, but even they were as delicate as spiderwebs. As far as Tarquin could tell, time had done little to change her otherwise. She still looked as lovely and fragile as a woodland sprite. The appearance, however, was deceptive. Lady Hythe possessed the fortitude of Juno.

At the moment, she was standing stock-still on the glossy parquet floor, eyes wide.

"Is something amiss, Mother?"

"Amiss? I would not know. Dearest, you were *whistling*."

Tarquin blinked in surprise. "Surely not, madam!"

"I am very much afraid so." The laughter now evident in the pale blue eyes made it clear she was not sorry in the least. "I do believe it was one of those regimental ditties Julius is always bringing into the house."

Now Tarquin grimaced. As unthinkable as the possibility of his whistling was, he could hardly suspect his mother of lying. And the very fact that the tune had been one of those his wild brother favored made the situation worse. "I apologize whole-heartedly, madam, for subjecting you to such base stuff. I cannot think where my sense has gone."

"Oh, Tarquin, *really!*" The countess rolled her eyes. "I cannot help but believe our lives would be a bit jollier if you would lose your sense completely every so often."

It was a familiar refrain. As much as the earl loved his mother, he was growing heartily tired of her suggestions that he was somewhat lacking in joie de vivre. Hadn't he just purchased a book so scandalous at the time it was written that all copies but four had been burned?

"To be sure," he commented dryly, "we would all benefit greatly should I take to whistling my way through the day. Let's see. . . . Perhaps I could then set aside matters of estate and take up juggling colored balls. No, even better, I could have a rope strung between the towers and hop along it on one leg. No safety net below, of course."

The countess waved a languid hand at him. "There is no need to be snide, dearest. I am simply of the opinion that one cannot help but be cheerful when there is whistling about."

In Tarquin's opinion, any act that often involved spitting was one to be avoided. "I shall take that under advisement

where their afternoon tea was already waiting, precisely as it always was, on the low Hepplewhite table. "In the meantime, I do play the pianoforte, so you cannot accuse me of being entirely without a musical nature."

He thought he heard her say something about dismal fugues, but let it pass. He couldn't imagine how anyone could find fault with a good somber Bach fugue, but his mother had been forever slipping Mozart concertos into his music case. Even now, there was Mozart on the music stand, Mozart spread atop the grand pianoforte. Tarquin made a mental note to relegate it to the depths of the hollow bench. He would certainly not be using it, and the copious sheets disturbed the neat lines of the instrument.

The countess commenced with what she liked to blithely call their "daily tea ceremony." Tarquin rather liked the term, ironic as she might mean it to be. Ceremony brought images of rule and order to mind. He accepted first the delicate napkin, then a single lemon cake on its tiny Wedgwood plate. The fork followed. His mother had always preferred to use her fingers, but there was a fork for her as well at his decree—just in case she should ever change her mind.

"You seem in good spirits, dearest," she commented as she measured a precise teaspoon of sugar into his cup. It was of the utmost importance that the sugar come before the tea. Otherwise, the earl insisted, it would not dissolve properly. "I take it you collected something expensive today."

Tarquin sipped appreciatively at the tea, brewed to the precise second, and sat back in his chair. "A most excellent addition to my library, madam. A Montefiore."

"How nice." The countess sipped her own tea, closed her eyes for a moment, then added a second dollop of cream, which, apparently, necessitated another spoonful of sugar. "More old pictures, I assume."

"Mother, it is a *Montefiore*, an illuminated manuscript from the fifteenth century!"

"Yes, dear, I quite understand. They usually are. What is this one about?"

"It happens to be a collection of the Greek myths. Quite scandalous at the time."

"Oh?" The countess selected a rather gooey cake and bit in. "Mmm. Marvelous. So sorry, dear," she added when a crumb landed on Tarquin's knee. "Greek myths. How splendid. I expect it was a vastly popular book when it was written."

"It was banned and burned," Tarquin replied dryly. "Monks were not meant to illuminate books about heathen gods."

"So why did they bother, if their work was only to end up fueling someone's evening fire?"

"Knowledge, madam. Someone had to pass on the Classical tales."

The countess polished off the cake before turning guileless blue eyes on her son. "So that is why you spend so much time with these books of yours, is it? To absorb the knowledge."

"I do not often read my antiquities. They are too fragile for much handling."

"Then why have them, dearest?"

"For the same reasons they were written, I suppose: enjoyment of their beauty and to make certain they are available for the next generation . . ."

"For the next generation *not* to read?"

Tarquin drummed his fingers against the arm of his chair. It would not do at all to engage his mother in a conversation about the values of either literature or the collection of it. Her idea of a good debate was winging an endless series of nonsensical questions at him. "My books are rather like everything else in this house. Rather like the house. I possess them during my lifetime, admire their glory, then pass them on for the next earl to possess and enjoy."

"You take that responsibility very seriously, don't you, dearest?"

"Of course I do." It was galling to even consider it otherwise. "I will do everything in my power to keep the line going."

"Everything?"

"To be sure. I could do no less."

The countess brushed several crumbs to the floor, ignoring her son's scowl. Then she neatly folded her napkin and linked her hands in her lap. "I am so very glad to hear

I assume this upcoming event will be the *last* of your shopping parties?"

"Shopping parties, madam?"

"Exhibitions, then. Less vulgar."

Tarquin was appalled. "We are hosting a *house party*, Mother. We have done so several times since the Season ended."

The countess's mouth thinned. "No, Tarquin, we have not. *You* have arranged to conduct several endless affairs that have amounted to no more than exhibitions for you to examine potential brides. And which have amounted to nothing!"

"You cannot expect me to choose a wife without proper deliberation, surely." The very concept was unthinkable.

"I do not, dear." His mother's face softened for a moment. "I want only for you to be happy. But"—the steel returned to her eyes—"the time has come for you either to make your choice or commence with another year of bachelorhood. I will not play hostess any longer to a train of simpering, cooing misses whose attempts to prove themselves the most beautiful, the most accomplished, the most sporting young ladies in the realm run the staff ragged and turn the house quite upside down. It is exhausting, Tarquin, and it is a thumping bore!"

Stunned, he leaned back in his chair. "I had no idea you felt this way."

"Of course you did not. *I* happen to be the most sporting lady in the realm and have tolerated your endless deliberations because it is time for you to wed, and because I love you. You are a big boy now, nearly one-and-thirty, and quite capable of coming to a decision."

Some of the vinegar went out of her then. "Sweetheart, you have managed to reduce the field to three. To that end, we will be having Lady Theresa Wardour, and the Honorable Misses Caroline Reynolds and Elspeth Vaer with their respective mamas, papas, maids, and quite possibly pets. Do you think you will be able to make an offer to one of them within the next fortnight?"

"One of the pets?" Tarquin asked blandly.

"Well, bravo, dearest. You actually made a jest." The countess returned an equally bland smile. "Well?"

Tarquin looked at the clock. A quarter past. Their teatime was over. "I will not be rushed in this decision, Mother. But if it sets your heart at ease, I will promise to make every effort to settle upon one of the young ladies during their visit."

"Thank you ever so much, Tarquin. I may die in peace now."

He shot her a look, but she was one of the few women of his acquaintance who could indulge in biting sarcasm with the expression of an angel. "Try not to expire before next Tuesday, Mother. We have guests coming, and I wouldn't have the slightest idea in which rooms to put them."

"Very *good*, my love. You have now graduated to witty." The countess rose and, when he followed, reached up to pat his cheek. "Do something for me, if you will."

"Certainly."

"Avoid the haircut this week."

Tarquin scowled down at her. His valet had trimmed his hair each Wednesday for the past ten years. "For heaven's sake, why?"

"You are too severe, dearest. You might frighten off your young ladies before you have the chance to choose among them. Besides, you used to have the most charming little curls above your ears when you were—"

"Mother."

"Oh, very well. But you will forsake the shears for a fortnight?"

He sighed. "I will consider it, though since our lovely trio has not been frightened off to date, I think the concept absurd."

"I know you do, dearest." The countess stroked the rigidly controlled black wings above his ears and sighed. "One more thing. I have invited a companion for myself."

"Oh?"

"Lady Leverham."

Tarquin closed his eyes briefly, counted five. "Mother, she is—and I say this with the utmost respect—a menace."

"Nonsense. She is my oldest friend and charming company."

"She prattles."

"She is a lively conversationalist."

"She pries."

His mother smiled. "I do so love a good bit of gossip. I get

Tarquin gave up. It would be wholly uncivil to do otherwise. "For your sake, I will be happy to welcome her."

"You are a good boy, Tarquin, if hopelessly stuffy." The

9

countess breezed toward the door. "By the way," she said over her shoulder, "she will be bringing Galahad."

"The monkey? Oh, Mother." He gritted his teeth, trying not to remember what the blasted creature had left inside his boots on its last visit. "Very well." He would simply remember to keep his chamber door locked.

"And Sibyl."

This time, Tarquin allowed himself the faintest of groans. "Must she?"

"Of course, dearest."

"God give me strength. Sibyl."

The celebratory Egyptian cheroot had suddenly lost its appeal.

2

SIBYL CAMERON PATIENTLY shifted an encroaching tail from in front of her eyes. "Aunt Alfie, do you think Galahad could perhaps spend the remainder of the journey in his cage? He is trying to consume my hat."

A twittering laugh came from the opposite seat. "It is the cherries. The silly darling must be hungry."

The silly darling had been perched atop Sibyl's head for the past hour, chattering ill-temperedly and tugging at the miniature fruit decorating the straw bonnet. If that were not enough, the roads were appalling due to recent, heavy showers and each time the carriage hit a rut, monkey and bonnet rocked with it. There was no telling what was left of the woven straw, and now Sibyl's hair, disarranged by the constant motion, was straggling from beneath it. She had never been an expert on monkeys, but had always assumed they were graceful creatures, well used to maintaining their balance on swaying jungle vines. Galahad possessed all the grace of a cow at sea.

"Perhaps you could feed him *in* his cage," she suggested hopefully. "Wax fruit will likely have the most distressing consequences for his digestion." The carriage lurched again. Monkey and bonnet slid to starboard, and Galahad reached out a back foot to get a steadying grip, on Sibyl's nose. "Aunt Alfie?"

"Oh, very well. Come along, Galahad."

Lady Alfonsine Cameron Leverham held out a piece of very real apple. Her pet leapt to her plump wrist, seized the fruit, and ~~passed to her shoulder, where~~ he proceeded to shred the treat. Some of it was consumed; the rest ended up making damp spots over his white belly and Lady Leverham's ecru bombazine. In Sibyl's opinion her aunt, with her pale face surrounded by still-dark curls and Galahad's tail curving beneath her nose like a fluffy black mustachio, rather resembled her pet.

"Should we not have arrived already, Sibby?"

Sibyl was doing the best she could to set her own appearance to rights. Not that it really mattered. The toplofty Earl of Hythe was hardly likely to notice that she was no longer a pinafored scattermuffin. "Soon, I trust, Aunt Alfie. The keeper at the last posting house said we were but five miles from Rome Castle."

"Nasty place, that inn," Alfonsine sniffed. "I expected better of a place called 'The Bard.' But then, that man Shakespeare was hopelessly stuck in the Renaissance. Men in silk and stockings . . . hmmph. Now, in King Arthur's time, men were men, all armor and jousting for honor. And they revered their ladies fair. Look what Arthur went through for his Guinevere—"

"Arthur chose his friends poorly," Sibyl interrupted the familiar speech wearily. "His wife ran off with one of them."

"Really, Sibyl. Must you be so terribly unromantic?"

"It appears so, Aunt. I know I am a disappointment, but there doesn't seem to be anything I can do about it."

While the ever-romantic Lady Leverham spent a good portion of her life in Camelot, her sadly practical niece could not seem to manage the feat. It was a curse, really, she had long since decided. The Cameron family was well known for its singular ability to live in grand Romantic fashion. A vast fortune helped, certainly, but Romance and Adventure seemed to come with the blood. Until Sibyl.

Alfonsine reached forward to pat her disappointing niece's hand. "Nonsense. We are all ever so fond of you, dearest. Perhaps if you simply worked a bit harder on your sensibilities . . ." She demonstrated with a heartrending sigh and fluttering eyelashes. "Now, you try."

Sibyl knew it was hopeless. She had tried to be a proper Cameron for twenty-odd years. From her toddler days, she had passed countless hours gazing up at the vivid portrait of Great-great-great-grandfather Kirkcormac, with his kilt and warrior's claymore. Later, she had spent even more time reading the epic poems he had written when taking the occasional holiday from reiving and sieging. She could recite each thrilling, blood-soaked Highland line. She could not, however, create a stirring rhyme to save her soul. To everyone's horror, she was discovered to be appallingly good with numbers.

Great-aunt Ophelia had coached her in the fine art of wearing a conical hat and veil—and mixing undetectable poisons. In her hurry to show off the marvelous purple potion she had concocted, ten-year-old Sibyl had tripped over her trailing, moth-eaten veil and spilled the liquid all over the floor. Before anyone could prevent the disaster, Ophelia's rheumatic pug had lapped up every last drop. An hour later, the animal had been cavorting like a puppy across the lawns. The mixture had eventually proven equally effective in easing the fits Great-uncle Machulus had suffered ever since the bloody day at Culloden Field.

And Sibyl's mother, a Cameron only by marriage, had lovingly taught her daughter to ride—bareback with lance in hand. That had gone very well. Until Sibyl, forgetting that a lance must always be held firmly aloft, had caught the dragging tip in a mole hole. She had remembered that a good knight never released her lance, and hence had ended up doing a relatively graceful pole vault twenty feet into a gorse bush. Iolanthe Cameron, her motherly sentiments temporarily surpassing her Romantic, had put an end to the jousting lessons. She had even managed a wan smile when her daughter produced a simple Archimedean diagram of her flight.

Even Sibyl's single laudable talent had been a fraud. Oh, the collective Camerons had rejoiced when she displayed an ability to foretell the future, gleefully labeling her the Oracle. She had never had the heart to explain that her predictions were based on simple logic and science. And she had conveniently "lost" the gift when it became obvious that her dire portents were proving more distressful than impressive to her beloved family.

Sibyl had spent most of her life battling the cruel joke Fate had played on her, ever trying in every way to substitute her dull, pragmatic nature with a dashing, epic one. She had honestly tried . . . until her rational inner voice could no longer be ignored. When, two years before, Uncle Ninian had been launched into the hereafter by an experimental catapult, she had questioned the safety of Adventure. A year later, when her beloved parents had gone down in the Firth of Clyde while reenacting Jason's storm-tossed travails in the Argonaut, Sibyl had abandoned Romance entirely. It no longer had seemed worth the effort—and she could not help but feel the tragedies were her fault.

It would have been a simple matter, after all, to inform Uncle Ninnie that the level of tension he had chosen was likely to catapult him right over the pile of straw he had laid out for his landing. And it had seemed perfectly logical that sailing a home-crafted Hellenic ship during a storm was not a wise choice. Sibyl had held her tongue both times, knowing her words would not only not be heeded but would also be one more disappointment to the devil-may-care people who loved her.

With the same good if ineffectual intentions, she chose to humor her aunt now and mimic the stirring sensibilities. "How is this, Aunt Alfie?" She raised a languid hand to her bosom, fluttered her eyelids, and managed a half-hearted sigh.

Even to her own ears, it sounded more like the weary groan of a beleaguered schoolmistress than the wistful whimper of a damsel in distress.

Alfonsine's responding sigh was, of course, perfect. "We shall work on it, dearest."

Galahad, perched now on the back of Alfonsine's seat, threw the last crumb of apple at Sibyl. It hit her chin and promptly slid into her bodice. The monkey gave a triumphant squawk and, rising onto his hind legs, clasped his hands above his head.

Even the Cameron pets possessed more Grand Spirit than Sibyl. She tried not to feel smug when the next lurch had Galahad tumbling headfirst into Alfonsine's lap.

"No matter, love. You will have ample time to hone your skills at Rome Castle." It was unclear which of her companions the lady was addressing, until she added, "The earl always did have an appropriate passion for times of old. You shall be able to practice quite nicely on him."

The earl, Sibyl silently corrected, had most often had his nose in moldering old books, and had never appeared passionate about anything save having those books lined up in perfect alphabetical order. Of course, she had not seen him in nearly three years, but she doubted he had changed during that time. He had always been rigid as a Knight Templar, even at sixteen, when they had first met.

Sibyl, nine at the time and still under the misconception that she would someday possess the Cameron Dash, had nonetheless fallen very passionately and appropriately in love. After all, what damsel could resist such a figure as Tarquin Rome? Even as a youth he had been uncommonly tall, with a face straight from the illustrations of the *Morte d'Arthur*: steel-gray eyes, lofty brow, and chiseled jaw, all beneath raven-black hair. On those occasions when he participated in outdoor activities, Tarquin was a bruising rider, never got less than a bull's-eye when shooting with a bow and arrow, and stalked the ancient paths of Cameron House's grounds with all the majesty of a feudal lord.

Even better, he had appreciated logic and science. Sibyl had learned that marvelous fact on hearing him fervently entreat his mother to shorten her visit by a sennight. When the countess demurred, Tarquin had informed her that, by his careful calculations, departing the very next day would add a notable amount of years to his life.

Oh, that first visit had quite conquered Sibyl's determinedly sentimental heart. Unfortunately, the young earl had not been equally struck. In fact, he had scarcely spoken to her at all. Matters had not improved much over the following years, despite Sibyl's every attempt to prove herself worthy of his lordly notice.

"I believe I see the Castle's towers, Aunt." Sibyl was somewhat less than overwhelmed with joy at seeing the grand edifice again. She was not ready to face the Earl of Hythe, despite having thought of him every day during the three years of separation— and for more than ten before that. Thinking of him necessitated recalling any number of disastrous encounters; seeing him would mean reliving them. Humiliations, she decided, were best experienced when one was very much alone.

This time, she vowed as the carriage rounded a last curve

and Rome Castle was revealed in all its crenellated, mullioned splendor, *this time* would be different.

"Oh, splendid!" Alfonsine clapped her heavily bejeweled hands in delight. "Is it not just the picture of Camelot, Sibby? I have always thought it just the picture. What a terrible shame they filled in what was left of the moat. I cannot imagine what Hythe was thinking. A castle is nothing without a moat."

Sibyl winced as she took in the fifty feet of flower beds that, even ten years past, had been the remnants of the Castle's defense. On her second visit with her aunt, it had still been a picturesque pond of sorts, filled with reeds and brightly colored carp.

Fresh from her success with the lance-as-pole, Sibyl had thought to vault the span and storm the ramparts. She had not taken into account the soft mud at the bottom. Her pole, pilfered from an outbuilding, had promptly sunk. Sibyl, striking her head against the hard wood, had tumbled headfirst into the pond, utterly insensible for perhaps the first time in her life. Tarquin had shown his true knightly character, jumping fully dressed into the waist-deep water and hauling her out. He had then settled her across his lap and thumped her back until her lungs were clear.

She had promptly fallen even more deeply in love. He had promptly commenced a quarter hour of calmly, icily berating her for her idiocy, her thoughtlessness, and the destruction of his impeccably polished boots. Then he had summoned his steward and commanded that the moat be filled.

Aunt Alfie had said nothing, but the message in her sad eyes had been more than clear as she gazed into the soon-to-be-lost moat. Sibyl was responsible, yet again, for the Death of Romance.

Shaking off the humiliating memory as the coach turned up the sweeping drive, Sibyl suggested once more that her aunt put Galahad in his cage. "He has not been here in three years, madam, and you know how he reacts to strange places."

"Oh, piffle." Alfonsine was cheerfully fluffing the dark curls visible beneath her hat. "Rome Castle is hardly a new place. Galahad has been here—"

"Once, Aunt, and he made his unease clear on several occasions, including his very first appearance in the grand salon."

"Had the earl not shouted, the dear creature would never have . . . er . . . And it was no more trouble than mopping up spilled tea, really."

Sibyl did not think the earl frequently spilled dank-smelling tea over his shoulder and lapel. "Please, Aunt Alfie, just until we have been shown to our chambers. . . ."

It was too late. The coach rolled to a halt, the footman jumped down to open the door, and Alfonsine, monkey on her shoulder, toddled onto the drive. Sibyl's sigh as she followed was really quite a good effort, but of course there was no one to hear it.

Hythe's formidable butler appeared through the massive, carved wood doors. With his long form, pinched lips, and heavy-lidded stare, Sibyl had always thought he resembled an arrogant lizard. Alfonsine, however, had long since decided he was the very image of King Arthur's father—and addressed him as such.

"Why, Uther Pendragon, you have not changed a whit since I last saw you!"

The butler bowed, then winced imperceptibly when she thumped him affectionately on the shoulder. "Welcome, madam. Her ladyship is—"

"Yes, yes. We know our way." Alfonsine hurried up the stairs. Galahad turned on her shoulder, shook a tiny fist at the butler, and chattered shrilly. "Come along, Sibyl!"

Sibyl paused on the marble steps and made a last, hopeless attempt to tidy her hair and dress. "Good day, Gareth."

"Welcome to Rome Castle, Miss Cameron," the butler replied.

Perhaps it was nothing more than her imagination, but Sibyl could not help thinking it was a particularly unwelcoming welcome.

At that moment, two shrieks—both distinctly simian—came from inside. They were followed by a barrage of canine barks and one feminine, human cry. Gathering her creased skirts, Sibyl rushed through the door. Gareth right behind her.

Her eyes adjusted slowly to the dimmer light of the Castle's Great Hall. Amazing, she thought sadly as she surveyed the

17

scene. In the mere minute it had taken her to follow her aunt, chaos had broken loose. Galahad was tearing about the Hall, leaping from one piece of furniture to the next in terror. Beneath him, baying frantically, was a pair of sturdy beagles.

Alfonsine stood in the center of the Hall, wringing her plump hands. Their hostess, the elegant and diminutive Dowager Countess of Hythe, was in determined pursuit of the dogs. She got a grip on one's flailing tail just as Sibyl reached her. Galahad, having miscalculated his leaping distance, missed a wall sconce and landed on the floor. He screeched and disappeared under a massive side table.

"Ah, Sibyl," Lady Hythe said with one of her lovely smiles. She got a tenuous grip on a canine ear. "How delightful to see you again."

"Thank you, Lady Hythe," Sibyl replied politely. "You are most gracious." Then, in familiar resignation, she ducked beneath the table in search of the monkey.

She almost had him when Lady Hythe's beagle struggled free and bounded toward them. Galahad scurried away from her hands and scampered up the carved wainscoting to the tabletop. From there, he jumped to the back of a massive chair nearby. Both beagles promptly leapt toward the leather seat. From her vantage point, Sibyl watched as the monkey curled into a quivering, furry ball and, with another strident cry, launched himself at a new, taller object.

This time, her sigh was drowned by a bellow from one of the interior doorways.

"What the devil is going on here!"

Sibyl, crouched beneath the table, did not need to look. She knew the voice. With ease born of much practice and a logical mind, she predicted that this beginning to their visit was only the dismal overture to a very long fortnight ahead.

Tarquin had heard the commotion in the Hall, but had chosen to let Gareth deal with it before making his own appearance. Gareth was invaluable at dealing with chaos. It was one of his many irreplaceable talents.

When the butler failed to appear with a report, however, Tarquin had reluctantly left the haven of his study. The sight that greeted him was enough to stop him dead in his tracks. A tiny, plump woman was fluttering around the butler, calling him Uther and twittering about being careful. More astonishing was the sight of the prim retainer standing calmly with a chattering monkey on his head while Master Julius's beagles clambered over his feet, howling with abandon.

"What the devil . . ." Tarquin demanded again as Gareth tried to walk forward through the dogs, becoming engaged for a moment in what looked like a Scottish reel with Lady Leverham before she finally stepped right and he left. *"Quiet!"* Tarquin bellowed at his brother's ill-behaved hounds, and they instantly collapsed into squirming silence at Gareth's feet. "Now—"

"Lady Leverham and Miss Sibyl Cameron have arrived, my lord," the butler intoned.

A full day early. "Of course. Lady Leverham, it is a pleasure, as always," Tarquin managed. Lying was not among his preferred practices. "You have not altered since last we met."

The lady blushed and tittered. "You always were the most outrageous flirt, Hythe! Lizzie, how did you ever manage to raise such a plush-tongued fellow?"

Tarquin looked wearily first to his mother, who was smiling, and then to Gareth, who was not. "I shall ascertain that Lady Leverham's and Miss Cameron's rooms are ready, my lord." Monkey aloft, the butler started to make his stealthy escape. Tarquin envied him.

"Where is Miss—" he began.

"And how very well *you* look, Hythe," Lady Leverham announced, beaming at him. "Quite the pink of fashion. Of course, you really ought to have a beard."

He blinked at her. "I beg your pardon, madam?"

"All good knights have beards." She gave a decisive nod, setting improbably dark curls into motion. "Do you not think so, Lizzie?" Before the countess could reply, Lady Leverham called out, "Uther Pendragon, you have my monkey!" and hurried after the fast-departing butler.

Tarquin's envy of his retainer's escape diminished somewhat.

"Sibyl, dearest?" Lady Hythe called.

". . . or . . . yes, madam?"

Tarquin turned slowly to see the bane of his existence

19

crawling out from beneath the Henry IV table. He forced himself to remember that it had been several years since their last meeting and hence he really should not regard her as such an annoyance.

At present, she looked as if she had met with a sudden storm. Her pale blue dress was creased and had a visible spot in the center of the bodice. Tarquin imagined the shredded object atop her head had once been a straw bonnet; her hair, half loose and straggling from beneath, was a veritable rat's nest. Mouse's nest, he corrected, noting that the rather ashy brown had not brightened in the least.

In short, Sibyl looked precisely as she always did.

"May I be of assistance, Miss Cameron?" he asked blandly as she extricated her second foot from the table gates. She was missing a shoe.

"Oh, no. No, thank you, my lord." She reached back and groped for a scuffed kid slipper. There was a bit of an awkward moment as she got the thing back on, then she rose gracefully to her feet.

One thing Tarquin had always been able to say for the girl was that she moved well once removed from tree branches, window ledges, ponds. . . .

She stepped forward, curtsied, and finally looked into his face. Each unpleasant escapade Tarquin recalled, but he had forgotten about her eyes. They were, quite simply, stunning: large, heavily fringed, and a rich golden brown. Gazing into those eyes, a man could easily overlook how very little he thought of the woman behind them.

She blinked. He blinked. And realized he had been staring. It was disconcerting, being caught by those eyes when there was so little else to note. From the freckled nose to the nondescript mouth and rounded chin, Sibyl was merely one more ordinary Scots-English face. But those eyes . . .

"I apologize for my unseemly appearance, my lord. Galahad was loose and I thought it best to contain him as soon as possible."

"I . . . ah . . . certainly." Tarquin was startled. In the past, Sibyl's greetings had been more along the line of Highland battle cries or appalling iambic pentameter verse. And she certainly had never apologized for anything. "I trust we will have no more such episodes."

Her brows rose at his tone, but she did not wilt in dejection as she always had in the past. "I will do my best to see Galahad is not often in your presence, my lord. You may be certain neither my aunt nor I wish to see your life disrupted."

Tarquin found he had nothing to say.

Sibyl gave him a very mature, rather dismissive smile and turned to his mother. "Thank you for your assistance, Lady Hythe. I cannot express how mortified I am by our arrival."

"Oh, pish. There is nothing quite so good for the stultified soul as a bit of chaos, my dear." The countess reached out to pat the girl's cheek. "And had Julius's dogs been properly confined to the kennels, there would have been no scene."

"Is Julius here, then?" Sibyl asked, all but turning her back on Tarquin.

"He arrived last night. I expected him to be here to greet you, but . . ." Lady Hythe smiled and spread her hands expressively. "With my younger son, one is always left in some uncertainty."

"Well, I am very much looking forward to seeing him. It has been some years, you know. I daresay we shall hardly know each other."

"Unlikely," Tarquin muttered before he could stop himself.

Sibyl merely gave him another brief, pleasant smile. "We cannot all remain as steadfast in our character as you, my lord. But how nice it is to have so solid a figure to emulate." While he was trying to decide if he had just been insulted, she addressed the countess once more. "I believe I shall repair to my chamber, my lady. I fear I am quite a sight."

"You are charming," was the warm reply. "But by all means, go have a rest. We will be a small party for supper tonight. The rest of the guests will not begin arriving until tomorrow." Lady Hythe waved for a footman. "Higgins will show you to your rooms."

"Thank you, madam. My lord." Sibyl made a graceful curtsy. "Until supper, then."

21

Tarquin watched as she followed the footman up the stairs, slender back straight and scraggly head erect. "Impossible," he muttered under his breath.

"What was that, my dear?"

"Gnats do not change their stripes."

"Is that not tigers?"

"Not in this case."

Lady Hythe tilted her head and regarded the departing figure thoughtfully. "Girls grow into ladies, dearest. It happens all the time."

"That is not a lady, madam. That is Sibyl Cameron." He scowled. "Blast. Did you remember to have the staff remove the Ming for safekeeping during her visit?"

"Oh, Tarquin." His mother gave a weary sigh. "Go play in your library. You are too tiresome for polite company." With that, she gave a thoroughly unladylike whistle to the beagles and led them toward the kitchens.

Tiresome? Tarquin dismissed the possibility. He was merely being a prudent host. His collection of Ming porcelain was unequaled in the realm and he did not relish the thought of losing any of it. Nor could he bring himself to believe Sibyl had changed a whit. No, she was merely biding her time until she could flutter about him like a gnat, spouting a multitude of silly questions and inane Romantic verse.

He very nearly felt sorry for her and the position in which she would find herself over the following days. Already a drab little package, she would be all but invisible in the company of the three Diamonds yet to arrive. And there was no doubt the ever-decorous, utterly sophisticated trio would find her customary dramatics less than seemly. Sibyl, he had long ago decided, could not seem to help herself; she was destined to absurdity.

Perhaps there was a higher reason for her presence at the house party. Perhaps, in the company of such charm and elegance, she would gain some small modicum of refinement. As Tarquin wandered back toward the library, anticipating his intensive perusal of Montefiore's illuminated Aeneas in Hades, he felt rather pleased with the possibility. He was really doing the girl a great kindness in exposing her to his future wife—

whichever of the three he should happen to choose. Now, if only Sibyl would allow herself to benefit . . .

Unfortunately, he could not help but wonder what nonsense was presently filling Sibyl's scattered little mind. And he could not forget that the only time her remarkable eyes had brightened was at the mention of his scapegrace younger brother.

That disturbed him.

Well, of course it did, Tarquin grumbled silently. Julius and Sibyl in league—perish the thought.

He was so distracted that he almost did not notice the chair. A gift from Elizabeth Regina to the first Tarquin, then merely Baron Hythe, it had resided in cordovan leather splendor in the Great Hall for more than two centuries. Countless aristocratic bottoms had occupied its seat, leaving a majestic hollow.

Tarquin grimly summoned a footman. Before the next patrician posterior sat, the small puddle would have to be mopped up. The Sixth Earl of Hythe was just optimistic enough to assume it had not been left there by one of his human guests.

3

SIBYL'S KNEES WERE knocking somewhat when she descended the stairs several hours later. For all her grand schemes, that first meeting with Tarquin had not gone well at all. She would have very much liked to blame the disaster on Galahad, but that was hardly sporting, and merely convenient. She knew she would do far better to curse Fate. In nearly fifteen years, she had not had a single positive encounter with the Earl of Hythe. Only Fate could be so perverse.

She passed a scalloped alcove on her way down and paused to examine the stone figure residing within. It appeared to be an image of Apollo: sixth century B.C. Etruscan, if her art lessons with Cousin Hesperia had served their purpose. She reached out to trace the graceful lines, then quickly withdrew her hand. She had just recalled the Venetian glass vase that had occupied the space three years earlier.

The vase had been brilliantly colored, sinuously sleek, and unexpectedly heavy. She certainly had not meant to drop it, only to examine it a bit closer.

Gareth was standing in the middle of the Hall when she reached the ground floor. Sibyl had the disconcerting feeling that he had been watching her descent. Of course, there would have been little he could have done had she taken a precarious grip on the Apollo, but he would have had a clear view had she dropped it, and hence could have given an incisive report. Hardly necessary, she mused somewhat crankily. It was not as if she ever tried to foist the blame for her accidents on maids or other innocent parties. No, she was scrupulously honest about such matters.

To his credit, Tarquin had not raged at her when she had

informed him of the vase's demise. Instead, he had merely thrust both hands into his immaculate ebony hair and closed his eyes for a moment. Then he had politely inquired, through a clenched jaw, whether she had cut herself on the shattered glass. On receiving a grateful negative, he had nodded once, spun on his heel, and quitted the salon.

The only words Sibyl had heard from him between that moment and their meeting upon her present arrival had been a terse and rather relieved-sounding good-bye.

She had been painstakingly careful during the mere hours of this visit. She did not think the earl would react too badly to the one small mishap. In fact, he would probably not even hear of it.

Gareth regarded her impassively as she approached. "You will find the company in the drawing room, Miss Cameron," he informed her. "Supper will be served precisely at seven."

"Thank you, Gareth." Sibyl followed him meekly across the marble floor. She knew perfectly well where the drawing room was, but was not about to mention the fact. The butler was not one to approve of familiarity from a Castle guest, and besides, he probably wanted to keep an eye on her as long as possible in case she was taken by the urge to touch one of the earl's precious possessions.

She took a deep breath as a footman opened the paneled door with a flourish. She had prepared carefully for supper, taking far more time than was usual with her appearance. Tarquin would probably never look on her as anything other than a menace, but she was determined that he would at least look on her as a presentable menace.

As it turned out, his view of her careful ministrations would have to wait. Lady Hythe and Aunt Alfonsine were there, sitting close together on a brocade sofa, giggling like schoolgirls. Tarquin, Sibyl noticed glumly, was not present. Galahad, she noted with some relief, was not present, either.

The countess looked up with a welcoming smile. "Sibyl, dearest. How very lovely you look this evening."

"Thank you, my lady." She accepted the proffered chair. "I do hope I have not kept you waiting."

"Oh, not at all. Alfie and I have been reliving our wilder

days. Did you know, my dear, that your aunt once quite stole the heart of the Duke of Corofin?"

Sibyl did, actually. Aunt Alfonsine, despite her epic love for her darling husband, was very fond of telling that particular tale. No one, most especially not the Romantic Camerons, ever bothered to comment that the Duke, elderly even in Alfonsine's zenith, had always been a bit otherworldly. The less kind among his peers called him mad as a hatter. He had been gallant, however—and besotted enough to temporarily exchange worlds: his habitual Xanadu for the lady's Camelot. It had been a match made in some incarnation of heaven.

"Ah, but he was nothing to Leverham," Alfonsine said dreamily. "How could I possibly have resisted such grace, such charm . . ."

Such a splendid inheritance, Sibyl added silently. Her Uncle Leverham was indeed gracious and charming. He was also the possessor of a picturesque ruin in Cornwall, reputed to have been a stronghold of King Arthur himself. The poor, gallant Duke of Corofin had never stood a chance.

"I am expecting Julius at any moment, Sibyl," Lady Hythe announced cheerfully. "Tarquin, unfortunately, has been detained by some estate business. He will join us as soon as he can."

Sibyl tried to feel relieved. Any reprieve should have been welcome. Instead, she felt vaguely dispirited. She had planned so *carefully.*

"I understand we are to be quite a large party as of tomorrow, my lady," she said, shoving both her nerves and her disappointment aside.

"Oh, goodness, yes." The countess's smile this time did not quite reach her eyes. "The Marquess and Marchioness of Broadford with Lady Theresa Wardour, Lord and Lady Vaer with Miss Elspeth Vaer, and Lord and Lady Reynolds with Mister George Reynolds and Miss Caroline Reynolds."

Ten more guests, Sibyl calculated quickly. Ten more aristocratic members of the ton, including two acknowledged Incomparables. Possibly three, she amended, not knowing Miss Elspeth Vaer. All in all, it promised to be an extremely elegant party—an accomplished, attractive, and elite party.

Sibyl had not felt quite so miserable since the time eight years earlier when she had tried to impress Tarquin with her prowess with a slingshot and had smacked his favorite hunter squarely on the flank. The horse had not been hurt in the least, merely startled. Tarquin, who happened to have been in the saddle at the time, had landed badly and had passed the remainder of the visit in bed. Sibyl had tried to get into his chamber to explain that Grandfather Daibhid had always instructed her with walnuts rather than rocks. Gareth, posted at the door, had refused to let her so much as poke her nose across the threshold.

It had always been a relief to Sibyl on subsequent arrivals to see that Tarquin did not limp. She was resigned to annoying him. Crippling him permanently would have been rather hard to forgive.

Tarquin gave a cursory glance to his cravat in the Hall mirror and strode briskly toward the drawing room. His tardiness was unfortunate, but it had been necessary to attend his steward. The thatch on several of the tenant cottages had been stricken by the recent inclement weather and required his examination. He had been quite forgiving of the time demanded. Beyond the fact that any leaks would be intolerable in the coming months, the damaged thatch was a terrible eyesore. He had made his perusal and immediately ordered that the stuff be replaced posthaste.

Now, changed into neat dinner attire, he hastened to attend his mother and guests. Gareth met him at the drawing-room door.

"I beg your pardon, my lord, but I have only just become aware of an unfortunate incident of which I feel you ought to be informed."

Tarquin took one look at the butler's taut features and felt his own innards contracting. "Yes?"

"It involves one of the suits of armor, my lord. It has been . . . er . . . dismantled."

"Armor?" There were precisely three suits to be found in the house. Tarquin's eyes slewed to the Flemish pair standing sentry beneath the gallery. Both appeared to be intact. The third was in his own private sanctum, the library. "Dismantled?"

27

"Yes, my lord. And I am afraid it gets worse."

With certainty born of rising fury, Tarquin fully believed that. "Well?" he snapped.

"As the one in the library toppled, the pike came loose."

He was already heading toward the library, one door away, Gareth right behind him. The scene in his sanctum was enough to have him cursing—silently, but eloquently. A footman was seated on the floor beside the desk, surrounded by pieces of embossed metal. The fellow was, at the moment, reattaching the codpiece to the base of the central plate.

"Was she hurt?" Tarquin asked in a voice that was little more than a growl. There was no doubt in his mind that Sibyl was the culprit and, despite his anger, he felt compelled to ascertain her state.

"Quite unscathed." Gareth almost sounded disappointed. "Your desk, however . . ."

There was no need to complete the statement. The pike was quite visible on the desk. Or rather *in* the desk. It had landed bladedown and was embedded, albeit loosely, in one corner.

The desk had belonged to Tarquin's great-grandfather and the maids did not even dust the surface without his permission. He completely forgot that minor fact as he rushed forward. He had left the Montefiore spread open on the blotter.

It was intact, a good foot from the blade, yet he still had to lean against the desk for a moment as the blood returned to his head. Then he straightened, carefully closed the book, and, on reasonably steady legs, removed it to the safety of a high shelf.

"Is she in the drawing room?" he demanded.

"Indeed, my lord," the butler replied promptly, something that could almost be called a smile creasing his severe features as he watched the earl stalk from the library and back to the drawing room. The attending footman scuttled wisely out of his way.

"Sibyl!" Tarquin bellowed as he hauled the door open.

"Yes, my lord?"

He jerked to a halt on the edge of the Tabriz carpet. His mother and Lady Leverham were seated on one of the settees, regarding him curiously. Sibyl, in a nearby chair, was gazing

28

somewhere in the vicinity of his boots, looking decidedly guilty.

She was also, he noted, looking rather different than usual. The mussed blue dress had been replaced by a very neat one in pale pink. The current style, with its high waist and low bodice, displayed what had mysteriously become a perfectly acceptable figure. Tarquin noted the pale swell of generous breasts, the hint of a narrow waist, and promptly jerked his gaze properly upward. Sibyl's hair, free of its shredded straw topping, was drawn into a glossy collection of curls atop her head.

He still could not see her eyes clearly, but the rest of the picture was startling enough without them. Sibyl was looking different, indeed. She was looking almost pretty.

"Tarquin, dearest. I take it you have dealt with your business."

Remembering his manners, he turned and offered his narrow-eyed mother a faint smile. "I have, madam." He tried an even breath. "Good evening, ladies. Please accept my apologies for the delay. I regret that you were kept waiting. It was most discourteous of me to allow myself to be so long detained."

"Oh, fustian!" Lady Leverham waved a filmy handkerchief in dismissal. "You must see to your demesne, dear boy! We have only just gathered, ourselves."

"Ah, well . . . I am pleased. . . ." Tarquin's eyes strayed back to Sibyl.

"I see you have noted how very well Sibby looks this eve," the lady twittered. "Why, I could tell from the moment you walked in and said her name how very struck you were with her appearance. She has grown into such a lovely young lady, has she not?"

"Aunt," Sibyl murmured, a distressed flush rising in her cheeks.

The blush suited her, Tarquin found himself thinking. Then he recalled the matter of his desk. "Sibyl, I should like to speak with you."

"Oh, dear."

"Perhaps we ought to step outside . . ."

"I am so terribly sorry, my lord!" she blurted, fixing her lovely eyes directly on his face.

"Yes, well, I . . . er . . ."

"Had I known the thing was not entirely steady, I would never have—"

"Sibyl," he said, recovering most of his poise and all of his ire, "you are my guest and hence are entitled to certain liberties. There are, however, some places that are not meant to be entered!"

Her brow furrowed. "I beg your pardon?"

"Tarquin, really!" his mother chided. "Whatever are you talking about? I am certain Sibyl would never intrude—"

"Mother, please." He gestured toward the door. "Sibyl, if you would be so kind."

She did not budge. "You may scold me here, my lord. There is no need to spare my pride. I take full responsibility for the carpet."

"The carpet?" he repeated. Gareth had not mentioned any damage to the library carpet. Then he remembered the full inkwell on the desk. "Oh, hell."

"The maid assured me there would be no stain, but I suppose she could have merely been consoling me. Tea certainly leaves a mark."

"Tea? What on earth were you doing taking tea in my library?"

The countess rapped her hand against the sofa's gilt-painted arm. "Tarquin, you will stop this right now! I will not have you reprimand Sibyl for a bit of spilled tea!"

"Library?" Sibyl repeated. "I was not in the library."

"But the armor . . . my desk . . ." She was staring him in the eye now, and Tarquin had the distressing feeling that she might be telling the truth. For all her faults, Sibyl had never been a liar.

"I tipped over the little japanned table in my chamber. I had set my cup there, and what tea was left splashed onto the carpet. It really was but a few drops."

His mother, Tarquin noted when he glanced her way, was not looking at him kindly. "I . . . I beg your pardon. I had assumed . . ." Well, damn, he thought confusedly, Gareth had said . . . He closed his eyes for a moment, counted five. "May I

As her host reached for the bellpull, Sibyl disengaged the monkey's hands from her hair and addressed the countess. "Please, go ahead into supper. I will join you in the dining room after I settle Galahad."

Lady Hythe nodded. "Thank you, dear, for . . ." she said softly, spreading her hands expressively. Then, to her son, "Tarquin, I would have a word with you."

He crossed the carpet and bent over to listen. From the look in his mother's eyes, Sibyl half expected her to swat at his posterior. Taking advantage of the opportunity, she murmured to her aunt, "What happened in the library, madam?"

"Why, nothing terrible, love. I merely disturbed some fascinating armor."

"Oh, dear."

"Really, Sibby, there is no need to look at me that way. I merely wanted to see inside the helmet. The falling pieces missed me entirely."

"Oh, Aunt Alfie," Sibyl shook her head despairingly. "No wonder Lord Hythe was so upset."

"Pooh. Merely a nick in a piece of wood. A true knight wouldn't have noticed it." Alfonsine sighed dramatically. "Whatever is the matter with young men today? One would almost think that chivalry is quite dead."

Sibyl couldn't help it. She laughed. "I would imagine," she commented cheerfully, "that women have been saying those very words since the term was invented."

Galahad on her shoulder, she slipped from the room. And was nearly flattened just outside the door. The Honorable Julius Rome was moving at his usual speed—a dead run. He skidded to a stop just inches from Sibyl, shoved black hair from his brow, and regarded her through familiar steel-gray eyes.

Julius, when standing still, looked rather a lot like Tarquin.

"Sibyl!" A brilliant smile lit his handsome face, quickly removing much of the resemblance to his older brother. "My God, it must be a year since I last saw you."

"Three, actually."

"Has it? Damn. Well, you look splendid. And Sir Galahad in tow. How are you, old chap?"

The monkey, like every other living creature, adored Julius.

He tried to leap from Sibyl's shoulder, aiming, no doubt, for the gold cord decorating Julius's blue uniform. Her quick grip on his tail held him back, so he contented himself with chattering a greeting.

Julius listened quite seriously for a moment and nodded. "I see. Well, Galahad, I shouldn't take it personally if I were you."

The monkey, apparently satisfied, subsided to a contented silence on Sibyl's shoulder. She laughed. "You have not changed, Julius."

"Mmm. Much to the distress of His Lofty Lordship. But you've changed, Sibby. You look marvelous. I take it the London Seasons agreed with you."

She did not need to ask how she had looked before; his comment was far less unintentional insult than simple truth. "I never had a Season after the first one, actually."

"No? But I am six-and-twenty . . . you must be . . ." Julius grinned again. "Sorry. Dashed rude of me, calculating a lady's age."

Sibyl grinned right back at him. "I am just four-and-twenty, a good few years from despair. But no, I was unable to return to London. My Great-uncle Machulus passed away three years ago March."

"Oh, I am sorry. I always liked the old coot . . . er . . . fellow."

She nodded. "I miss him. But he was ninety-six and went peacefully. Then, poor Uncle Ninnie a year later."

Julius, unlike his brother, had always welcomed visits to Cameron House and its madcap residents. "The catapult, was it?"

"I'm afraid so, though I expect he would have chosen to go in such a way."

"I'm sure." Julius reached out then and clasped her hand. "I did hear about your parents last year. Oh, Sibby . . ."

"Thank you," she said softly. " 'Tis the life of a Cameron."

"Well, it's a grand life, isn't it? I always envied you."

"You did? Good heavens, why?"

He swept one arm in a wide arc, gesturing to the splendor of the Hall. "Dull as dirt, my girl. No dash, no drafts, and the Living Marble Statue ruling over it all."

"Julius!"

"Oh, don't misunderstand me. I'm terribly fond of my brother, but he's hardly . . . Well, speak of the devil. Hail, Tarquin!"

Sibyl spun about, cheeks flaming, to see the earl, his mother, and Alfonsine just quitting the drawing room. She reminded herself that it had not been she calling Tarquin a living statue, but could not help wondering if he had overheard. His expression—like marble, she was forced to admit—displayed nothing.

"Julius. Just in time for supper." Tarquin's eyes roved disapprovingly over his brother's undone coat buttons and dusty boots.

"Always," Julius said cheerfully. "Sorry I'm late, Mother. I quite lost track of time. Ah . . . Lady Leverham. The sight of you has made this sorry day bright again."

Alfonsine giggled as the young man made a courtly bow and actually kissed her plump hand.

He straightened, gave her a deliberately dreamy smile, then turned back to the countess. "I say, Mother, by the by, a bloody huge coach just pulled around the drive. Are we expecting more guests tonight? Thought the Great Exhibition didn't start till tomorrow."

Sibyl caught the quelling look his mother sent him. Great Exhibition? She darted a glance at Tarquin, but his face was still expressionless as . . . stone.

Later that night, she would consider what a picture they must have made to the Vaers as that family entered the Hall. Lying in her canopied bed, feeling some slightly scandalous comfort in knowing Tarquin was asleep on the other side of one wall, she was able to giggle at the image. As it happened, however, giggling had not been advisable at the time.

Lady Vaer appeared first, a stunning matron in a mauve gown of the highest fashion. Her daughter was behind her, an equally stunning young lady with mahogany hair and the roundest, greenest eyes Sibyl had ever seen. Bringing up the rear was the viscount. Most notable about him, once one got past the puce, rose-embroidered waistcoat, was his vividly red nose.

The trio glanced, in admirable unison, from Julius's windswept appearance to Alfonsine's floating violet gauze to Sibyl . . . with her monkey epaulet. Just as Lady Hythe swept forward to greet her newest and also early guests, there was a quiet gasp from the lovely Miss Elspeth. Greener-than-emerald eyes going rounder than Sibyl would have thought possible, she turned her head into her mama's shoulder. Lady Vaer, suddenly rather pink in the face as well as gown, gave a pinch-lipped frown and averted her own eyes.

Lord Vaer continued staring. Sibyl, following his gaze, could see why. The ever-proper, determinedly decorous Earl of Hythe was scratching. In a perfectly scandalous spot. And he most certainly did not realize he was doing it.

Sibyl promptly removed Galahad from her shoulder and held him at arm's length. It was not the monkey's fault that he had caught fleas from the Rome beagles, but she was not taking any chances. After all, no one with a modicum of grace and decorum would scratch in public.

4

TARQUIN STOOD ON the terrace two days later, surveying the west lawn with great satisfaction. It was, he decided, a picture to rival even the trio of Gainsboroughs he had recently acquired. Perhaps even better at present, as the tableau before him was delightfully visible, while the paintings were still in their crates, waiting to be hung. He supposed he could move the Rubens from the dining room, the Caravaggio from the Great Hall, and the El Greco from the great staircase. They were, after all, already renowned and well documented as being in his possession. Then the Gainsboroughs could be arranged for most advantageous viewing. . . .

A trilling laugh came from the boules court. Apparently Miss Reynolds had made a good toss. As Tarquin watched from his vantage point on the terraced rise, she did a graceful pirouette, caught his eye, and waved gaily, half greeting and half summons. In a moment, she was joined in her silent entreaty by her companions. Three lovely young ladies, perhaps more Fragonard than Gainsborough, were charmingly demanding his attention.

Yes, they were a picture, indeed. And rather elemental, Tarquin thought fancifully. Elspeth Vaer, her brunette beauty enhanced by her decorous, earnest character, was steadfast as the earth. Lady Theresa Wardour, with her flaming auburn hair, smoky blue eyes, and lush curves, put one in mind of fire. Blonde, delicate, hands always in graceful motion with the breezy, pale blue gowns she favored, Caroline Reynolds was decidedly airy.

It only took water to complete the tableau.

Tarquin's eyes flitted over the edge of the lawn and encountered Sibyl. He sighed, the brief moment of fancy lost. She was seated by herself on the grass some twenty feet from the boules court, a still image in white muslin. The glossy curls were in neat order, the smooth skin sheltered by a frilly parasol. She looked perfectly acceptable, if rather colorless.

Tarquin was not fooled for a moment by the quiet picture. There was nothing bland about Sibyl Cameron beyond her outward appearance, and as much as he had always loathed pithy proverbs, Tarquin knew those still waters ran deep indeed. He started down the slope, intending to discover just what schemes were brewing in the girl's labyrinthine mind. He changed his mind halfway. This was Sibyl. She was clever enough to evade his questions, and daft enough to put such a twist in her plans as to make prevention of disaster impossible.

Besides, his future bride was requesting his attendance, and it would not do at all to keep her waiting. He turned again to face the stunning trio. All he had to do was choose a countess from among them. And he had just over a sennight in which to do it.

Perhaps Lady Theresa had the slimmest of edges as far as looks were concerned. She was, quite simply, perfect. Tarquin had never had much of an interest in redheads; he equated them with temper and trouble, but this one had caught his eye and held it. The lady was spirited, certainly, but her behavior had always been impeccable in his presence. And, equally important, she had once, during a predictably brief and bland chat at a long and torturous ball, expressed an interest in the antiquities of ancient Greece. Yes, if the consistent glitter in those splendid blue eyes did not make him slightly uneasy, Tarquin would certainly be leaning toward the luscious Lady Tess.

Of course, Caroline Reynolds was beyond lovely, too, and far smoother on the various senses. She had rather the look of a Renaissance madonna: pure, gentle, and dutiful. Her pale beauty would certainly go well among the vibrant Hythe possessions. Of course, the charming, airy fluttering might not bode well among the more fragile of those possessions, but Tarquin had never seen the girl so much as upset a teacup. He thought his Ming would be perfectly safe.

And then, of course, there was Miss Vaer. The glorious Elspeth had been properly overwhelmed upon her arrival at Rome Castle, and that recognition of the honor he was paying her had quite strengthened Tarquin's approval. As wealthy, powerful, and respected a family as the Vaers were, marrying a Rome would be a major coup. And the viscount happened to possess a truly stunning collection of jeweled Venetian daggers. Tarquin, having his own truly stunning collection of Florentine swords, thought the union of the two a rather nice idea.

Three lovely forms dipped into graceful curtsies as he reached them. "Good afternoon, ladies," he offered, unable to keep from noticing that Lady Theresa's leaf-green bodice was a tad lower than was perhaps perfectly seemly. But he could not help noticing, too, that she quite did it justice.

"My lord." Her eyes sparkled sassily as they met his. "Have you come to play with us, or only to watch with a discriminating eye?"

Tarquin blinked. "Well, I had thought . . ."

"Oh, you must play!" Caroline skipped to his side in a waft of blue gauze wrap and proffered two heavy, wooden spheres. "You must have a pair of b—"

"No, no, I vow Lord Hythe meant only to watch." Elspeth's gaze skittered from his grip on the boules. "Tess has been trouncing us soundly and I daresay would not care to relinquish her command."

Tarquin offered the balls to Lady Theresa. "By all means, my lady, continue. I would not detract from your pleasure in the day."

"You are too kind, sir. But I have already done my pitch for this round." She gestured to the court, then flashed him a brilliant smile as she returned the boules to Miss Reynolds. "Your turn, Caro."

"Actually, I believe it is mine," Elspeth said softly as she stepped into place. "We would not want to upset the proper order of things."

As Tarquin watched approvingly, pleased that the girl had a regard for order, she swung her arm in a graceful, underhand arc and let go. The ball flew an impressive distance, then dropped to smack soundly into one of Theresa's, sending it skidding to the edge of the court.

"Oh, good toss, Elly!" Caroline cried. "I fear I shall never be able to compete with the two of you."

She looked almost too fragile to throw the heavy boule. When it cracked into the one just tossed by Miss Vaer, Tarquin quickly amended his opinion and decided he would do far better indeed just to watch. His glorious trio were admirable competitors.

From her seat, Sibyl studied the tableau with some amusement, but a decidedly heavy heart. Tarquin had certainly chosen an impressive selection of Diamonds. She had been watching them at their game, not having been invited to play. In truth, she had been watching them since each had arrived—all a full day early and clearly not pleased to have been preempted in that plan.

Yes, it had been a fascinating two days. Meals were an exhibition of high fashion and elegant wit. Most other hours had been filled with various displays of ladylike accomplishment. Miss Reynolds had proven to possess a voice as angelic as her visage, surprisingly strong enough not to be drowned out by Miss Vaer's supremely talented if loud performance at the pianoforte. Lady Theresa had, with a combination of clever play and brilliantly witty conversation, been quite unbeatable at all of the card games organized.

The entire party was entranced by the trio. Tarquin, though his face had shown nothing but familiar granite politeness, had clearly been dazzled as well. Sibyl knew him too well to miss the pleased sharpening in his silver eyes when Miss Vaer had chosen a Bach sonata from the music stand. Nor had she missed the fact that he had sat up a bit straighter when Miss Reynolds fluttered her delicate fingers over the grotty old Italian harp in the corner and cooed at its beauty. Yes, Sibyl was well aware that the thing had once graced the palace of a Medici and quite appreciated its value and history. She was simply peeved that Tarquin had been so impressed by Miss Reynolds's notice of it. If the airy Caro had an iota of knowledge about the Medicis—or history—Sibyl was the Queen of Sheba.

Worst, by far the worst, was Tarquin's expression when Lady Theresa had greeted him just minutes earlier. His formidable jaw had actually gone a bit slack. It was quite obvious why, of course. The lady had the figure of one of the earl's precious Greek Aphrodites, and was a great deal warmer and softer than any stone sculpture. That was until one took her heart into consideration. That would be hard as marble.

Well, meow.

Sibyl groaned quietly, rather ashamed of herself. She knew nothing of Lady Theresa's emotions. But she could not help the jealousy. The three splendid creatures currently occupied in impressing the Earl of Hythe with their prowess at handling boules were placing their lovely forms directly in the way of her dreams. Hopeless as the desire might be, she wanted Tarquin Rome for herself, and no amount of logic was going to turn her own, hopelessly soft heart in another direction.

It did not help matters in the least that the man in question had apparently abandoned his customary too-good sense for a sort of moonstruck blindness. As beautiful and accomplished as the fawning trio was, each displayed a dismal want of integrity.

Well, she was forced to amend, Caroline and Elspeth seemed singularly lacking in that important feature. The musical sparring the night before had been blatant—even if she had been the only one to notice it. Their behavior at the present game was no better. Sweet-tongued, smiling, enviably graceful, and deferential as to turn, the pair had been far more concerned with knocking each other's boules from the court than landing them close to the target. Lady Theresa, to her credit, took the game more seriously. She aimed for the heart of the court, never for the playing pieces of her opponents.

Sibyl sighed. How very hard it was to dislike a woman she admired rather desperately. Of the three, Theresa was the only one who had not dismissed her with a satisfied smile. Yes, the lady had no doubt dismissed her as a potential rival, but it had been more honest than calculating. Sibyl was not a rival.

Theresa had taken a moment to speak to her, however, a

seemingly genuine inquiry as to her presence at Rome Castle. And had expressed a seemingly genuine delight in the mention of Argyll.

"Ah, Scotland," she had sighed in that annoyingly, appealingly husky voice. "How I long to go." She had leaned closer then, the dreamy smile turning impish. "I fell rather passionately in love with Walter Scott last year in Bath, you know."

"I . . . er . . . did you?" Sibyl had wondered if Mrs. Scott knew of this.

"Oh, completely! My brother carelessly left his new *Waverley* lying about and, as I had nothing else to do, I began reading. It vexed Mama to no end, but I would not go to the Assembly Rooms that night. I was far too involved."

"Were you?" That, Sibyl had mused, must have been fodder for the papers: Lady Theresa Wardour missing an opportunity to blaze in public.

"Of course. But then, I find those evenings dreadfully dull. Don't you? Everyone shoving and preening, and having nothing more interesting to discuss than which lordling's corset strings burst in the Pump Room. Deathly, if you ask me, but I can only defy Mama so far. . . ." As Sibyl sat, startled into speechlessness, Theresa had flashed another of her famous smiles and risen from the settee. "As she is shooting daggers this way now, I suppose I have to leave you. Time to perform. We shall have to discuss Scotland later."

Sibyl had watched in awe as the lady crossed the room. A less observant person might not have noticed, but Theresa seemed to don a glow as she approached the card table, almost as if it were a veil. By the time she reached the party and playfully tweaked Mr. George Reynolds's quizzing glass from his lifted fingers, the wistful aura of *Waverley* was quite gone, replaced by a dazzling, simmering elegance.

Sibyl, despite her best intentions, had been awed and utterly impressed.

Now, as she watched Theresa graciously accept her companions' dubiously gracious congratulations on a victory, she decided she had not felt quite so badly since a visit some nine years earlier, when she had been forced to watch Lord Kitcheley's widow in pursuit of Tarquin. That lady, though nothing compared to Lady Theresa, had been lovely and lush enough to make Sibyl quite hate her. And to chip away much of the stony ennui in Tarquin's eyes.

Sibyl had not meant to shatter the window of his bed-chamber late that night. She had simply thought to ascertain, by means of the ledge outside, that he was alone. He had not been there at all. He had, however, appeared in response to his valet's shouting, looking slightly flushed, decidedly rumpled, and not in the least pleased to see the glass fragments spread over the floor. He had stayed just long enough to inquire as to whether she had injured herself and to scold her soundly. Then he had quickly disappeared.

When Lady Kitcheley had committed expectedly ineffectual suicide a year later, Sibyl had heard her aunts and mother twittering over the tale. Of course, they had hustled her out of the room first, but the parlor had a large keyhole. *Insufficient laudanum*, she had heard. *Clever boy refused to answer her letters.*

The clever boy, she'd realized, had been Tarquin. Even as his rejection of the amorous lady cheered her, the utter hopelessness of her own situation had been quite afflicting. She had promptly removed herself to Great-aunt Ophelia's workroom, where she had proceeded to concoct a potion that would be fully sufficient at ceasing her woes.

Of course, she'd had no intention of actually swallowing the evil-smelling, green stuff, but had been prevented from even pretending a sorrowful farewell when Grandfather Cameron had tottered into the room. Before she could stop him, he'd downed the beaker in a single gulp. He had announced that since her purple rot had done so well for his ancient brother's fits, the green would serve delightfully for his gout.

Poor Grandpapa had been rather vilely ill some quarter hour after, but had not suffered so much as a twinge of gout until he was carried off a year later, victim of a fever he had collected while kite flying in a storm. Sibyl had tried to tell him that Mr. Benjamin Franklin's experiment with kite and key had been effected in a lightning storm, rather than torrential rain, but he had been adamant.

He had left this life grinning happily, key clutched in his

hand, already planning the smug debate he and Mr. Franklin would be having in the Great Celestial Taproom.

"Tears and smiles, Sibby?"

She blinked away the former, broadened the latter, and patted the grass at her side. "Do join me, Julius. I was just remembering my grandfather."

Tarquin's brother flopped down beside her, grinning. "Got myself the devil of a shock once, playing with his electricity machine. I thought I was done for, then was convinced he was. Never seen an old codger laugh like that."

"Mmm. Yes, he did take rather too much pleasure in seeing people with their hair on end and eyes wild. Grandmama was forever trying to warn their guests. And speaking of . . . Have you tired of Mr. Reynolds's company already?"

Julius followed her gaze over the lawn to where the young man, the epitome of Town elegance from his crimped blond hair to his champagne-polished boots, was haplessly winging arrows above, below, and to both sides of a massive target. "Told him his coat was far too tight for archery, but he snootily informed me that it was a Weston and nearly took out Lady Vaer with his next shot."

"Terrible."

"What? That he missed?" Julius laughed. "Oh, don't try that reproving look on me, Sibby. Doesn't suit you by half. You're no more enamored of this group than I."

"True. They're rather dampening on one's spirits."

"Rot. Nothing dampens your spirits."

Sibyl glanced back toward Tarquin. He was standing beside the tea table now while his fair trio took their refreshment. Caroline handed him a napkin, Elspeth a plate of cake, and Theresa pursed her lush lips and blew on the steaming tea before passing him the cup. He did not even blink at the outrageous act, but promptly lifted the cup to his own mouth.

Sibyl wondered if her spirits could be any more dampened.

"Stunning, aren't they?" Julius was regarding the scene with interest. "Care to make a wager on which he'll choose? Don't suppose it makes much of a difference one way or another, but my money's on La Wardour."

"Yes, she's very beautiful."

"And very clear on the matter. Not to my taste at all."

No, Sibyl thought, Julius would no doubt prefer Miss Reynolds. He had always liked ethereal blondes. They made such a splendid contrast to his devilish dark looks and character. "I do not think I care to wager on the matter, Julius."

"Smart girl. One never knows when an offhand comment about dusty old books or crumbling statuary will send old Tarquin into raptures. Yes, we'll just have to wait." Julius carelessly shoved a shock of hair from his forehead and grinned. "Another wager, then. A sovereign says Lady Reynolds murders Lady Broadford within the hour."

Sibyl glanced at the far end of the tea table where the matrons were gathered. The marchioness was watching her vibrant daughter and Tarquin with a smile suited to a cream-fed cat. At her side, Lady Reynolds was gripping the cake knife with knuckle-whitening force.

"My sovereign says it will be within the next five minutes."

"Not a chance" was Julius's complacent reply. "Reynolds will trot off to change her dress first. She's wearing pink, you know, and wouldn't be caught dead with bloodstains. Red and pink just *clash* so."

The statement was made in such a perfect imitation of Lady Reynolds's nasal drawl that Sibyl burst out laughing. "Oh, Mr. Rome, you are wicked!"

"And you're a glorious sight when you laugh, Miss Cameron."

That pronouncement, made with all the solemnity of a judge, set Sibyl into such helpless laughter that she half expected to join her dear grandpapa in the hereafter.

"Good Lord, don't tell me that's Sibyl Cameron!"

Tarquin jerked his gaze from the pair on the lawn and turned. "MacGregor. I thought you were on your way to Edinburgh."

Adam, Lord MacGregor, shrugged broad shoulders. "I decided to take a short detour."

"In precisely the opposite direction? Confess, man, you've come to have another go at my gun collection."

"If you would but let me try the one from the Cromwell trove . . ."

"That pistol is nearly two hundred years old and not to be

used. It is also not for sale, so you may cease badgering me about it." In truth, Tarquin was delighted to see his friend. The young lord, despite his complete irreverence for anything sacred or studious, was good company and more than welcome. "As it happens, you've come at a perfect time to join the party." He motioned MacGregor away from the table, where six pairs of speculative eyes—three marriageable and three matronly—were eyeing the new arrival. "I will be glad of your judgment."

"Judgment? On what?"

"My upcoming nuptials, actually."

MacGregor's shrewd hazel eyes narrowed under his unruly shock of auburn hair. "So you're really going to do it, are you? Don the shackles?"

"Take up the mantle of familial responsibility," Tarquin corrected blandly. "And I have the field narrowed to three. An impartial view would be welcome."

"Impartial, hmm? Forgive me for being so blunt, Hythe, but I would venture to say there is no view so impartial as your own. You're damnably detached about this whole matter."

"I am merely—"

"Yes, yes, approaching matrimony as you do everything else." MacGregor flashed the notorious grin that had loosened men's grips on their wagering money and set a multitude of female hearts to thumping. "It really should have crossed your oh-so-rational mind that I am hardly the person to ask for advice on such matters. I have but one requirement in a wife. When I get around to taking one, of course."

Tarquin cursed himself silently. He found it altogether too easy to forget that his friend had little more than lint in his pockets. MacGregor was a cheerful and acknowledged fortune hunter, at least as far as matrimony was concerned. With heiresses scarce as dodos, he lived on his wits and entertained his frequent female companions with amusements money did not buy.

"Fine," Tarquin said gruffly. "But you know I value your judgment in all matters."

MacGregor gave another careless shrug. "As you wish." His

gaze swept from table to lawn. "So, I'm to help you get the number from four to one, am I?"

"I said three. Lady Theresa, Miss Reynolds, and Miss Vaer."

"And Sibyl . . ."

"Sibyl?" Tarquin gave a short laugh, slightly amused and wholly horrified by the thought. "Good God. Sibyl. Perhaps I ought to take your advice and not ask for it on the subject. Good God. Sibyl."

"Well, I must say she's in fine looks. Your brother seems quite taken by her and, if I'm not mistaken, young Reynolds appears to be making an eager trot in her direction."

As Tarquin watched, George Reynolds did, in fact, join Julius and Sibyl, carefully lowering his tightly encased rump onto the grass beside them. "It's a wonder he didn't split his breeches," he muttered. "Preening fop."

"Indeed. But I believe he is quite a popular fop. Sibyl seems reasonably diverted. What do you say to joining their merry little party?"

"I say it would be terribly impolite to my . . . other guests. Beyond the fact that I have nothing to say to Sibyl, I have no desire to slight the other ladies. As it is, I'm having enough trouble finding ample time with the three to ascertain their true characters and suitability."

MacGregor rolled his eyes. *"Impolite,"* he mimicked. *"Slight. True Characters.* Use your head, man. Let your future wife, whichever she might be, see you expressing some interest elsewhere. A woman never shows her true character until she sees competition coming from an unexpected quarter."

"Hmm. You might be right." The theory was logical enough. And Tarquin did not quite like the way Mr. Reynolds was eyeing Sibyl's bodice. If he did not interfere, she was likely to pop the man in the nose, and it was against his principles to allow violence at his home. "Very well."

He noticed, as he followed MacGregor across the lawn, that Sibyl's hands were not fisted in preparation for a strike. On the contrary, they were settled neatly in her lap, both free as Julius was now gallantly holding her parasol over her head. Nor did she appear bothered by Reynolds's annoying presence. She listened intently to whatever rot the man was imparting, tilted her head, and gave a gentle laugh. Julius's response elicited another. Sibyl looked well amused. Her companions both looked bloody well pleased with themselves.

Julius glanced up at their approach. "Well, damme! The troops have arrived." He passed the frilly parasol to a willing Reynolds, bounded to his feet, and pumped the new arrival's hand cheerfully. "Dashed good to see you, MacGregor. I'm delighted to see that gray you bought at Tattersall's in May hasn't broken your neck yet."

MacGregor raised one dark brow and drawled, "That gray has proven to be something of a disappointment. He does well enough over a six-foot gate, but balks at the eight. I don't suppose you'd care to take him off my hands."

"Honestly? Good Lord, man, I'd give my right arm for a chance at that beast!"

An apt statement, Tarquin thought. No doubt the steel-limbed, wild-eyed horse would break both of Julius's arms in seconds flat. He opened his mouth to inform the pair that pigs would be taking eight-foot gates before he endorsed such a transaction, but never got the chance.

Julius had flopped back onto the grass and reclaimed the parasol. MacGregor was bent over Sibyl, lifting her hand to his lips. "This is indeed a pleasure, Miss Cameron."

And Sibyl, rather than gushing—or clumsily smacking this one in his nose—gave him a serene smile before gently reclaiming her hand. "You are too kind, my lord. I am afraid our past meetings could hardly reside pleasantly in your memory."

Tarquin clearly recalled the time some ten years back when she had crept after them as they went off to hunt grouse. When she had popped, shrieking but unscathed, out of a bush where MacGregor had just aimed a shot, the man had nearly keeled over. He had passed a shaky few minutes, crouched on the ground, before finding enough breath to shout.

That had been the most dramatic encounter, but certainly not the only one. Tarquin recalled several, none pleasant. MacGregor, however, seemed to have developed something of a selective memory, as he was now smiling easily down at Sibyl. "You will allow me to know my own pleasures, Miss Cameron. I very much look forward to conversing with you during my sojourn here."

"Thank you, my lord. I would be honored." Sibyl returned the affable smile. "Will you be staying for the duration of the party?"

"Yes, my lord," Tarquin muttered, "will you be staying for the duration?"

MacGregor regarded Sibyl for a long moment, then turned. "You know, Hythe, I think I just might. I assume you have room for one more guest."

"I'm sure we can locate something under the eaves. You might have to stoop a bit, but I daresay you'll manage."

"I daresay I will. Though if I ask very nicely, I imagine Gareth will find me a closet somewhere with a higher ceiling." MacGregor nodded to Julius and bowed again to Sibyl. "Until later, Miss Cameron."

"My lord."

"No need for you to come," he announced to Tarquin. "I'll speak with Gareth. You stay here and enjoy the . . . delights of your party."

He was striding briskly off before Tarquin could respond. There was little wonder why. The ladies, having finished their tea, were rising from the table and showing every indication of approaching. The future Lady Hythe—all possible three of her—watched the Scottish baron's departure. Tarquin noticed, but wasn't particularly bothered. MacGregor, with his devil's smile, had been the cause of countless feminine sighs over the years. But his lack of fortune made him a Detrimental. Even the most title-hungry of Society mamas balked at the thought of making their daughters Lady MacGregor.

No, Tarquin knew, his friend's presence would not interfere with his own plans. And the man would certainly take a bit of the pressure off in the evenings. Tarquin was not fond of dancing, but the ladies all seemed terribly keen on the idea. With the addition of MacGregor to the party, there would be less reels required of the host. Perhaps the fellow would even dance with Sibyl once or twice. Well, once would be sufficient. . . .

He glanced down to find her watching the trio. Apparently they had decided a bit of archery was in order, for they were donning the leather gauntlets provided and choosing arrows. Sibyl's expression was unreadable as she watched.

"Charming, are they not?" Tarquin had no idea why he felt compelled to make her note how very perfect the three were, but he could not help himself. "Graceful, decorous, lovely."

"Indeed," she replied agreeably.

"A credit to their sex."

"Mmm." She turned away and addressed Mr. Reynolds. "I believe I left my wrap near the tea table, and I am feeling a wind. I do so hate to ask . . ."

"It would be my pleasure, Miss Cameron." Reynolds was already awkwardly raising his stiff and padded self to trot off.

"Thank you." Sibyl, Tarquin, and Julius watched as the fellow headed straight for the cleared luncheon table some fifty feet in the wrong direction. "Oh, dear. Mr. Reynolds—"

"No matter." Julius handed her the ridiculous little parasol and sprang to his feet. "I'll get it."

Sibyl waited until he was out of earshot, then asked pleasantly, "So, which are you going to marry, my lord?"

"I beg your pardon?"

"That is why they are here, is it not? You are displaying them in the proper location, seeing how they suit the Hythe environs."

"For God's sake, Sibyl," Tarquin snapped, "that is a wholly unseemly thing to say!"

"Yes, I suppose it is. Forgive me. I should have said, 'seeing how they suit Lord Hythe.' "

Annoyed as much by her faintly amused tone as by her words, Tarquin scowled down at her, a stinging tirade forming on his tongue. Politeness—and experience—stopped him. Sibyl did not respond well to his tirades. Never had. She always appeared deaf for the duration, and he always felt apoplectic in the wake.

Instead, he managed his own cool smile. "Have you an opinion on the matter? I am of a good age to start thinking of filling the nursery, after all. Assuming I were to marry one of

50

these ladies, which would you suggest? They are all perfectly suited to the role of countess."

For the first time that day, Sibyl met his gaze squarely. "Do you really want to know what I have to say on the matter?"

He was so busy trying not to note how very splendid those large brown eyes were that he was not listening. "Hmm? I . . . er . . . What?" But she promptly dropped her gaze to her lap. He had not noticed the sketchbook there earlier. Now she was busy scratching away at a blank page with a drawing pencil.

After making something that looked like a list of nine or ten lines, she tore the page from the book, folded it three times, and waved it toward him. "My opinions, though I suppose predictions would be more apt. I have given three for each young lady. How much will you pay me for them?"

"Pay you?"

"Of course. When one asks for advice, one must be willing to pay for it."

The concept, of course, was galling, but Tarquin could not halt the surge of curiosity. Nor could he forget, absurd as it was, that Sibyl's family called her the Oracle. "What do you want?"

"The Montefiore."

"What?"

"I want the Montefiore," she repeated.

"Impossible!" he snapped. "Unthinkable! Why . . . How do you even know of the book?"

She gave him a small, vaguely pitying smile. "How dull life must be for you, Tarquin, having no one remotely close to your intelligence with whom to converse." She sighed at his responding snarl. "I am not wholly ignorant of the rare classics, you know. When your mother described your latest purchase, I knew it had to be a Montefiore."

Vastly impressed despite himself, Tarquin was no less appalled. "And you thought to trade a few ridiculous prophecies for it? I never thought you ignorant, Sibyl, but you are certainly mad."

"You are declining, then?"

"Damned right I'm declining!"

She shrugged. "Very well, then." As he watched she neatly tore a third of the paper off, ripped it into tiny pieces, and scattered it over the grass. His jaw clenched at both the mess and the blitheness of the act. "I believe it is time for you to join the Three Graces, my lord. They seem to want you."

She gestured to where the trio were, in fact, gazing in his direction. The blonde—Miss Reynolds, he corrected grimly—beckoned. When he glanced back at Sibyl, she had risen. Tucking her parasol and sketchbook under her arm, she gave him a polite smile and set off to meet Julius, who had located her wrap and was trotting back with it.

She was whistling as she went.

5

HOURS LATER, HE was contentedly holding a glass of port and not thinking of Sibyl at all. One of the few pleasures of house parties was the uncomplicated company of gentlemen after supper. Three satisfied papas and one indolent son lounged comfortably in their seats, MacGregor and Julius were bickering amicably over the merits of Scotch whiskey versus good English ale, and there was not a woman in sight.

The meal had been a trial. Some fluke of seating had placed all three potential wives at varying distances down the table. Tarquin had found himself with Lady Broadford to his left, Lady Vaer to his right, and Lady Leverham just close enough that he had been able to hear every word she nattered.

She had been lauding his very great merits. That, in itself, would not have been a bad thing had she had better aim with her commendations.

The woman had commenced by regaling Lord Reynolds with tales of Tarquin's legendary residence at Christ Church College, Oxford, where he had read no less than sixty-two complete volumes of the Greek classics—in Greek, of course. Not that it wasn't absolutely true, in fact he had read closer to seventy, but Tarquin had no idea where Lady Leverham had obtained the information and rather wished she had kept it to herself. Reynolds, a sporting man, was often heard to say that the only acceptable use for paper was to record bagged game. He was also, despite never having set foot in a university hall, the scion of a resolute Cambridge family.

The woman had followed by describing to Broadford Tarquin's youthful visits to Cameron House. The dearest laddie, she insisted, had been so gracious as to spend his time closeted in the library, cataloguing Kirkcormac Cameron's epic sixteenth century works. The marquess's face had become slightly red in the middle of the narrative. The Broadfords, originally border lords, had lost several massive estates to the stronger, cleverer Scots. The current marquess was well known for voting against Caledonian issues on the floor of Lords.

Lady Leverham had then soured the final course, a pristine cherry soufflé, by announcing to Tarquin, "I often wonder why you haven't married, dear boy. But then, I suppose you find few women equal to your fascinating pursuits. Ah, well, if the bachelor life appeals to you, we can always count on Julius to do the spawning."

He had managed a weak smile for his pensive guests before stabbing his fork into the soufflé with unnecessary force.

To top off his unfortunate dining experience, in those quiet minutes while Lady Leverham tucked heartily into her meal, Ladies Vaer and Broadford had handily filled the conversational space. While they had refrained from mentioning him at all, their chosen topic had done little to improve Tarquin's already waning appetite. They had, understandably perhaps, chosen to discuss their daughters.

In truth, it had not been much of a discussion at all. Each had merely presented her case with narrow-eyed zeal worthy of the realm's finest barristers. Tarquin, caught in the middle like a presiding judge, had fortified himself with nearly twice as much claret as he usually consumed.

"My darling Theresa declined *six* proposals during the Season," the marchioness announced proudly over the turbot, "and not one from less than an earl."

Lady Reynolds's appropriately congratulatory nod came simultaneous with, "Caroline is such a sweet girl, really. She was quite overset at receiving nods from all seven patronesses of Almack's. She simply could not decide which vouchers to carry."

"I was so grateful to have Theresa by my side when we had the honor of hosting the Princess Spogliama in our opera box. It was Gluck, you know, *Iphigénie en Aulide,* and rather difficult to understand, even for those with excellent French. The dear girl translated everything for Her Highness into Italian."

"We've had to replace our pianoforte twice. Both were exceptional pieces, of course, but not nearly grand enough to suit Caroline's talent. It was rather sad to have to turn down the Duke of Cambridge's offer of the instrument Handel used while here in England, but even Caroline could not coax the full majesty of Bach from it. . . ."

And so it had gone through the meal.

Now, in the company of other men, Tarquin felt decidedly relaxed, if still a bit windblown. One could always count on the male faction to speak of something comprehensible and proper. Like estate business.

"I tell you, Hythe, you've never seen the like. . . ." Broadford's cheerful voice drew Tarquin's attention back. Apparently he had been forgiven for any pro-Scottish sentiments. "Splendid little property just south of York: a mere four hundred acres, but prime cattle grazing. Paid a pretty penny for it, mind you, but the return will be tenfold."

"A fortunate acquisition," Tarquin replied solemnly.

The marquess leaned in till his formidable belly was pressed against the table. His eyes sparkled beneath hoary russet brows. "Ain't the half of it, my boy. Prime stud in situ, a splendid little castle, and I'm handing over the lot, tip to tail, to my gel as part of her dowry."

"Added another thousand quid to Caro's ten," Reynolds announced casually as he topped off Tarquin's port glass. "Peerless chit, you know, and a papa must see to her future."

Vaer was in the fray before Tarquin could do more than blink. "You haven't seen my latest acquisitions, Hythe. By pure luck, I managed to purchase old Paisely's sixteen pieces from the Gubbio Castle arms collection. Medici," he said slyly, wrinkling his reddened nose and giving a conspiratorial wink. "Quite a history there, sir."

"Of course, there's the box in Wales. . . ." Broadford added.

Reynolds settled his bony frame into the closest chair. "Chit's grandmama left her a tidy little sum. . . ."

"Blades like a razor, hilts dripping with glittery rocks . . ."

Tarquin supposed it could be worse. He could be in the presence of Lady Leverham and her monkey.

"Now, Galahad, you silly boy, release Lord Hythe at once!"

Sibyl glanced up from *Waverley* at her aunt's giggled command and winced. The monkey was attached to Tarquin's waistcoat again, this time upside down with his head inside the coat and his tail waving in Tarquin's face.

Several members of the party were stifling laughter. Julius wasn't bothering; he was holding his sides and gasping for breath. Tarquin looked ready to spit nails. He suffered Galahad's company in the drawing room since his Three Graces had decreed the beast to be adorable. He did not, however, invite the monkey anywhere near his own person. Galahad, of course, needed no invitation. In the conspicuous absence of the butler, the earl had become the object of his great affection. The moment the gentlemen had arrived from their after-dinner port and chat, the monkey had made a familiar beeline for Tarquin.

One small concession had been made. A length of twine now ran from Galahad's jeweled collar to Aunt Alfie's jeweled wrist. When Tarquin had first commented on the excessive length of the lead, Alfonsine had sweetly reproached him for insensitivity. The dear creature, she had informed him, had once been accustomed to the spacious jungles of Africa. Such confinement as a three-foot lead would be cruel.

Tarquin, to his credit, had refrained from mentioning that the ornate gilt cage Alfonsine had brought was a good deal smaller than any jungle. Sibyl had seen no reason to comment that Galahad was a product of the Duchess of York's rotating menagerie and had been born in Surrey.

Right now, half of the eight or so yards of twine were coiled neatly in Alfonsine's lap. The rest was tangled around Tarquin's leg, wrist, and watch fob. "Madam, please summon your pet," he demanded through clenched teeth. He had, Sibyl mused curiously, been a bit stiff-jawed since halfway through supper. "He is chewing on the lining of my coat."

Alfonsine beamed at him, then turned to Lady Broadford, who was seated beside her. "So gallant of Hythe, is it not, to show such kind attentions to my little darling. Of course, a truly chivalrous soul is always kind to creatures smaller and more helpless than he."

The marchioness, whose quintet of pampered poodles had not been invited to join the festivities, eyed Tarquin with some doubt. He was presently scowling fiercely and muttering inaudible invectives as he tried to haul Galahad away from his chest by the tail.

Sibyl knew very well that she could have him free of his unwelcome companion in seconds should she choose. She was enjoying her reading, however, and had managed to snare one of the better chairs in the room. Bathed in the soft light of a large wall sconce, it was a perfect seat for reading. It would also be a perfect display pedestal. After three days in the trio's company, Sibyl was well trained to recognize such important issues. There was little doubt in her mind that, should she relinquish the seat, one of Tarquin's ladies would have her silk-swathed bottom in it posthaste. Central location and flattering lighting were at a premium.

Miss Reynolds had stood in the middle of the room for a moment, staring expectantly. When Sibyl had merely smiled pleasantly and opened her book, Caroline had given an audible sniff and flounced away.

In lieu of sitting, the trio had ultimately posed themselves in various spots within Tarquin's line of vision. Now they abandoned their posts to gather around him, laughing and tickling Galahad's furry sides to make him release his grip. The monkey briefly poked his head from inside Tarquin's coat to have a look. Sibyl imagined the various, glittering gems decorating the ladies' ears and throats offered serious temptation, but apparently he was finding the coat lining particularly tasty. His mustachioed face disappeared again.

"Diverting, is it not?" A hand came to rest on the back of her chair, just brushing her shoulder.

Sibyl had not noticed Lord MacGregor coming up behind her and now tilted her head to look into his face. His eyes were bright with amusement beneath the shock of auburn hair. She had caught his gaze upon her several times during supper, direct and . . . speculative, perhaps. It had been a bit disconcerting and . . . rather nice. What a pity that MacGregor's need to marry money was as infamous as his heartstopping smile.

Well, she thought, a bit amused herself, both her heart and fortune were safe enough from his charm. A clever heiress, especially one whose accomplishments and physical charms were not remotely sufficient to outshine her gold, was always on alert. But Sibyl liked MacGregor; she couldn't help herself, and saw no reason not to enjoy the mild flirtation while it lasted.

"What is so diverting, my lord?" she asked, matching his conspiratorial tone.

"Why, the pageant, of course. Best of the year, actually."

Now she followed his gaze to where Tarquin stood, surrounded by beautiful, chattering women, and decorated by a small primate. "There have been others?"

"Oh, aye. This is the third . . . no, fourth, I believe. And, I daresay, the last. Old Hythe will make his choice this time."

Lady Tess's laughter rang out. Sibyl's heart slid downward. She managed, however, a light "You think he is in imminent danger of falling in love, then?"

"Love?" MacGregor chuckled. "Our Hythe? Not at all. I think he is in danger of being severely inconvenienced by the time and mess inherent in finding his countess. Ergo, I expect a decision within the sennight."

Another glance at the tableau showed Miss Reynolds's hands fluttering delicately around tumbled curls. Apparently Galahad had come out of Tarquin's coat long enough to have a go at one of the lady's hairpins. The monkey had a taste for silver hairpins. He looked quite content. The earl, gingerly pulling the pin free, looked disgusted. Caroline, with several thick gold curls decorating her shoulders, looked quite lovely. And not in the least upset with her disarray.

Sibyl sighed quietly. "Lord Hythe could not have chosen more beautiful inconveniences."

"Mmm." MacGregor's smile, though still undeniably wicked, held a hint of gravity. "But beauty's the first thing to go, isn't it? Why, it can vanish between the chapel and wedding luncheon." He looked back to Tarquin, then leaned down and, cheek brushing Sibyl's hair, whispered, "If Hythe must choose from that lot, I'd advise him to go for the monkey."

58

Sibyl smiled. She had no doubt that, if forced to choose for Tarquin among his current adoring circle, she would gladly pick Galahad as well.

"Lady Leverham . . ." Only a practiced ear would detect the rising anger in Tarquin's well-modulated voice. "If you would be so kind as to employ the lead." Apparently Galahad was back to sampling his coat.

Sibyl heard the annoyance quite clearly. Aunt Alfie's ears, not surprisingly, were out of practice. "You know," she murmured to Lady Broadford in a confidential tone, which could probably be heard in the kitchens, "all of the Camerons are ever so fond of Hythe. Why, we'd even had such hopes for a match between dearest Si—"

"Aunt Alfie!" Sibyl hissed, mortified, before her aunt could complete the unmistakable and unsubtle sentiment. Behind her, MacGregor chuckled.

"Lady Leverham," Tarquin repeated, voice louder still.

"Yes, dear boy?"

"If you would be so kind . . ."

"You see, Regina?" Alfonsine beamed at her companion. "Such a polite young man. Such courtly manners, such indulgence, such—"

"Stop at once, you blighted bit of fluff!"

"Such passion." Aunt Alfie sighed, and tugged on the lead, just as Tarquin took a step toward her.

Perhaps had he not been moving, perhaps had she tugged a bit less forcefully, disaster could have been averted. But he was and she did, and suddenly Tarquin's arms windmilled frantically. A second later, he went down like a felled oak. As Sibyl watched, one hand halfway to her mouth, his knees hit the floor, followed by his flattened palms, and finally by his chin.

The tea table shook with the resulting tremor. One empty cup tottered daintily along the slick surface before dropping over the edge to bounce on the thick carpet an inch away from Tarquin's nose.

There was a complete silence. Or rather, not quite complete. Another empty cup continued for a moment to rattle against its saucer. When it settled with a tiny click, silence reigned. Briefly. The proper behavior in the wake of an earl going tumbling onto

59

his face in the midst of a drawing room, Sibyl assumed, was not covered in either ladies' or gentlemen's guides to deportment.

Then the Three Graces squealed in unison and rushed to Tarquin's side, all but obscuring him from view in a multitude of petticoats. Lord Vaer cleared his throat awkwardly, Lady Reynolds gave a faint moan, and Julius, face a brilliant red and shoulders shaking, bent over double and clasped both hands to his face.

Above all came a sudden shrill chattering. Galahad's furry face poked from beneath Miss Vaer's skirt. To Sibyl's experienced eye, he looked unharmed but distinctly out of sorts. Apparently he'd had the sense to let go of the earl's coat during the fall, but had been taken along anyway by the lead.

"Oh, you poor boy!" Alfonsine was out of her seat and scurrying toward the prostrate Tarquin. Elbowing Miss Vaer out of the way, she demanded, "Oh, dearest, are you hurt?"

"I think—" Tarquin began.

"He did not land atop you, did he?" Alfonsine had scooped up her pet and was haplessly tugging at the taut lead, trying to free him. "Did he?"

Galahad gave a piteous squeak, then quite ruined the effect by chattering again, louder this time, and waving a tiny fist.

"Hythe, you must get up! The poor creature is near to being strangled by your weight."

As Sibyl watched, Tarquin raised unfocused eyes to her aunt. "Only near?" he muttered hazily, then his forehead dropped to the carpet again.

Alfonsine reached out a plump hand to shove at his shoulder. "Up!" she commanded.

And he got up. It was a slow process, hampered as much, Sibyl decided, by the fact that all three young ladies insisted on helping, as by the fact that it had been a hard fall. Tarquin got himself onto his elbows, rested there for a moment, then slowly sat up. His half-hearted attempt to rise farther was prevented by the twine wound round his ankles.

Sibyl, as usual, had the instinctive urge to go to his aid. She didn't think the Graces would allow her within five feet of him, however. Beyond that, she was determined to stay right where she was, conspicuous in her location. This was one mishap in which she'd had no part, and she was not about to take the blame for it. Beyond *that*, Lord MacGregor's hand had somehow come to rest firmly on her shoulder, holding her quite still.

In the end, Lady Tess untangled the lead from around his watch fob and Miss Vaer from his wrist. Miss Reynolds, hands fluttering in customary style, was left to deal with the fateful tangle around Tarquin's ankles. He might have stayed hobbled for rather a long time had he not reached out with his free hand—the other was pressed to his jaw—and handled the matter himself.

He did, however, accept the fluttering hand Caroline offered once she had risen to her feet. Sibyl's faint envy turned to guilty amusement as the girl nearly went onto her pert nose when Tarquin tried to pull himself up. Caroline Reynolds couldn't lift an infant, let alone a large man like the earl. She gasped and promptly let go. Tarquin, several inches off the floor, thudded onto his posterior. Only when Caroline took a new, rather tentative grip, and Tess and Elspeth positioned themselves at each of his elbows, did he finally regain his feet.

Sibyl swallowed a giggle when Miss Vaer let out a wholly unladylike grunt.

Staggering slightly, knowing he would do something violent if anyone so much as coughed, Tarquin made it to the brocade sofa. His mother, cheeks suspiciously pink, shifted to make room for him. He grunted as he bent his knees and lowered himself carefully onto the cushions. Two of the young ladies— the blonde and the brunette—Caroline and . . . the other— hurried toward him, and he wearily waved them off before leaning back with a quiet groan and closing his eyes.

Everything hurt. Had he been in a court of law, he would have sworn that he had shattered every bone from the kneecaps upward. And he was still seeing faint stars behind his eyelids.

"Ow!" he snapped as his mother prodded at his chin. "Mother—"

"Well, I suspect you'll have quite a lump come morning," she announced matter-of-factly. "You might want to employ a cold compress."

61

Tarquin gingerly opened one eye, expecting to meet a maternally concerned gaze. She had already turned away and was addressing Lady Leverham. "How is Galahad, Alfie?"

"Not at all well" was the mournful reply. "He is in a terrible state of shock, and I fear he bruised one of his little paws."

A chorus of sympathetic murmurs came from the assembled guests.

Tarquin's gaze swung in disbelief to the monkey. The blasted beast was perched on his mistress's shoulder, chewing contentedly on a large gold button. A quick glance downward gave Tarquin a very good view of the dangling threads in the middle of his waistcoat.

His head snapped up at the sound of a muffled chuckle. No one met his eyes as they slewed around the room in search of the culprit. It hadn't been Julius; the bounder was past chuckling—doubled over and wheezing. George Reynolds was studiously studying his shirt cuff, Lords Broadford and Vaer were hunched over their interrupted game of vingt-et-un, the elder Reynolds gripped an estate-game book from the previous century.

The sound came again, just as Tarquin located MacGregor across the room. The bounder was leaning against Sibyl's chair, lips twitching and eyes alight. When he broke into an unrepentant grin, Tarquin scowled. The scowl deepened when he noted that his friend's hand was shaking slightly with suppressed laughter where it rested on Sibyl's shoulder.

She did not meet his gaze at all, but promptly dropped her head and lifted her book, quickly enough to hide her expression. Not that it mattered. No doubt she'd just shared a smile and giggle with the blasted Scotsman.

Tarquin felt a dull flush rising in his cheeks. Bumped chin and bruised knees forgotten, he now had a thoroughly unpleasant pricking sensation at his pride. He looked from the monkey, who had half the button poking from his mouth, to Lady Leverham, who was solicitously stroking the little cretin's furry paw.

"Madam," he growled with as much dignity as he could muster, "would you be so kind as to send your pet upstairs?"

She turned round blue eyes upon him and blinked prettily.

"Oh, he will be quite all right, dear boy. He just needs a few moments to recover."

"He may take whatever time he needs out of my sight."

"Really, my lord—"

"Lady Leverham." His jaw was throbbing now, right up through his gritted teeth, making speech decidedly uncomfortable. "At present, I am . . . disinclined to act. But I assure you that should your pet come anywhere near me in the foreseeable future, he will find himself with more than a bruised paw."

It took a moment for comprehension to dawn. When it did, the lady gave a shocked gasp and clasped the protesting monkey tightly to her ample breast. Tarquin grunted when his mother poked him hard in the ribs, but managed to keep his gaze firmly on Lady Leverham. She stared back for a full minute, the picture of childlike hurt, then rose slowly to her feet.

"Very well, my lord." She offered him a strained smile. Then, as she crept from the room, she murmured to the monkey, "He did not mean it, sweeting. It was merely the fall that made him speak so. Perhaps had he had a helmet . . ."

Once the door closed behind her, Tarquin took a look around the room. His mother, icily rigid at his side, gave him a reproachful glare. MacGregor's face was somber. Sibyl still had her face in her book. The other young ladies watched him, three pairs of eyes wide in three beautiful faces.

Lady Broadford who had, a mere hour before, been extolling her daughter's charms to him as eloquently as an Eastern silk merchant, would not meet his gaze now.

It was hardly as if he had kicked a puppy, he grumbled at the obvious disapproval. Or even a monkey, for that matter. He was the wounded party, after all. The persistent aching from knees to chin told him just how wounded. Of course, his guests could not know about the pain, but that still gave them no call to be staring at him as if he had committed some heinous crime.

He glanced back to his mother. "Can you see a lump?" he demanded.

She closed her eyes for a moment, shook her head, and sighed. "Oh, *Tarquin*," she said wearily, and turned away.

Grumbling to himself, Tarquin raised a hand to rub at his jaw. His fingers never made it to his face. Instead, they made a hasty detour to scratch at the sudden, intense itch around his ribs.

6

SIBYL REMAINED AS long as possible in her room the following morning, listening to the rain pattering against the windows. She was usually up and active by eight, but she managed to linger until nearly ten with some effort. Hunger finally pushed her out the door. There was little chance of having to share the breakfast table with any of the Graces. They did not quit their beds until the sun was well up in the sky. Tarquin, however, was an early riser and she did not particularly want to meet him, either. Considering the weather, it was likely everyone would be trapped inside, at least for the morning. How very small a very large house could suddenly become when Mother Nature decided to water her gardens.

Despite the fact that she'd had nothing whatsoever to do with the debacle of the night before, Sibyl could not help feeling that Tarquin would somehow hold her responsible. He always did. Beyond that, she was certain he would be sporting a colorful bruise on his chin, and she didn't want to see it. Free from blame or not, she had seen him sporting too many bruises, plasters, and slings throughout the years.

She had invariably been responsible for those.

An ominous crash reverberated up the stairs just as she closed her chamber door. Skirts in hand and heart in throat, she rushed down the long hall. She thought she heard a door closing, but when she reached the landing, no one was in sight below.

At the bottom of the staircase, facedown on the stone floor, was a massive painting. Several pieces of the gilt frame were scattered nearby amid a dusting of plaster. As she descended toward the scene, Sibyl looked up. A chunk of the molding was missing from the wall.

She gingerly picked her way over the debris and reached for an undamaged corner of the frame. She was just bracing herself to lift the painting when a voice thundered, "Miss Cameron!"

Sibyl jumped and spun to find Gareth hurrying across the floor. Before he reached halfway, the morning-room door opened and Lady Hythe came rushing out. She skidded to a halt some twenty feet away, just avoiding a collision with her son, who came bolting from the dining room. Hot on Tarquin's heels were Lord Broadford, both elder Vaers, and George Reynolds. And behind them, a stunning tableau in pale pastels, were Caroline, Elspeth, and Lady Tess.

Apparently everyone had been hungry that morning.

Tarquin's chin was indeed painted with an interesting combination of blue and faint orange, Sibyl noted. What she saw immediately after was the fierce fire in his eyes. He stalked toward her, face drawn and eyes blazing, and Sibyl found herself imagining a dragon. With a crimp in his tail.

"Are you hurt?" He demanded brusquely as he reached the base of the stairs.

"Not at all. I—"

"Fine. Gareth!" He all but shoved her out of the way. "Help me."

Sibyl scuttled back a few feet and watched as the two men lifted the painting. Once it was upright and leaning against the wall, they huddled in front of it, blocking her view. Tarquin's shoulders jerked as he ran his hands over the canvas.

Several seemingly endless minutes later, both straightened. Gareth stalked off toward the kitchens. Tarquin studied the painting a bit longer before announcing, "The only damage appears to be to the frame."

The Graces oohed in appropriate, if careless, gratification.

Sibyl could see the painting clearly now and felt her own stomach give a slippery lurch. She wasn't sure that any of the trio could tell the difference between what was before them now and a child's dabbling, but she could.

"My goodness, what an ugly, po-faced creature!" Elspeth had stepped in for a better view. She wrinkled her own pert nose at the hawk-faced, black-garbed figure. "Hythe, do not tell me this is an ancestress."

"Donna Benedicta di Rizzoli," Caroline read from the little plaque on the frame. "Why is it that all Italian women seemed to be named Donna?"

"It is, I believe, a form of address, not a name." Lady Tess tilted her head and examined the portrait. "She is rather long in the face, is she not? And they call English ladies horse-faced."

Sibyl rolled her eyes as discreetly as possible. "It is an El Greco," she announced to no one in particular. The painter's distinctive, elongated forms should be perfectly obvious to anyone who had bothered to spend an afternoon studying Continental art. She suspected the Graces were unconcerned with any portrait not of themselves.

"When you are ready, Sibyl," Tarquin muttered, bruised jaw outthrust and arms folded over his chest, "you may tell me what happened."

"I have no idea."

"It simply jumped from the wall?"

Some things really never changed. Ignoring the gathered company, Sibyl faced Tarquin squarely. "It was already fallen by the time I got here."

"Sibyl—"

"Lord Hythe. Do try to give me a bit of credit here. I take responsibility for my actions. This was not one of them."

His brows drew together and she could see him trying very hard not to believe her. In truth, she had no idea if he ever *did* believe what she said. When his eyes swept over their audience, she steeled herself for an icy request to attend him in a more private setting. With one or two notable lapses, he had always scolded her in private.

"Where is your aunt?"

"What?" She blinked at him.

"Have you seen her this morning?"

"I . . . er . . . no."

Apparently no one else had either.

"You will locate her, please, Sibyl," Tarquin commanded tightly. "I will be in the library for the next hour. Mother—"

Lady Hythe was already herding the guests back into the

dining room. The look she shot her son over her shoulder was cool enough to create icicles. Sibyl decided Tarquin had missed it. He was back to bending over the painting.

Whether to be helpful or spiteful, Sibyl couldn't tell, but she was unable to resist giving him a brief lesson in physics. "The chain was too long," she announced.

"I beg your pardon?"

"For the painting. The chain was too long for the painting, the painting too large for the hook, and the molding too delicate for them all." She peered up at the wall for a moment. "Shorten the chain by a third and increase the hook size by half."

When she looked at him again, he was wearily rubbing a hand over his eyes. "As a matter of fact, the painting is going elsewhere."

"Because it fell? Just replace the—"

"Because of the Gainsborough," he muttered vaguely. "This was meant for the rear gallery."

"Well, the maths will be the same anywhere."

"Sibyl," he said quietly.

"Yes, my lord?"

"Go find your aunt." Then, shoulders somewhat less rigid than usual, he trudged toward the library.

He skimmed half-heartedly through a stack of estate documents, realigned his collection of early Shakespeare printings on their shelf, and tried various rearrangements of his blotter and writing implements. That was a waste of time; he had long ago found the most efficient placement of each piece. He inspected the suit of armor for new dents or loose pins, checked his desk drawers for stray papers, and even bent down himself to straighten the fringe on the rug.

For once, Tarquin found no satisfaction in ascertaining the order of his sanctum. Nor did he have the requisite energy to conduct any business there. He just didn't particularly want to venture anywhere else in his home.

It was unforgivably rude, he knew, closeting himself away from his guests. It was also necessary. His pride still smarted from the previous night's disaster, and the unexpected presence

68

of half the party at breakfast had not helped. The eyes darting surreptitious glances at his chin were, he was convinced, also noting Lady Leverham's absence. It was hardly as if he'd had her locked in one of the towers, but he had the sneaking suspicion that the possibility had crossed the mind of more than one of his guests.

The lady was a menace. Perhaps her inappropriate chattering was simply a matter of henwittedness; the physical mishaps, unfortunate accidents. Regardless, she was making him look very bad indeed in front of his prospective brides and their respective families. It was usually Sibyl behind the chaos, but he was more than willing to assume it was a family trait.

Sibyl. He really shouldn't have barked at her; he knew that. But finding her, pale in the Hall's limited light, so soon after hearing the crash, had given his heart a painful jolt. True, she had been standing, but he had been waiting nearly fifteen years for her to end up flattened by some sharp or heavy object and was certain each calamity was the One.

He was relieved that the El Greco was unscathed. He was even more relieved that Sibyl had not been beneath it when it fell.

He was also furious, relief be damned. All he had wanted was a nice, peaceful sennight in which to arrange a nice, peaceful future for himself. Instead, he was bruised, crazed, and had developed a devilish itch under his arm. And it seemed to be spreading.

When the knock came at the door, he hurried back behind the desk. He smacked his knee in the process, and his "Enter!" was rather closer to a pained wheeze than a firm command. He did manage to resist rubbing the afflicted spot, so that when the door swung inward, he had both hands clasped neatly on the blotter. If he had to face the Cameron ladies, he wanted to be at a safe distance and in visible control of the interview.

The wrong Scot appeared in the threshold.

MacGregor, looking rather like a reiver in a loose coat and scuffed boots, raised a thick brow as he entered. "I swear to you, Master Rome, 'twasn't me who ran Archie Fremont's drawers up the flagstaff."

Tarquin scowled and unlinked his fingers. "Very amusing."

"Not half so much as that headmaster's pose you were holding, my friend." MacGregor strode over to the leather sofa and dropped cheerfully onto the cushions. Tarquin's frown deepened when the bounder leaned his shoulders against one padded arm and propped his crossed ankles on the opposite. "If I remember correctly, it was Conovar who actually ran the drawers up the pole."

"If I remember correctly, I was the one who took the hand-lashing for it."

"Well, Fremont took *his* shot at me."

"He did, didn't he? Was that the first time your nose was broken, or the second?"

MacGregor ran a lazy finger over his nose. As far as Tarquin could see, it was just crooked in an otherwise even face. According to the Scot, women found the flaw irresistible. "Second. And he'd never have gotten that shot if he hadn't had three of his flunkies holding me down. The first break was at a far abler hand."

"Let me guess. The able back of your father's hand."

"Not at all. The victor's name was Katie and she was wielding a broom handle. Ah, she was a treat."

Tarquin was intrigued in spite of himself. They'd been no more than fourteen at the time of the drawers-up-the-staff school episode. "How old were you?"

MacGregor thought for a moment. "Twelve or thirteen," he replied, then grinned at Tarquin's raised brows. "I was an early bloomer."

"So said the broom handle."

"Well, I was just testing the waters and they were rougher than expected. But Katie came around eventually."

They usually did—at least for MacGregor. To be honest, Tarquin had always been slightly awed by his friend's easy success with the fairer sex. He wasn't jealous, just awed. His own appeal inevitably seemed connected to his money or title, usually both, and he wasn't certain he would recognize genuine interest on a woman's part if it, or she, smacked him in the face.

MacGregor, on the other hand, attracted women like honey. Oh, he had a title, to be sure, but it was little more than a courtesy. He was a well-enough-looking fellow, but hardly an Adonis. He had absolutely no money whatsoever. He also rarely spent a night alone.

"I don't suppose you've come up with some fail-safe advice for me in my own quest," Tarquin said wearily.

"Throwing your hands up already? That's hardly like you, Hythe."

"I am most certainly not giving up. The goal was to choose a wife, and I fully intend to do that. It is simply that between the monkey and flying household objects, I cannot seem to concentrate on romantic endeavors."

MacGregor rolled his eyes. "There you go again, implying that there's any romance to be found in the situation. I would say your biggest problem lies right there."

"What would you have me do? Draw lots? Choose the first one I see tomorrow morning? Correct me if I am wrong, but a man ought to have some feelings for the woman he marries."

"Fine, then." MacGregor lifted his arms and wiggled his fingers in the air. "Use the touch test. Put them all in a room, close your eyes, and see which one feels best."

"And that is your idea of a romantic endeavor?"

"No, but it can be a very good beginning."

"Well, thank you very much for that pearl of wisdom." Tarquin decided to ignore the fact that MacGregor was now idly unraveling his frayed cuff and dropping the pieces onto the sofa. "I flatter myself by thinking I know what to do with my hands."

"Oh, no doubt of that." The words were followed by a sly grin. "Rumor has it Miss Wilson's tears on your departure had nothing whatsoever to do with the lost allowance."

Tarquin winced. Yes, his parting from the volatile demirep had been messy. But so had she, forever bringing foodstuffs into her bed. Actually, he mused, he hadn't minded the sweet cream so much. . . . But that was neither here nor there. Once he had decided to enter the Marriage Mart, the lady and her cream jug had had to go.

"Assuming I am to keep my hands to myself, have you any suggestions? Thus far, I am having a devilish time finding any of my three prospects more appealing than the rest."

"Fancy that" was his friend's dry retort. Then, "I daresay you'll just have to get each of them alone for a spell. See whose figurative scent lingers with you after you've parted."

That, Tarquin decided, was not a bad idea at all. It would give him the opportunity to get to know the ladies better individually, and would forestall any interference from other members of the party.

Leather creaked as MacGregor levered himself into a sitting position. "Damn this rain. I'd fancied taking my pick from your glorious stables this morning. Ach, well. What say you to a game of billiards?"

Tarquin was busy shuffling hours, locales, and prospective brides in his head. "Hmm? Oh, yes. Why not?" He was sure Gareth would have seen to removing the canvas dustcover from the table and polishing the cues. They were a rather splendid set, purchased some years ago to replace the ones Sibyl had warped while practicing miniature vaults throughout the house. "Oh, hell."

"What?"

Tarquin braced his elbows on the blotter and, forgetting his sore chin, dropped his jaw onto his palms. "I am waiting for Sibyl and her aunt. They really ought to have been here some time ago."

"To receive a dressing-down, I assume. For pity's sake, Hythe, it is merely a painting."

"It is an El Greco," Tarquin corrected, and found himself smiling as he recalled Sibyl's obvious scorn of the other ladies' ignorance. "You missed quite a show."

"I feel safe in assuming there will be another. Anyway, if I were Sibyl and La Leverham, I would hasten myself to the deepest recesses of the house for the rest of the day."

"Another person might," Tarquin agreed. "Sibyl, however, despite her myriad faults, is rather good at facing the unpleasant tasks. She'll arrive soon enough."

She tried. For nearly an hour, Sibyl tried to locate her aunt. Alfonsine, unfortunately—or fortunately, perhaps—was nowhere to be found.

The lady was not in her bedchamber. Galahad was. He

shrieked ill-temperedly and made a dash for the door when Sibyl poked her head in. Praying he would not cause any damage of his own, she hurriedly pulled the door shut, ignoring both the indignant chattering and the faint thump against the wood.

Aunt Alfie was not in the front gallery, with its portraits of long-ago Romes. She was not in the music room, with its grotty old harp. Sibyl fervently hoped she was not anywhere near the library, with its priceless books and reassembled armor. And resident irate earl.

Before dismantling the suit of armor in Tarquin's library, Alfonsine had apparently discovered a copy of George Ellis's *Specimens of Early English Romances in Metre* and had spirited it out of the room in her pocket. The lady's Romantic spirit had been overjoyed and further convinced that there was indeed the soul of the gallant knight in their host's body. Sibyl doubted her aunt would find anything gallant about Tarquin should the two come face-to-face just now.

After the end of an hour, she was flummoxed. She was also struggling between concern and annoyance. Cringing at the necessity of the act, she went in search of the one person most likely to be of service. She deliberately quashed the conviction that he would also be one of the persons least willing to help.

She eventually tracked Gareth to the rear gallery, where he was overseeing the removal of the El Greco from its ruined frame. One look at his rigid back and Sibyl very nearly tiptoed back out the door. Instead, she squared her shoulders and approached.

"I beg your pardon, Gareth," she began, losing much of her courage when he swung about to glower at her. "Have you seen . . . I, er . . . cannot seem to find my aunt."

The butler promptly grunted—twice—and turned his back on her. Startled, Sibyl opened her mouth to repeat her query but quickly changed her mind. All the better, she decided now, if Gareth stayed put. Her aunt's chances of remaining unscathed seemed far better if neither he nor Tarquin were involved in the search. As she backed away, she mused that coming from any other man, the grunts might have resembled a chuckle. There was no doubt in her mind, however, that Gareth did not chuckle.

Another quarter hour later, she was on the verge of panic. She had coaxed several servants into helping, and together they had managed to cover a good portion of the huge house. One footman had even gone out in the rain to scour the park and stables. Despite the fact that she was loath to call attention to the dismal situation by summoning more staff, Sibyl was nonetheless on the verge of doing just that when the maid who had been scouting the back halls came rushing in.

"I've found your aunt, miss," she announced breathlessly.

"Thank heavens!" Then, noticing that the girl looked far more distressed than exultant, Sibyl felt her own relief wane. "I take it," she said wearily, "that there is still a problem."

"There is, miss."

"Has she . . . disturbed something else?"

"Well, no, miss. At least not as I can see."

Sibyl's heart lurched. "Oh, God, is she *hurt?*"

"I—I don't think so. 'Tis hard to tell . . ."

The girl was now twisting pleats into her apron and Sibyl's patience snapped. "For pity's sake, where is she? You must tell me!"

"I think, miss, it'd be much better if I showed you."

The maid turned back toward the recesses of the lower floor; Sibyl and the rest of the search party following close behind. Soon they were in a rather dim and extremely crowded back hall. It seemed that every belowstairs servant was there, not to mention several grooms and chambermaids, all talking at once. Straining her ears, Sibyl was relieved to hear her aunt's distinctive if muffled voice coming from the far end of the crowd.

"Aunt Alfie?"

"Sibby? Oh, good morning, dear." The voice became slightly clearer as Sibyl wriggled her way through the tightly packed audience. "I seem to be in a bit of a muddle, though I must say everyone has been offering the most helpful suggestions. . . ."

Sibyl suddenly found herself flat up against a door. Whirling about, she looked for her aunt, knowing she must have pushed right past her. "Where are you, Aunt?" The only faces in sight were those of the staff. "I don't see you."

"Of course you don't, dearest. It would be odd indeed if you could."

Sibyl turned her head slowly, not quite trusting her ears. By this time, the young maid had slipped through to stand at her side. "What is this room?" Sibyl demanded, finding the door locked.

"Room, miss?"

It was clear enough that the girl was honestly trying to be helpful. Closing her eyes, Sibyl took a calming breath.

"Sibyl, my dear, it's a bit dark in here," she heard from behind the door. "If you could perhaps—"

"We'll have you out in a moment, Aunt Alfie." Then, patiently, to the maid, "What is your name?"

"Gertie, miss."

"Well, Gertie, you've been very helpful. Thank you. Now, can you tell me what is inside here?—other than my aunt," she added quickly, anticipating that response.

"Brooms, miss."

"Brooms?"

" 'Tis the broom closet."

"The broom closet. I see. Aunt Alfie," Sibyl called with brittle cheeriness, "how did you come to be locked in the broom closet?"

"Oh, merely a mistake, love."

Yes, I would certainly hope it was not deliberate. "How, Aunt?"

"Well, you see, I asked Uther if there were any tapestries in the house. Where one finds armor, one often finds tapestries, you know. He was more than eager to point me toward this chamber. . . ."

"I'm sure he was," Sibyl agreed dryly. "Gertie, who has the key? No, don't answer that." The collective muttering told her exactly where the key was to be found. "Does anyone other than Gareth have one?"

"I don't think so, miss. The door's never locked."

Now the staff was regarding her sympathetically, and Sibyl managed a weak smile. "Aunt Alfie?"

"Yes, dear?"

"I have to go fetch the key. Will you be all right for a few minutes?"

There was a pause, then Alfonsine gave a twittering laugh. "I will have to be, won't I? But you are an angel to ask." Sibyl stepped away from the door, shaking her head in bemusement. Her aunt picked the most unpredictable times to be sensible.

"Sibyl?"

"Hmm?"

"I am sorry, dearest. Really. I shall speak to Lord Hythe if you like."

Sibyl couldn't help but smile. *That* would certainly be an interesting conversation. "Thank you. But I'll tackle the dragon."

"He might be a smidgen annoyed. His temper these past few days does not seem quite as mild as usual. Perhaps you ought to wait before playing St. George."

"Don't worry, Aunt. I shall be fine."

Sibyl made her way slowly down the hall, too concerned with the possibility that she would not be fine to notice that the crowd had parted, clearing a path for her. "Pardon me, please," she murmured when one figure blocked the way.

"Certainly, although a gentleman really ought to do anything in his power to prevent a lady from accosting a dragon."

Glumly, Sibyl glanced up past the pristine scales of London's finest tailor to a color-mottled jaw. Unable to face Tarquin, she opted instead to stare at his shoulder. Moments later, she wished she had kept her gaze at his feet. Behind him, bringing the total number of witnesses to a good three dozen, was the entire house party.

7

IT HAD BEEN some years since anyone had called the Earl of Hythe onto the carpet. He was there now, in the middle of a pale Aubusson, receiving perhaps the most stinging dressing-down of his life.

"While this is *your* party, Lady Leverham and Sibyl are *my* guests, and I am appalled by your treatment of them!" His mother paced her sitting room angrily, preventing him from sitting and leaving palpable fury in her wake. "How *could* you be so callous, Tarquin?"

Resisting the urge to scuffle his feet on the carpet, he muttered, "Once more, Mother, I did not lock Lady Leverham in the broom closet, nor did I command, request, or even hint that Gareth should do so."

"Honestly, Tarquin. Gareth would hardly take it upon himself to lock a guest in a closet."

"Gareth was not responsible, either." He'd had his own interview with the butler. The man's dignity had been sorely affronted, and Tarquin had all but crept away from his icy glare. "The only reasonable explanation is that the lock was somehow engaged when Lady Leverham closed the door behind her."

"You call that a *reasonable* explanation?"

"In the absence of any other, madam, it must be."

The countess ceased her pacing and faced her son, hands firmly planted on her hips. "Your logic frequently escapes me, young man. This time, you have succeeded in quite rattling my brain. But, as it happens, that is neither here nor there at the moment. What I would like to know is how you plan to make amends to the Camerons."

Tarquin was far more concerned with how he was going to convince the Vaers, Reynoldses, and Wardours that he was not a churlish, petty lunatic. He was not particularly concerned with the Camerons. Hadn't he, in light of the situation, graciously excused them from the parley in the library? It seemed, too, that the matter of the El Greco would go unattended.

A sheet of rain spattered against the window. Summer storms tended to hit Kent fiercely, then vanish as quickly as they appeared. This one seemed content to remain just where it was, strong and steady, battering the ancient walls of Rome Castle and driving the castle's rapidly aging lord and master stark raving mad. Another day cooped up inside with the motley collection of people and animals was one more than Tarquin was ready to contemplate.

"I will deal with the Camerons," he said grimly, silently adding *when necessary*.

"Cordially?"

"Really, Mother. With your current opinion of me, one would think I had turned into a strange creature in a matter of days."

"You know, Tarquin"—his mother gazed at him bemusedly, all temper vanished—"one would think just that, indeed. You do not seem quite like yourself of late."

"I do not much feel like myself at the moment," he muttered. "But I am certain it will pass. Now, if we are finished here, I believe I will rejoin my guests."

"A commendable idea. We are not finished, however. I have a question for you before you go." His mother settled herself gracefully on the edge of a Hepplewhite writing desk. Tarquin, ordinarily a firm believer in putting one's posterior only on pieces of furniture designed for it, wearily propped his hip against the solid, marble-topped console table. He was feeling a bit edgy himself.

"Ask away, madam."

"Thank you. Now, when can I expect you to make your monumental decision? This house has become something of a circus and I am presently debating running off to join a peaceful, civilized establishment."

So was Tarquin. "We are not even through the sennight.

The other two held their own, however. Miss Reynolds's first shot, languid and limp-wristed, had ended up in the carpet beneath the target. Lord MacGregor had obligingly taken her tiny hand in his much larger one and demonstrated the proper method. The lady's second round had resulted in three darts imbedded firmly in the outer ring.

Elspeth collected the darts and passed them over. Caroline aimed and came very close to the bull's-eye. "Oh, dear," she trilled. "I just cannot seem to grasp the right way of it. My lord, you must come show me again."

At Sibyl's side, MacGregor shook his head and demurred. "You have no need of my assistance, Miss Reynolds."

"Oh, but I do! You must come tell me what I am doing wrong."

"Your modesty equals your talent, my dear." MacGregor crossed his arms and offered the girl a slow, stunning grin. "If you insist, I shall watch carefully from here and provide what comments I can."

Caroline twitched and wiggled for a moment, lining up her next shot. She glanced back over her shoulder and batted her lashes. Sibyl supposed it was meant to be a shyly questioning look. MacGregor nodded. The next two darts landed solidly next to the first.

"Very nice," he drawled. "Very nice indeed."

Miss Reynolds giggled. "You are too kind, sir. I am such a complete novice at this."

Sibyl disagreed. Caroline was not a novice at all. In the matter of targets and aim, the lady was more than proficient. "Impressive," she said on a sigh.

"Isn't it?" MacGregor watched idly as Caroline stepped aside for Tess. "One might almost think we had three sharps in our midst."

The target shivered slightly as three darts thudded into the center in succession. "One might indeed."

Julius stepped in for his turn now and was promptly surrounded by three Graces, correcting his grip and offering helpful suggestions. Sibyl had seen Julius at darts before. He was not much of a shot on a good day. Now, his shots would have disgraced a blind man with palsied hands. The lovely trio was only too happy to laugh and pet and show their own skill.

"Are you certain you won't have a go, Sibyl?" MacGregor nudged her with a friendly elbow. "I daresay you'd do well enough."

"You would be wrong." She gave a rueful laugh. "I would probably strike the ceiling."

"And few would blame you for it" was the gentle reply.

"I beg your pardon?"

This time, there was a wry edge to the man's smile. "I would think no less of you for it. But my opinion is hardly the one of import here. Come along and take your turn with the darts."

"I don't think so. I am content to watch."

"Are you? I'm not certain of that, but then, you haven't much of a competitive spirit, have you?"

Sibyl stared glumly into MacGregor's handsome face. "No, I don't suppose I do."

"That, Sibyl, was a compliment. Stop frowning. I expect you get what you want without any scratching and shoving."

Miss Vaer discreetly elbowed Lady Tess out of the way and aimed a dart. Sibyl shrugged. "I cannot complain. I have a very good life, everything I need." The second dart slipped out of Elspeth's fingers and rolled across the carpet. George Reynolds and Julius both scuttled after it. "And most everything I want."

MacGregor propped one shoulder against the wall and gazed down at her. "Most everything, is it? Pity, that. I don't suppose I'm allowed to ask what you are missing."

"I would rather you not. It is always so humiliating, discussing one's shortcomings."

"You mean these unnamed things you lack are within you? What rot, Sibyl. You are perfectly delightful the way you are."

It was very hard, even for a woman of good sense, to resist the flattery of one of the ton's most accomplished flirts. Sibyl smiled and waved away the gallant words. "You are too kind, sir," she announced, unable to resist mimicking Caroline's breathy little voice, "and I am too old to worry overmuch about improving myself—and to have my opinions of myself changed by a glib tongue. Or a pretty smile," she added when her companion flashed her a boyish grin. This Scottish laird, she decided, had more variations to his smile than the Regent had corset stays.

Unabashed, MacGregor reached out and chucked her under the chin. "If you're too old, lass, I'm half dead. And I don't think you should change a thing; just allow yourself more time in Society. Experience life and all, get yourself a good . . . er . . ."

"Husband? Is that what you were going to say?"

"It wasn't, actually, but why not?"

"I am past three-and-twenty and—"

"Not yet out of the first bloom."

She rolled her eyes. "I never had a first bloom, but it isn't a matter of years, really. It is a matter of . . ."

"Money?" MacGregor supplied after a moment, eyes twinkling.

"No, I have plenty of that."

"So you do. Cleverness?"

"I am not wholly deficient there, either."

"You are not deficient in the least. Common sense?"

This time, she sighed. "I think I have rather too much of that."

"No such thing. So, let's see." He ticked the words off on his fingers. "You are young, wealthy, clever, and sensible. I would say you can have whatever you ask for, Sibyl. It's simply up to you to ask for the right things."

"Mmm. Well, that's the rub, isn't it?" She gazed at the far wall. There was a painting there of some past Lord Hythe garbed in a bizarre combination of Classical armor and more modern hunt clothes. "Do you know the story of the Cumaean Sibyl?"

"Ancestress of yours?"

"No, she was a figure in mythology. . . ." Realizing MacGregor was teasing, playing the careless, undisciplined character that suited him so well, she demanded, "Do you know the story?"

"Prophetess, wasn't she? And Apollo's mistress. He kept her settled in a snug little cave near Olympus for a few hundred years till he tired of her."

"That," Sibyl said tartly, "is just the sort of faulty male memory that pervades the schoolroom and guarantees that the

83

Classics lose something from one generation to the next. No, she was not Apollo's mistress, but it was not for lack of his trying. She was smart enough to resist his amorous advances, but not quite so clever when it came to accepting his gifts."

"Is there a poisoned apple in this story?" MacGregor chuckled when she glowered at him. "Go on. I appreciate the education."

"Hmph. Well, in any case, Apollo promised to grant any wish—"

"Best way for a fellow to find himself in the suds, that."

Sibyl ignored him. "She was perfectly comfortable with her portion in life, so she asked for as many years of life as grains of sand she held in her hand."

MacGregor nodded approvingly. "Clever girl. I wouldn't mind a good slice of eternity."

"Ah, but she forgot to ask for eternal youth. Believe me, after a few years and some wrinkles, Apollo lost all interest in her. She lived out a thousand years in that snug little cave you mentioned."

"Interesting." MacGregor tilted his head and studied her thoughtfully. "I hope you are not comparing yourself to the wrinkled Sibyl, Sibyl. You've a fair number of sand grains left to you before that point."

"I was merely telling a story about knowing what to ask for."

"Ah, well, if that's all . . . As for the cave woman, I imagine she got some comfort out of foretelling the trials her godling would go through with the women he chased. He never did show much sense there."

Another dart thunked into the bull's-eye. "Perhaps not," Sibyl agreed, "but he always chose beautiful creatures to chase. Now, if you would excuse me, I really ought to go see to my aunt. She has had a difficult day."

She and MacGregor were standing near the door. It should have made for a quick and easy exit. And perhaps it would have had Sibyl not run straight into Tarquin as she crossed the threshold. She had no way of knowing if he had been standing there for some time, or if he was just arriving. Either way, she trod on his toes.

"Oh. Oh, I am sorry, my lord." Sibyl hurriedly stepped back

and bumped her elbow against the jamb. She had rather hoped to avoid him for the rest of the afternoon, or at least to not speak to him. He had not looked happy earlier about having been called a dragon, even less so when he had been forced to see Aunt Alfie released from the closet. "I was not watching where I was going." She edged along the wall, determined not to bump him again as she made her mortified way off.

"No matter." He stepped back as well, no doubt in self-protection. "You have had enough of darts?"

"I was not participating. . . ." She noted that he looked relieved. "And it is not a sport for spectators."

"No, I don't suppose it is." He gazed through the open door. "Who is winning?"

"Lady Theresa."

"Of course. Quite an accomplished young lady."

Sibyl followed his line of vision. The very accomplished young lady was looking particularly stunning that day, her pale gold dress a perfect foil for her flaming hair and creamy skin. At the moment, she was waiting her turn, sliding the feathered end of a dart absently along the edge of her bodice. She had abandoned her filmy shawl sometime past, nonchalantly draping it over the mounted fox in the corner. The creature seemed to be snarling less than usual. In fact, it looked ready to drop onto its stuffed haunches, roll its glass eyes in ecstasy, and beg.

Tarquin's own eyes had gone slightly glassy and Sibyl very nearly decided to have a go with a dart after all. The fact remained, however, that she might do injury to someone if she threw one, and attempting to duplicate Tess's enticing little motion would only send her into a ticklish fit of the giggles.

She scooted another several steps, hoping Tarquin would not notice her leaving. His eyes were on Miss Vaer now as she made a toss and laughed happily at the result. Elspeth really was a beautiful creature when she smiled. Sibyl decided Tarquin wouldn't notice if a herd of elephants went tromping down the hall. Abandoning subtlety, she plodded away.

"Sibyl." His voice stopped her before she had gone more than a few yards.

"Yes, my lord?" She turned to see that he had followed her.

"I . . ." A thunderclap rattled the mullioned windows at the end of the hall. "God, I am tired of this storm."

"It will end sooner or later."

Tarquin ran one hand through his hair, making one black lock stand quite upright. The gesture—and the result—made Sibyl's heart do a little skip in her chest. If there was one thing more appealing than Tarquin Rome at his dignified best, it was Tarquin Rome slightly rumpled.

He promptly ran his palm over the crown of his head, smoothing his hair into customary order. "It was not supposed to rain. The almanac said . . . Ah, bother it. Mother Nature never had to host a house party."

Sibyl liked rain. She didn't think this was the best time to admit it, however. "It does put a damper on a party. But I suppose it also gives us all a chance to get better acquainted. Characters are never so well exhibited as during a long storm."

She was sorry he had not been in the room when Elspeth and Caroline had had a bit of a tiff over who ought to fetch Lord MacGregor's darts from the board. Neither girl was quite so beautiful when jostling and arguing.

Both were back to their charming, exquisite selves now.

Tarquin was glowering at the rain-spattered window. He looked absolutely beautiful regardless of the situation. Sibyl sighed. "At least you do not have to worry about the moat flooding," she offered.

"No," he replied distractedly. "No, I don't have to worry about that."

"Well, then, I'll just be on my way. . . ."

"Sibyl."

"Yes, my lord?"

"Do you think me rigid?"

He certainly appeared so, standing with his chin up and shoulders straight. "I . . ."

"You do. You think me incapable of flexible thoughts and whimsical actions."

"I . . ."

"Rubbish. I can be as outrageous as the next man. I simply choose not to be. Well, don't let me detain you. I believe I will go play darts."

Mystified, Sibyl watched him stroll into the room. No, she did not think of him as an outrageous man, nor did she think he had any aspirations toward outrageousness. He would certainly get a response, however, should he greet his Graces with his left hand where it presently was.

Sibyl couldn't help herself. She felt marginally better about her own disastrous place in the party, knowing the Earl of Hythe had a case of fleas.

8

M ISS VAER APPEARED to be in some physical distress. Her
feet, as she trod the garden path, remained rather close
together with each step, her arms were close to her sides, and
her mouth was pinched into a tight line. Tarquin, much as he
hated to even contemplate such matters as they related to a
lady, was fast coming to the conclusion that she was suffering
from an intestinal ailment. During his much younger years, he
had been known to move just as she was. It was always in
polite company. And always accompanied by a silent plea to
his body not to embarrass him.

He had no idea how to broach the subject. Deciding to heed
MacGregor's advice, he'd brought Miss Vaer out into the gardens as a means to see how they suited. He had wanted to
speak with her away from the party, to discover what went on
inside that pretty head. He had hoped they would *talk*. Instead,
for the past few minutes, he had talked. Miss Vaer, eyes darting furtively from side to side, had done little more than nod,
hum in response to his comments, and giggle nervously at his
lame wit.

The rain had stopped abruptly during luncheon, leaving the
grounds green—where they were not abundantly muddy—and
bursting with life. Tarquin had hoped to walk his companion
through the leafy paths to his mother's rose garden. That, he'd
thought, would be the perfect setting for a tête-à-tête with a
lovely young woman. Women liked roses.

Now he had his doubts as to whether they would make it that
far. Miss Vaer had certainly accepted his invitation to walk
eagerly enough. Now he had the strong impression that the

lady wanted nothing more than to be escorted back to the house immediately.

"Er . . . Miss Vaer?"

"Yes, my lord?" She flinched as they passed a lilac bush and bumped into his elbow. "Oh, pardon me."

"It's quite all right. I . . . are you well, Miss Vaer? You seem a bit . . . pale."

She was not especially pale. In fact, her cheeks bore a distinct flush. But decorum prevented him from using another word.

"Perfectly well, sir." She gave him a strained smile. "Exceedingly well, in fact. Thank you."

Tarquin was ready to ignore her demurral and return her to the house. It had been difficult to get her away from the rest of the party, however, with her two friends never more than a step away, and he was determined to make use of the time. He gently guided her onto the narrow south path. She bounced off his side again, nearly pushing him into the encroaching arms of some flowerless bush.

"Do you care for gardening, Miss Vaer?" he asked, willing to try even the most inane conversation.

Her eyes darted over the vast expanse of the castle's rear gardens. "Oh, I adore it, my lord! Positively . . . adore it."

"Well . . . er, splendid."

"Oh, yes. Adore."

"Shrubberies? Herbs? Perennials?" He scoured his memory for any of the names his mother had babbled at him over the years. "Bipedals?" No, he thought. That was biology, not botany. The word for which he was searching would be some-thing-*petals*. He wondered distractedly if the cursed monkey qualified as a bipedal and whether he could see the flea-bitten beast strung up by its opposable thumbs.

"Most certainly bipedals!" Miss Vaer squeaked, interrupting his pleasant contemplations. "My very favorite!"

"I see."

"Such colors, such fragrance, such . . ."

Utter rot. "Do you spend much time in the garden, Miss Vaer?"

She twitched. "As much as I possibly can, my lord. Why,

hours on end, month after month." Tarquin deftly guided her around a large puddle left in the gravel path. "Though perhaps not when it is so . . . damp."

They were approaching the roses now. His basic disinterest in all things floral could not prevent Tarquin from smiling at the sight. Even now, on a cool September afternoon, there was a profusion of blooms. Such color, from the most translucent cream to the deepest red. Such fragrance, a combination of delightful perfumes.

Miss Vaer's eyes were fixed firmly on her feet. Her nose twitched. "Shall we sit?"

Her head shot up, panic blazing from the emerald eyes. *"Sit?"*

"There are several benches available nearby. I trust the gardeners were by earlier to dry them off. We could rest on one for a bit. Unless, of course, you would rather return to the house."

"Oh. Oh, no. Not at all. I should not care to return . . . Benches, you say, sir?"

They rounded a corner in the path. As promised, a stone bench stood among the roses. It looked dry. Tarquin ran a hand over the surface. It was cold, but not damp enough to signify. He gestured to Miss Vaer to be seated. She glanced dubiously at the stone, then gingerly lowered herself onto it. It occurred to Tarquin as he sat beside her that perhaps, in her state, she would prefer to continue walking. Unfortunately, he had no idea how to ask.

"Are you comfortable, Miss Vaer?"

"Oh. Oh, yes. Quite comfortable. Thank you."

Her expression belied her words. She looked as if she had just settled her posterior on a nail.

"Are you certain? We could stroll to the park—"

"No!" She bit her lip and said, more gently, "This is perfectly . . . delightful. Right here."

"Well. Good. Splendid." Tarquin ignored her faint wriggling, and looked away as she tugged discreetly at her pale skirts. "I . . . er . . . I hope you are enjoying your sojourn at Rome Castle."

"Immensely, my lord. Thank you."

"It can be a beast of a place in poor weather. Modernization has its limits in a four-hundred-year-old castle."

"Yes, I daresay it does."

Tarquin cleared his throat and stared at the sky. "I fear the rain has lessened the number of available entertainments."

"Lessened? Oh, no. Well, perhaps it is as you say. Yes."

"I had thought to arrange an excursion to some local ruins today. Pity there will be too much mud."

"Yes, indeed. A pity."

Tarquin waited for her to offer her own banal topic of conversation. And waited. He prided himself on being a patient man. He also had confidence in his ability to blather away as well as anyone. He did not care for blathering, however, and felt faint annoyance prickling like a rash at the back of his neck. It was going to be extremely difficult to determine whether he liked Miss Vaer enough to marry her if she refused to carry on any sort of interesting conversation.

He had no idea what sort of girl she really was. Twitchy, he decided, but perhaps that was only a circumstantial trait. She clearly did not care for gardening. Neither did he, to be honest, but he liked his gardens and his grounds. They made for a very nice alternative to the pleasures of his library. Rome Castle was a haven, his frequent respite from the trials and chaos of Town.

"Do you spend much time in the country, Miss Vaer?"

"Not a great deal, my lord." She was now peering intently at her feet. "Mama keeps the London house open year-round."

"You prefer the city, then."

She darted a quick glance at him. He kept his face impassive. "I . . . er . . . I am equally happy in both. There is so much more society to be found in Town, but the country is so . . . restful."

Tarquin nodded approvingly. Yes, the country was restful. He enjoyed his town house and his clubs, strolls along the Serpentine, and soirees with London's literati and Classical scholars. But he was most content here, with his estate and his books. One could relax in the country, take deep breaths, and move with leisure.

"Oh. Oh, dear!"

He was nearly jostled from his seat when Miss Vaer sprang

91

to her feet and all but leapt atop the bench. She stood there, face white, pale hands gripping her skirts well above her ankles.

"My dear, whatever is the matter?"

She did not answer, but instead released the muslin long enough to point one trembling finger at the ground near his feet. Tarquin glanced down, half expecting to see some large, hairy rodent. There was nothing there.

"Miss Vaer, I am afraid I do not—"

"There! Oh, dear heavens. *Dozens* of them! *Hundreds!*"

He looked again. Then he bent over and examined the ground carefully. "I still do not . . . Ah. They are merely earthworms, nothing to be feared."

"Where did they come from?"

"The earth," Tarquin replied dryly. "The rain flushes the smaller ones to the surface."

"Well, get them away! Stomp on them. Anything!"

He glanced over the path. Now that he was looking, he could see hundreds of the little worms, wriggling among the gravel. They were not attractive creatures, certainly, but he could not understand how they could cause such hysteria. With neither teeth nor legs, they were surpassed in harmlessness only by rocks. And rocks, of course, could be thrown.

So could worms, he recalled. To be fair, he did not think ten-year-old Sibyl had meant to shower him with the things. She had merely taken exception to his using them for fish bait and had attempted to set them free. He had attempted to stop her and had ended up with earthworms wriggling in his hair and collar. It really had not been Sibyl's fault that he, in his fumbling to rid himself of the worms, had tripped over his fishing pole and ended up going bottomfirst into the stream. Nor could he blame her for the fact that, as he tried to climb from the water, his boot had skidded on a slippery rock and he had gone headfirst into the bank. He still had the scar beneath his chin.

Sibyl, for all her harebrained schemes and pesty shadowing, had never gone into hysterics over anything, least of all an earthworm.

"There are too many for me to deal with, Miss Vaer. Beyond that, they are beneficial for the earth. If I were to have them eliminated, the soil would suffer. They are," he added, "rather more important to my land than we are."

"Well." She swung her elegant head from side to side, studying the ground. "I hate them. They are filthy and slimy and . . . What are you doing?"

Tarquin had lifted one worm and now held it aloft. "Ugly, yes, but hardly—"

Miss Vaer's shriek sent a family of blackbirds flapping out of a nearby pear tree. It sent the fine hairs rising at Tarquin's nape. "I cannot abide it! I cannot abide the rain and the dirt and mud and the . . . the . . . wildlife! I detest walking on paths where there is always some . . . some . . . bush reaching out to ruin one's dress! I loathe the country!" With that, she sprang from the bench. Panting, she rounded on Tarquin. "I am going inside, my lord!"

He hurriedly got to his feet. "Of course. I will escort—"

"No!"

Before Tarquin could take two steps, she took a last, horrified look at him, then was haring up the path and away, skirts nearly at her knees. Dumbfounded, he looked at his hand. He was still holding the worm.

"Well, for God's sake," he muttered, and tossed the thing aside.

Propriety would have had him trotting after the girl. Ordinarily, he would have done the proper thing in an instant. This time, however, he opted instead for preference and started strolling back to the house. Miss Vaer was undoubtedly already there, and he had neither the desire to run, nor to experience more of her hysterics.

Pity, he mused, that his impressions of the young lady had been so faulty. He had seen something solid in her, something calm and terrestrial. Like Demeter, the goddess of fertility, perhaps. He wasn't certain whom or what precisely she brought to mind now. The round eyes, white plumage, and screeching rather made him think of a barn owl. She ought to like worms very well indeed.

"Good Lord," he grumbled to himself. Along with his ears and bones, his brain had clearly been rattled in the past several days. There was no other excuse for the appallingly fanciful thoughts that kept drifting into his head. He had neither the time nor the inclination to be fanciful. He was a serious man, with serious matters to attend.

He was not ready to abandon Miss Vaer as a possible wife just yet. The hysterics were not a good sign, nor was the aversion to the country. In fact, he was of the rising opinion that she would not suit him at all. But he was ready to give her the benefit of the doubt—this once. A great many ladies did not care for dirt and damp; he expected none liked earthworms. Except Sibyl.

He glanced up at the sound of heels crunching over the gravel path. She had regretted her behavior, he decided, and was coming back to apologize. She would certainly have to prove herself after the incident, but if she was willing . . .

It was not Miss Vaer who came striding around the hedge corner, arms swinging pluckily, but the Savior of Things Crawly herself. Unlike the fair trio in their fragile and floaty apparel, Sibyl was garbed this afternoon in a sturdy dress and half-boots. The clear air had brought a brightness to her eyes and soft flush to her cheeks. Several ash-brown curls had come loose to frame her face. She looked, Tarquin decided, like a healthy, hearty country girl. She looked very well indeed.

She came to an abrupt halt when she spied him coming toward her. "Ah. I had wondered if you were about."

"Did you wish to speak to me?"

"No. No, I didn't." She tilted her head and regarded him thoughtfully. "In fact, I decided yesterday that it might be best if I were to avoid you entirely. But things have a way of changing, don't they?"

They certainly did. Had Tarquin possessed a fanciful nature, he would have thought there was some enchantment at work. As it was, he merely credited the fact that he was glad to see Sibyl to the fact that she neither shrieked nor twitched. "Why did you intend to avoid me?"

She gently pushed a tangle of worms to the side of the path with her toe. "I had grown tired of being scolded, actually. Not that you haven't had reason to be irritable lately—this party has been trying, I'm sure—but one does weary of being held responsible for things one did not do."

It was the second time in as many days that someone had criticized him for perfectly understandable behavior. Sibyl was slightly more subtle than his mother, but the message was equally clear. Tarquin opened his mouth to retort, then thought better of it. For once, Sibyl was quite right. She had taken the brunt of much of his anger and, as far as he could ascertain, deserved none of it.

"I am sorry," he said, sighing. "It has been a damnable few days."

"Mmm. Yes. Do you want to talk about it?"

He was astonished to find that he did. "Would you care to walk with me?"

She glanced back toward the house, brows raised. "Now? I would think you'd want to go after Miss Vaer."

"You passed her, I take it."

"Well, I think it would be more accurate to say that she passed me—at something near a dead run."

Sibyl had been quite startled to see the ever decorous Elspeth Vaer thundering up the garden path, eyes wild and skirts pulled up to an indecent level. The girl had not said a word, but continued past as if Sibyl were not there at all.

She had slipped out of the house not for the fresh air, as she'd explained to her aunt and hostess, but because she'd seen Tarquin and Elspeth from the drawing room window. Her best intentions to stay out of his way had vanished with a flash. No matter how heartily she scolded herself, and she found she was scolding herself as much as Tarquin was, she simply couldn't sit back and silently watch him choose Elspeth Vaer.

She'd had no idea what she would do if she encountered the pair in any sort of loverlike embrace. Shriek, most likely. But the possibility had become moot when she'd been all but bowled over by the galloping Miss Vaer.

"Whatever happened, my lord?" It was an overly bold question, but the worst he could do was snap at her for insolence. She was used to him snapping at her for other things; she would survive.

"I did not attempt to ravish her"—he did snap "in case that is what you imagined."

She had, in fact, imagined just that. She had abandoned the

thought immediately. The image of Tarquin as a ravening Lothario had been too absurd—if rather lovely in that moment when she had mentally substituted herself for Miss Vaer.

"Nothing quite so dramatic," she lied. "But I daresay the lovely Elspeth hasn't moved so quickly in her life."

The second thought had been more alarming than the first. Sibyl could only imagine Miss Vaer running like that for one reason: to announce her betrothal. Of course, most girls wouldn't look quite so wild after a proposal from the Earl of Hythe. But then, delighted hysteria could perhaps be mistaken for terror. . . .

"Worms."

"I beg your pardon?"

"Worms," Tarquin repeated grimly. This time, when he thrust his hands through his hair, he did not hasten to repair the damage. "She does not like worms."

So there had been no proposal. Sibyl's heart soared. "Well, now you know not to offer them again," she said blithely. And promptly bit her tongue. She did not want Tarquin offering Miss Vaer *anything*. Except perhaps worms, she decided.

"Very amusing, Sibyl."

"I am sorry, my lord. It is simply that the idea struck me as being so . . . so . . ."

"Amusing?" he offered.

"Yes, I suppose. Oh, well, no. Not precisely."

As she watched, cursing her loose lips, his twitched into a fleeting smile. "Very well, it was amusing." As she grinned back, his brows drew together in a fierce line. "But infernally galling. For God's sake, I do not want things to be amusing. I want them to be simple, sensible, and serious!"

"Yes, I know you do." Lamenting the lost moment, she gestured to the path leading toward the knot garden. "Shall we walk?"

"I would like that."

When Tarquin offered his arm, Sibyl hurried to accept it. It was no more than a polite gesture on his part, she knew, but she wasn't about to pass up the opportunity. The fine wool of his coat was soft under her fingers and she was convinced she could feel the warmth and strength of his lean muscles through the fabric.

She had not felt quite so content in his presence since the night some eight years back when she had concealed herself behind the sofa in his library and waited for him to arrive. He had, eventually, and she had spent a precious hour listening to the gentle rustling of manuscript pages, the clinking of decanter against bottle, smelling the faint aroma of his muted cologne.

It would have been a perfect, if not particularly social, interlude had she not fallen asleep. Even that wouldn't have been so bad had she not rolled over some time later. Her outflung arm had knocked into the little side table, upsetting the fragile, carved wood globe there. The thing had bounced once on the carpet before reaching the hard floor and breaking into pieces. Tarquin had bellowed, then promptly gotten a nasty splinter in his thumb when he picked up the Asian continent. Sibyl had crept off to her chamber in disgrace.

Now, walking peaceably at his side, she shoved the memory from her mind. "I am happy to listen if you wish to speak of these past days."

"Hmm? Ah, no. I don't think so. It is simply that *nothing* has gone as expected."

"I see."

Tarquin waved his free hand impatiently. "I really have no need to speak of it."

"Fine," Sibyl said quietly. "As you wish."

"You know, I cannot fathom what has gone awry, precisely. Other than the monkey and the painting and your aunt-in-the-closet, of course."

"Of course," Sibyl murmured, hoping he wouldn't choose to harp on those particular items.

"All I want is a nice, comfortable life. Seems reasonable enough to me."

"Entirely reasonable."

"And there is no reason I shouldn't be able to orchestrate it."

"None at all," she agreed.

"I planned so carefully. Of course, I should have known better than to rely on the almanac. It is notoriously faulty."

"Notoriously."

Tarquin muttered something inaudible. Sibyl might have thought it a curse. But the Earl of Hythe never cursed. "I really don't need to talk about it. Whining . . ." He paused and muttered something else. Sibyl thought it sounded suspiciously like *bloody itching*. "Whining serves no purpose."

"You were not whining."

"Wasn't I?" He looked pleased for a moment. "Complaining, then. I don't need to do that, either."

"Complaining can be a relief," Sibyl replied. God only knew how often she had lamented her lack of Cameron Dash into her pillow. "I don't mind listening. Truly."

"Well, I mind. We'll talk of something else." They had rounded the knot garden now and were approaching the little carp pool. The house rose proudly above the four tiers of stone steps. Tarquin's eyes drifted along the rows of sparkling windows. "Tell me what you think of Miss Reynolds."

Sibyl's heart, which had grown so light in the last few minutes, plummeted. "She is very lovely." *And rather stupid.* A truly adventurous spirit wouldn't have hesitated to express that opinion. Sibyl, however, was far better at answering direct questions with the response desired.

"Yes, she is, isn't she?"

She rarely bothered to answer rhetorical questions at all.

"Graceful, soft-spoken, accomplished," Tarquin continued.

Flighty, Sibyl added silently and kicked at a loose stone. She had not quite envisioned this conversation when she offered to listen. It was decidedly difficult to offer a generous ear when the topic was so painful. So, before Tarquin could launch into a rhapsody on the lovely, graceful, stupid Caroline's further charms, she said, "Tell me about the Montefiore."

"Incomparable," he murmured. "A treasure for any man's home. Such a beautiful creation is priceless and must be revered."

"The Montefiore," Sibyl insisted irritably. She was past tired of Caroline Reynolds.

"Of course the Montefiore. It is an extraordinary work."

Only Tarquin, Sibyl thought with some amusement and great pleasure, her annoyance gone, would speak of a book as most men would a woman. "You are very proud of it."

98

"Proud?" He narrowed his eyes thoughtfully. "It isn't my achievement to be proud of. It is, I suppose, my honor to have it."

"Honor," Sibyl whispered.

"Oh, the thrill of possession is tremendous, I assure you. But there is more than that in the value of the objects I collect. There is beauty—in both the ornate and the simple. There is the education to be found in workmanship and content. There is the pleasure in knowing I will be leaving something precious behind for future generations, making one little step toward immortality . . ."

"Go on," she urged, charmed.

He shrugged. "The Montefiore is a work of art. The illustrations are remarkable, the writing superb." He stopped walking then, pulling Sibyl to a halt. "But you already know that, don't you?"

"Yes, I do."

"And had the gall to demand it as payment for . . . what was it? Some predictions? You must be very certain of your skill as a prognosticator."

"An unwelcome achievement to be proud of," she said grimly.

"Perhaps. So, what did you predict for me, Sibyl?"

"Do I get the Montefiore?" she shot back.

To her surprise, Tarquin's face creased into a stunning smile. "Heaven help us if you ever take up dealing on the 'Change, my dear. You know exactly what you are getting, yet demand blind payment." He patted the hand she had curved around his arm. "No, you do not get the Montefiore, and I suppose I'll never know if my fate is to end up headfirst in the Thames or driving camels in the Sahara."

" 'Tis goats in the Alps, actually."

He laughed. It was, Sibyl thought, as glorious a sound as musical Alpine yodeling. She had never heard Alpine yodeling, of course, but she could imagine. "So, tell me how you came to learn of the Montefiore, Sibyl. It is hardly a common book."

"An uncle told me all about it."

"A Cameron?"

She smiled at his incredulous expression. "Camerons do read occasionally, my lord, when taking a respite from the

99

grand life of Adventure. But no, as it happens, I am speaking of an honorary uncle. When I was younger, he used to entertain me with detailed descriptions of rare books."

"Good Lord. That must have been terribly dull fare for a Cameron child."

"Sarcasm doesn't suit you, my lord." Sibyl closed her eyes for a moment, recalling the hours she had spent at Uncle Percy's knee, listening as he methodically and reverently catalogued the contents of Oxford's rare book archives. "'The world's finest books are more beautiful than nature itself,'" she quoted from memory, adding wistfully, "true beauty isn't always found in the obvious places."

"You always had a good head," Tarquin announced. Sibyl blinked, surprised and gratified by the rare compliment. "On those very few occasions when you chose to use it."

"You are too gracious, my lord."

"Sarcasm doesn't suit you, Sibyl, any more than a habitual lack of sense. But, as I said, you are a perceptive creature." His eyes drifted to the house once more. "So, tell me what you think of Lady Theresa."

"She is very lovely," Sibyl replied dully. Men, she reminded herself, could always be counted upon to find beauty in the most obvious faces.

9

"DON'T BE SUCH a goosecap, Regina!" Lady Vaer snapped. "Of course she did not make a fuss over nothing. There were *worms*!"

"Well, my Tess would not be frightened off by something so piddling as a worm," Lady Broadford huffed. "Why, she is never so missish as to behave in a ridiculous manner because of a mere insect."

Lady Theresa glanced up from the brightly bound novel she held. "Not a mere insect, surely, Mama," she remarked languidly, "but I have been induced to flight by the occasional spider."

"Oh, hush!" her mother hissed.

"Can't be certain of it," George Reynolds drawled, apparently having been roused from his habitual stupor on the settee, "but I believe spiders ain't insects."

"Well, what are they, then?" Lady Broadford demanded.

"Spiders" was his pithy response. He leaned back again and closed his eyes.

"Young men today!" Lady Vaer passed a trembling hand over her brow. "No manners whatsoever."

Lady Reynolds glared.

In the doorway, Tarquin sighed. By all appearances, the comradely atmosphere had soured a bit. He had delayed his entrance into the drawing room as long as possible. For the first time in his life, he had been deliberately, discourteously late. He had felt rather good, in fact, striding those last, tardy yards across the Hall. He was planning on a few glasses of wine, a superb meal, and easy conversation with pleasant company.

What he'd gotten, it seemed, was a room full of squabbling guests.

When Vaer, red-nosed and sharp-eyed, spied him and snapped, "Worms, sir!" Tarquin actually considered backing out the door and sneaking into the kitchens.

His mother halted him before he could make an escape. Piercing him with a withering gaze that clearly said she'd read his intentions, she announced, "Good evening, my dear. How nice of you to join us."

He resisted the urge to scuff his feet against the carpet. "My apologies to all. I was . . . delayed."

"Of course you were. Well, as it happens, so is supper. Do come in and sit." She subtly pointed her little chin at the chair next to Miss Vaer's. He subtly wandered in the other direction.

The Ladies Vaer and Broadford were seated at opposite ends of one sofa, eyeing each other fishily. Lady Reynolds occupied a nearby chair, resembling a pale, pinched little storm cloud. The rest of the party was arranged about the room, none looking particularly cheerful.

Miss Vaer spared him a brief, wounded glance and a faint sniff. Sibyl alone offered him a fleeting smile. She made a small gesture toward the seat beside her, but he declined with a quick shake of his head. She was sitting altogether too close to the sulking Elspeth.

Bland-faced, MacGregor was leaning against the large pianoforte. Julius, settled on the bench, was plunking rhythmically at the lower keys. It was a dismal, depressing sound, and Tarquin wondered just how long he had been vexing the group with it. Now, apparently in his brother's honor, the sod began picking out a tune from Handel's *Messiah*.

"All they that see him, laugh him to scorn," he sang in his subdued but perfectly audible tenor. Tarquin cursed himself for insisting that his brother practice his music more.

He managed to maintain his composure until Julius, having tired of Handel, launched into the "Lacrimosa" from Mozart's *Requiem Mass*. Enough was enough. Tarquin strolled over to the pianoforte and closed the lid with a snap, forcing Julius to move his fingers in a hurry.

"Really, Tarquin," their mother announced, "I was enjoying that."

Julius's hands snaked back toward the instrument.

"Ah, sorry," Tarquin remarked smoothly, propping his hip against the lid to keep it closed, "but I was finding it a bit too grim for such a pleasant evening."

"Well, then, perhaps you will grace us with something more lively, dearest."

"Perhaps a madrigal," Lady Leverham said hopefully. Then, "No, that will not do, will it? One sings a madrigal; one does not play it. Perhaps a nice hymn?"

"Or some Mozart." His mother accompanied the suggestion with her best, cool-eyed smile. "I should very much like to hear you play some Mozart."

Tarquin would just as soon have eaten worms.

"Oh, do!" Miss Reynolds urged. "We shall all be ever so pleased to hear you!"

The Vaers looked skeptical; the Broadfords disinterested. Julius was already springing to his feet. "Yes, do, old man. We've plenty of Mozart here." He riffled the music sheets on the stand. "But of course, you always did prefer Bach. Just spare us the fugues, if you please."

Tarquin decided he could either indulge in a good, churlish tantrum or play. He lowered himself to the bench. The temptation to crawl his way through a fugue was strong, but he resisted it. A quick-tempoed *presto*, perhaps. The fourth Brandenburg Concerto would do nicely. Tarquin was confident he could play it with no concentration whatsoever.

One advantage to the placement of the pianoforte was the ease with which he could see the rest of the room. Sibyl happened to be directly in his line of vision. So, as his fingers danced through the familiar notes, he watched her.

She was wearing yellow, a silly, frothy dress that was several years out of fashion and made her resemble a gorse blossom. Or a tormentil, he amended, rather pleased with himself for having recalled that piece of botanical minutiae from his mother's lectures. She had forever been pointing out various plants in the garden. He had always pretended to listen. Tormentil had caught his attention, probably because the name had seemed so beautifully apt to the lengthy discourse that had preceded the identification. What a pity, he thought, that he had not seen any of the creeping plants earlier that day. It would have made for a delightful topic of conversation with Miss Vaer.

To be fair, he had to admit that Sibyl was not nearly so much of a torment as she'd been in the past. She had been a calm, humorous companion that afternoon. In fact, she'd turned into an amazingly tolerable young woman all around. And, if one simply noticed the color of the dress rather than the style, and how it gave her skin a faint golden glow, an almost pretty one as well.

She looked up, met his gaze. His fingers faltered. When Sibyl Cameron fixed a man with those extraordinary, velvet-brown eyes, he completely forgot that she was not beautiful. As Tarquin fumbled for the next chord, he decided that, should a man be caught unawares by those eyes, he might damn well forget his own name.

It was no use. He had no idea where he had been in the movement before hands and brain had gone in separate directions. He gave a few more tentative pokes at the keys, then gave it up. Julius was back in an instant, before the scattering of excruciatingly polite applause could falter and end.

"Try this," he suggested, drawing a single sheet from the stand. "Bit more recent than Herr Johann, but slightly reminiscent, in my opinion. Delightful tune."

It certainly appeared simple enough. Determined to keep control of his hands and eyes, Tarquin launched into the piece. It was bold, rollicking, and short. He reached the end in a minute. There was no second sheet. There was no applause, either.

"What in God's name is this?" he demanded.

Julius grinned. "Oh, something a chap in my regiment wrote. Jolly, isn't it? Better with the words. Play it again, old trout."

"No."

"Now, Tarquin, be a good fellow and humor me. Then you may go back to Bach."

Tarquin had a feeling he would regret it, but he started the piece again.

"When I arrived in London Town," Julius sang, *"I was poor and I was humble. I could not get a horse to rise, nor a pretty lass to tumble."* Tarquin glanced up sharply. His brother nodded for him to continue. *"My pockets now are filled with gold, and every day I bless my luck. I have a stable, grand and full, and many a lovely lass to—"*

"Julius!" Tarquin bellowed, turning the last chord into a loud clash of notes.

"There are three more verses."

"No. There are not." Tarquin seized a random piece from the stand and started playing without much enthusiasm. Julius, grinning broadly, strutted away.

The sounds of Mozart drifted through the room. Delighted, Sibyl watched Tarquin's long, blunt-tipped fingers sliding across the keys. This was a side of him she had never seen: the one who seemed so easy, so comfortable in front of the pianoforte. He was accomplished, too. She didn't know much of this Bach, but the piece Tarquin had chosen had been beautiful and, until he'd faltered, most impressive.

"Do you play, Miss Cameron?"

Sibyl was forced to scoot to the edge of the settee when Caroline Reynolds decided to take over the central cushion where she had been sitting. It only took a moment to comprehend why. The position put the other girl directly in Tarquin's line of vision.

"Play at what?" Sibyl returned dryly. "I have never been much for parlor games."

"No, silly. I meant the pianoforte."

"Did you? Fancy that." She tugged the edge of her skirt from beneath the other girl. "No, I do not."

"The harp, then."

"Not that, either."

"Surely you must play some instrument."

Sibyl allowed herself a quiet sigh. She'd had far too many of these conversations with far too many young ladies just like Caroline Reynolds. "I do not. Nor do I sing." Unless, she amended, she wanted to clear a room. Perhaps she ought to try a madrigal now. "I enjoy music a great deal, but have no skill at it."

105

"None whatsoever?" Caroline blinked enormous, pale eyes and fluttered her hands in apparent dismay.

"None whatsoever."

"Well, goodness. What do you *do* with yourself?"

"Do you draw?" Elspeth Vaer had perked up slightly and was now leaning into the conversation. "I have seen you with paper and drawing pencil."

"I draw. A little." Trees, mostly, though leaves tended to defeat her.

"Paint?" Elspeth queried.

"Not often." Sibyl had long since abandoned paints. She was more likely to end up wearing them than getting them properly on the paper.

"Well, goodness," Caroline repeated. "Have you no skills?"

Sibyl was tempted to reply that she mixed a very good poison. But that wasn't true, either.

"Miss Cameron is a bruising rider. Takes jumps like no other woman."

She had not seen Julius approach, and gave him a grateful smile. She was a decent rider, to be sure, but he could not have known that. On the one occasion when they had ridden together, he had spent most of the time carefully extricating her from a holly shrub. She had been haring after Tarquin, who was truly a bruising rider. Julius had not been altogether lying, however. She had taken the jump like no other woman: head-first without her mount, right into the holly.

"Our Sibyl is a fine poet, too." MacGregor had left his position at the pianoforte and now propped a hip against the back of the settee. "Her verses have moved me."

Right out of the room, Sibyl added. She had been trying her hand at composing epic verse like Great-great-great-grandfather Kirkcormac Cameron. Tarquin had promptly closeted himself in the library. MacGregor, at Rome Castle for a visit, had been polite enough to listen through the first stanza of her poem about Culloden Field. He had hurriedly excused himself before she could launch into the second.

"*The Brave-hearted Jacobite Laddie* was your favorite, wasn't it?" she asked with an impish smile. "I do believe I could recite a stanza . . . or two for you now."

He grinned back.

"I do not much care for reading poetry. . . ." Caroline announced, batting her lashes at MacGregor.

"No?" Sibyl murmured. "Fancy that."

". . . but I am never averse to having a gentleman read it *to* me."

MacGregor inclined his head politely. "We take it as our duty to vanquish the difficult words for you, my dear. Soldiers of the page."

"Oh, I do like soldiers," Caroline breathed. How very nice it must be, Sibyl mused, to be wholly unaware when one had just been insulted. "Were you on the Peninsula, my lord?"

"I consider the Sound of Jura to be my very own peninsular domain, Miss Reynolds."

"Are there many French there?"

"Not a one," he replied solemnly. "I take it upon myself to keep the area free of them. Ask Miss Cameron. She will confirm what I say."

Caroline blinked at Sibyl. "You have been to Jura?"

"I have indeed. Many times. And, as Lord MacGregor asserts, a lady need not fear for her safety there."

There was a long pause as Caroline digested the information. Then she lifted her little chin into the air. "Well. Have you been to Paris?" she demanded.

"No," Sibyl confessed. "I have not."

"I have. Mama and Papa took me twice. Of course, I have not been recently, but I daresay I shall return soon enough now that Napoleon has been routed. French fashion," she said with an arch look at Sibyl's dress, "is absolutely necessary for any young lady of style and intelligence."

Sibyl glanced down at the sunshine-yellow muslin. She was not particularly fond of the dress. The ruffles at the bodice and hem made her feel rather like an oversized daffodil. It had looked so charming in the modiste's book. She could never quite understand why dresses always seemed to change their own appearance between the fashion plate and her possession.

She noticed that the music had stopped. She could not recall having heard it end and glanced at Tarquin. He was still seated on the bench, elbows resting on the closed pianoforte lid. He met her gaze and gave her a faint smile. Humiliated that he had quite probably heard the entire, dismal exchange, she flushed and looked away.

Some things never changed. She always appeared at her very worst in Tarquin's presence.

Caroline, too, had noticed the end of the music. Abandoning the lesser company, she rose and fluttered over to the pianoforte. "Do you know any duets, my lord?" she asked sweetly. Sibyl sighed.

Julius took her place on the settee. "I know as a fact that you have never left the Isles, Sibby. So where is this Jura? It certainly is not Portugal."

"No," Sibyl replied with a wry smile. "It is not Portugal. The Sound of Jura is on the western coast of Scotland."

"Well, good on the pair of you!" He gave MacGregor a smart salute. "Wonder if old Tarquin knows that."

Caroline was chattering away. The word "Jura" carried clearly. Yes, Sibyl decided, Tarquin probably knew exactly where it was. But with the lovely Miss Reynolds smiling and simpering mere inches from his side, he probably didn't care.

Tarquin retreated to the library after everyone else had taken themselves up to bed. He was exhausted and slightly irritable after an evening of entertaining his guests, but was not yet ready to retire. He had neglected his correspondence shamefully during the past several days. Now would be as good a time as any to see to the matter. He settled himself at his desk, drew the latest letter from his London solicitors from the pile on his desk, and reached into a drawer for a sheet of his crested paper.

He had ignored the faint itching throughout the evening. Now he indulged in a good scratch under his arm. Rather than offering relief, the act simply made him want to scratch harder. And he could feel an insistent prickling under the seat of his breeches. Gritting his teeth, he reached for his pen. Moments later, he was using it to reach a flaming spot beneath his shoulder blade.

"Agh," he grunted, and shifted the quill point to the other side.

This was absurd. He had bathed several times since his last encounter with the monkey, scrubbing each inch of itchy skin. He had seen no fleas on his body. There was, however, a constellation of small red bumps running under his arm, across his chest, and, though he could not see, over his back and posterior.

By now, the tickling had run a distinct pattern from his shoulders to his hips. It was a galling thought, but he was fast becoming convinced that somewhere, somehow, he had picked up a single flea and it was dancing a minuet down his back. He could feel it at the base of his spine, then an inch lower.

"Bloody hell!" he bellowed and, springing to his feet, made a headlong rush for the glass doors.

Moments later he was sprinting his way across the west lawn. Through the small copse of apple trees at the base of the hill, he could see the lily pond glittering in the moonlight. He had not swum there in years, not since he and Julius had splashed there in adolescent abandon. But he was going for a swim now, and nothing short of lightning in his path would stop him.

He tore off his clothing as he reached the copse, piling boots, breeches, and all in an untidy heap. He would give everything a good shake later. For now, all he wanted was to immerse himself from head to toe. Hopping along on one foot as he dragged off his second stocking, heedless of twigs and pebbles underfoot, he headed for the pond's edge and dived.

His belly skidded through the mud at the bottom. The icy temperature of the water took his breath away. But as he surfaced, gasping and shoving a dislodged bulrush from his forehead, he was in ecstasy.

For a good half hour, he wallowed in the cold water. Even after his limbs went numb, he continued diving and splashing, occasionally pausing to float contentedly on his back. In the still moments, he could hear frogs piping in the reeds and remembered why he and Julius had enjoyed the spot so much. They had waited impatiently through long summer afternoons in the schoolroom, then bolted to the pond, returning home hours later with mud between their toes and captive frogs in their shoes.

For a fleeting moment, Tarquin debated going back to the house, rousing his brother, and dragging him back to the pond. Actually, he knew no dragging would be required. Julius had never lost his pleasure in simple, carefree acts. He would be out the door and galloping half-naked down the lawn before Tarquin could finish the invitation.

With a sigh, he flipped onto his stomach and began a lazy crawl back to the bank. He had a house full of guests to entertain on the morrow and a wife to choose. Pleasant as this little interlude had been, it was time to return to sober adulthood.

He climbed from the pond and shivered in the night air. His stocking waved gently from a clump of reeds. He retrieved it and wandered toward the spot where he'd left the rest of his clothing. He dreaded having to don the lot. Perhaps he would make due with only his breeches and shirt. After a thorough shaking, just in case there had been a solitary flea, they would do well enough for the trek back to the house. He was unlikely to run into anyone. Even the staff would have long since vacated the main hall and family rooms.

Single stocking in hand, Tarquin paused beneath a gnarled apple tree. There was nothing beneath it save a half-dozen shriveled apples. He glanced around in confusion. This was the place where he had dropped his clothes. Wasn't it?

He moved to the next tree, and the next. More apples. No clothing. The copse was illuminated by moonlight, well enough that he could see the ground. He wandered among the trees for several minutes, growing more frustrated with each step. One promising mound turned out to be an abandoned badger hole. The next—and Tarquin nearly leapt from his skin at the discovery—turned out to be one of Julius's beagles. The beast must have followed him out of the house. It wriggled at his feet now, occasionally giving a friendly lick at one of his bare knees.

"Sit!" he commanded sharply. The dog sat, thumping at the damp earth with its eager tail.

By this time, Tarquin knew damn well that his clothing was not to be found. Eyeing the dog suspiciously, he demanded, "Was it you?"

The stupid animal wagged its rear end so hard that it toppled over. It promptly rolled onto its back, waved all four paws in the air, and grinned up at him, tongue lolling happily.

"Well, hell." If the dog had, in fact, taken his clothes, it had hidden them so well that not so much as a sleeve had turned up during Tarquin's search. The second possibility, that some non-canine member of the household had removed the items while he swam, was at the same time a great deal more likely and far less tolerable.

Either way, there was nothing to be done but to return to the house. Stark naked. Well, he mused, he did have one stocking. The idea of putting it on one foot was ludicrous. The other option was worse.

Grumbling, cursing each sharp object he stepped on, Tarquin plodded back up the hill. The beagle trotted comfortably at his heels, clearly unconcerned with the fact that it was following a nude, limping, muttering earl. It paused briefly to bark at some invisible animal in the shadows. Tarquin's sharp command silenced the yapping. The last thing he wanted was for the blasted hound to wake the household. As it was, he was counting his lucky stars that all of the lights were out in the front of the house. Chances were good that he could get inside and up to his chamber with no one the wiser for his state of undress.

He shushed the dog again as they went through the front door. Spurred by muffled domestic noises from the back hall, he hastened up the stairs to the first gallery landing. Now there was only another short flight and a length of hall between him and his rooms.

He'd just passed the portrait of Great-grandfather Hildebrand, snug in copious wig, heavy doublet, and ermine-trimmed cloak, his bedchamber door a mere twenty feet away, when he heard the scream. Or shout. It was impossible to tell, as it shattered the night silence, whether it was male or female, or from which room it came.

The origin hardly mattered. The noise did. Tarquin heard the first click of a door handle as he scrambled up the last few steps. It was only when he was standing in the middle of the hallway, with a row of guest-room doors stretching on either side, that he realized he had made a severe tactical error. Had he barreled back down the stairs, rather than up, he could have hidden. As it was, he was trapped. Several yards ahead, a door was swinging open.

10

SIBYL NEARLY SWUNG the door shut again. Prudence had her bracing her hand against the wood in preparation to push. Some far more potent impulse had her gaping, jaw slack, at the very large, very naked man in the hallway.

Tarquin had hurriedly shoved a strip of white cloth across the area where, by all rights, the placket of his breeches should have been. It didn't hide much. With an impressive force of will, Sibyl dragged her eyes upward. She took in an expanse of broad chest, decorated with a fascinating sprinkling of dark hair. Above that, though the temptation to keep examining his torso was strong, she saw a rigid jaw. That was familiar. His jaw was often rigid in her presence.

"For God's sake. Sibyl!"

His eyes, when hers met them, were blazing in his unusually pale face. The message there was as clear as if he'd spoken.

Help.

Several voices were audible from other chambers now. Several feet down the hall, there was the click of a handle. Without thinking, Sibyl pulled her door wide and stepped aside. Tarquin sprang past her, shoving the door closed behind him with a swift kick.

Sibyl counted five before turning. Tarquin had gone all the way to the other side of the room, where he was now crouched behind the bed, visible only from the nose up above the counterpane. A giggle welled in Sibyl's throat, and she struggled to contain it. The situation was not laughable. In fact, it was rather alarming. From the sounds outside the door, most, if not all of the party was gathered in the hall. It would not do at all for

Tarquin to be found in her bedchamber, especially without any clothing.

"What on earth—"

"Shh." He scowled at her. "We must be very quiet."

"We must be very smart," she corrected, and started toward him.

"Stay where you are!" His nose disappeared, leaving only his eyes and the top of his head in view.

She debated telling him that his modesty was far less important than their respective reputations. Dealing with the situation at hand, however, was more important than making a point. "I have to go out there."

"No!"

"Think, my lord. If I do not, someone is bound to come in here to ascertain that I am all right. You may take your chances of remaining concealed if you wish, but . . ."

"Fine," he hissed. "And you may stay out once you leave. Tell your aunt you wish to spend the rest of the night in her chamber."

"She snores," Sibyl informed him tartly.

"Sibyl, for pity's sake!"

"I am not going to spend the night with my aunt. She does snore and, as I believe you have noticed, Galahad has fleas. Don't move. I shall be back as soon as possible."

He popped halfway up in protest. Then, as if only then realizing that he was naked, he dropped back again.

"By the way"—she paused by the door—"did you scream?"

"No, I did not."

"Curious. Very well, then. Be quiet and stay there."

"Sibyl . . ."

Her last view as she slipped from the room was of his eyes glaring fiercely at her over the edge of the bed.

True to her expectation, everyone was in the hall. Lord Broadford, a diverting figure in a garishly striped dressing gown and nightcap, was herding the rest of the party back against the wall. Lady Reynolds was clinging to his arm and wailing about being murdered in her bed. From the look on Lady Broadford's face, Sibyl decided it was a distinct possibility.

The Three Graces were huddled together, looking far too

lovely for anyone dragged out of a sound sleep. Lady Tess, her red hair spilling in fiery abandon over a gauzy white dressing gown, looked rather as if she had been engaged in a less restful activity.

Could Tarquin have been . . . ? Sibyl felt her jaw dropping once again. She knew little of such matters, but had heard enough gossip to know that a man rushing naked down a hallway usually implied an interrupted tryst. It often also implied a possessive husband. Or an irate papa. Lord Broadford, silly nightwear or not, looked fully capable of violence.

But Tarquin was hardly the sort to be caught with a respectable young lady. . . .

He had not been caught. He had, it seemed, gone flying from one young lady's chamber to another's. The very nerve of such an act was shocking. Sibyl had a vision of herself storming back into her room and coshing him over the head with the chamber pot. She knew a prostrate and naked Lord Hythe would be harder to explain than a conscious one, of course. And no one would believe he had been in the process of seducing the plain Miss Cameron. No, the miserable truth would quickly come out and Tarquin would most likely find himself betrothed to the lovely Lady Theresa Wardour before the sun rose.

Quite simply, Sibyl could not bear that thought. She knew very well that Tarquin might end up engaged to Lady Tess in any case, but she would crawl naked over broken glass herself before she would play any part in hastening the event.

There was a faint clatter from her chamber. The cumbersome Argand lamp, she thought, coughing to explain the noise, and hoped Tarquin had not set himself or the furniture on fire. Modernization was all well and good until it burned a stately old home to the ground.

Julius appeared in his doorway then, gripping a practical candle and rubbing his eyes with his free hand. "What's all the ruckus?"

"Someone screamed," Caroline Reynolds announced, shivering. "It was horrible."

"Like a hell-fiend," her mother added.

"Or a ghost," was Elspeth Vaer's contribution.

"What rubbish," Lord MacGregor snapped. His dressing gown, Sybil noted, was in need of repair. The hem was dragging on the floor and there appeared to be a tear in one sleeve. "It was someone very much alive and, I would say, in some distress."

"Did you scream?" Lord Vaer demanded of his daughter.

"I most certainly did not." She turned to Tess. "Was it you?"

"Of course not. Mama?"

Lady Broadford shook her head and stared daggers at Lady Reynolds. "Frances?"

"Not I," the lady insisted, but she did release Broadford's arm. "It was *not* a sound that a lady . . . or gentleman would make."

And so it went, half of the group searching for the screamer, the other half arguing over the presence of supernatural elements in Rome Castle.

"Where's Hythe?" Broadford asked suddenly.

Twelve pairs of eyes swept the hall. Sibyl fought the urge to examine her toes.

Lady Hythe stepped forward. "Tarquin," she called loudly. Sibyl flinched. "He must be downstairs in the library. Julius, would you—"

"It was me," Sibyl blurted before the young man could move. Now a dozen gazes swung to her. "I was the one who screamed. I . . . er . . . had a terrible nightmare."

"Nightmare?" Reynolds demanded. "Sounded like you were being set upon by thieves, girl!"

"It was a most unpleasant vision, sir." A quick glance at the disheveled Lady Tess, paired with an image of Tarquin bounding from the girl's bed, brought on a convincing shudder. "I would rather not speak of it, if you don't mind."

"I should say not!" Alfonsine trundled forward, Galahad perched on her shoulder. "Nasty things, nightmares. Best to put them out of one's mind as quickly as possible." She enveloped Sibyl in a warm hug. Galahad gave an ill-tempered squeak when his tail got in the way.

"Thank you, Aunt." Sibyl stepped back as quickly as was seemly. She didn't want to risk accepting a flea along with the comforting embrace. "I shall be fine."

116

"Of course you will, dear girl. But you must come and spend the remainder of the night with us."

Sibyl considered the offer for a moment. It was just what Tarquin had suggested. She had a few words to say to him, however. "I don't think that will be necessary, Aunt Alfie."

"Now, dearest, you mustn't worry about intruding. We would not be put out in the least. Would we, Galahad?"

The monkey chattered a response. It did not sound particularly welcoming to Sibyl's ears.

"Truly, I shall be fine," she insisted. "And I really think it best if I do not join you. I doubt I shall be able to sleep any more tonight and I refuse to keep you awake." To the rest of the group, she announced, "I am so terribly sorry. I am quite mortified about it all. I do hope you will not have trouble getting back to sleep."

"Sorry business," Reynolds muttered under his breath, "dragging a fellow from his bed because of a silly dream."

He shepherded his daughter and wife back to their rooms without further comment. One by one, the others wandered back to their rooms. Julius gave her an encouraging grin as he disappeared. Lord MacGregor winked. Lady Theresa, Sibyl noted, gave her a long look before shrugging and disappearing into her chamber. Alfonsine made another attempt to change her mind. Galahad yawned.

Lady Hythe remained in the hallway after everyone else had retired, arms crossed, one tiny foot tapping against the runner. "Perhaps you ought to think of consulting a physician, my dear."

"Good heavens, madam, it was merely a dream. I assure you I am quite healthy."

"Mmm. Yes. Well, it was quite a bellow, Sibyl. I was certain one of our male guests had been shot. I am surprised you can still speak at all."

"I . . . ah . . ." Sibyl coughed again. "Now that I think on it, my throat is a bit sore. If you will excuse me, madam, I think I will return to bed. I should keep my . . . throat warm."

"Of course, dear." The countess started down the hall. "You are a sensible girl. I'm sure you know to do what's best. Sleep well and may your dreams be pleasant."

"Thank you, my lady." Cringing, Sibyl groped for her door handle. That had not gone quite as well as she'd hoped. "My lord?" The room was dark, the only light coming from the glowing embers in the hearth. She couldn't see much more of the bed than its hulking shape. "Are you . . . Ow!" She knocked her knee into a hard-framed chair.

Then she nearly did give a loud scream as a shadowy figure rose from behind the matching chair. Or rather, half rose. Tarquin's head only reached the level of hers. "Be quiet, Sibyl, or you'll have everyone at the door again."

"You know," she said through clenched teeth as she groped her way around the chair and limped toward the hearth, "you really ought to be thanking me for getting them all back to bed, rather than snarling at me."

"Thank you. What in the hell are you doing now?"

She paused in the act of hefting the fireplace poker. "I am stoking the fire."

"It is perfectly warm in here already."

"Yes, it is," she agreed. "You really have a splendidly built home, you know." She felt for a piece of applewood in the copper bin and tossed it onto the embers, sending up a shower of sparks. The room was illuminated enough that she had a fairly decent view of Tarquin ducking down behind the chair again. She had never seen a man's naked chest before and was intrigued by the V of wiry-looking hair. "Warm or not, I suppose you really ought to put something on. It would be most unfortunate were you to catch a chill." She had not noticed before, but his hair appeared to be damp. How that happened was not something she cared to contemplate.

"I was just going to avail myself of a blanket when you came bursting back in."

"I did not burst anywhere. Besides, this is my bedchamber." She did fetch him a blanket from the armoire, tossing it over the chair. "If I had any sense, I would demand that you leave right now."

"Don't. Please. I'll go when I can be certain I won't be seen." Tarquin emerged from his corner, wrapped from shoulder to knee. Sibyl decided he looked perfectly splendid in whatever he was wearing . . . or not wearing. He waited for her

118

to sit, then awkwardly lowered himself into the facing chair. She got a glimpse of hair-sprinkled thigh. It was not quite as interesting as his chest, but she was sorry that he covered it as quickly as he did. "Whatever you said to get everyone back to bed, I do appreciate it."

"I told them I screamed because of a bad dream. Somehow, I don't think your mother was fooled. I almost felt she knew I had you hidden."

"Nonsense. She would never in a thousand years suspect me of being in here with you. What a thought. Preposterous."

Oh, that stung, but Sibyl let it go. "Lady Theresa gave me an odd look, too." She gave Tarquin a very intent look. He simply shrugged. "In fact, she appeared a bit . . . miffed."

"Miffed? Hardly surprising. As far as she knows, you woke her from a sound sleep with your screaming. I would be miffed, too."

He had no idea why that statement made Sibyl grin. She always did seem to take her amusement from the strangest sources. At the moment, he couldn't have cared less. She had saved him from an extremely awkward situation—handled the matter, in fact, with impressive calm and intelligence. It was the first time he had ever felt grateful to her. Oddly enough, it was a rather nice sensation.

She continued to grin at him. With her hair in an unraveling braid over her shoulder and her bare feet poking from beneath a prim white nightgown, she looked very young and thoroughly pleased with herself. There was nothing childish about Sibyl, though. She was a grown woman—a not unappealing one—and he was suddenly altogether too conscious of the short distance between their two scantily clad persons.

"I suppose I owe you an explanation," he said, shifting carefully in his seat.

"I would not mind one."

Heedful of the state of the blanket, he stretched his feet toward the now blazing fire. His toes were still slightly numb. "I went for a swim in the pond—"

"You did *what*?"

"I went for a swim in the pond. It seemed," he explained defensively, "a very good idea at the time."

Sibyl grinned again. "I think it a very good idea at any time."

"Do you?"

"Certainly. I have always wanted to take a midnight dip in our great pond, but never quite manage to actually do it. Uncle Ninnie insisted there was a water serpent the size of a cow living in the center."

"He would."

"Very like him," she agreed, unoffended. "But the fact remains that no one has ever caught a carp there, no matter how frequently the pond was stocked. And several sheep have gone missing from the vicinity over the years. But that is neither here nor there. You went for a swim . . ."

"Someone took my clothing while I was in the water."

"Good heavens. Deliberately?"

"Well, it would be a hell of a mistake, wouldn't it?" he retorted. "Yes, deliberately. I left my garments near the bank. For whatever reason, someone came along and absconded with them."

"It wasn't me."

Tarquin blinked, startled by her sudden vehemence. "It did not occur to me for a second that it was."

"Truly?"

"Do you think me likely to lie about the matter, Sibyl?"

She actually slumped back in her seat. "Well. That is a relief."

"I think it must have been Julius. I expect he saw me going down to the pond and followed."

"Why on earth would he take your clothing?"

Tarquin gazed thoughtfully into the fire. "We used to play such tricks on each other. A great many years ago."

"Why did you stop?"

"I . . . I suppose it was because our father died. I was the earl."

Sibyl drew her feet up and wrapped her arms around her knees. "Ah. I think I understand."

Tarquin wasn't sure he did. He also was not certain it was worth contemplating. "Why did you think I would blame you for it?"

She smiled, but it did not reach her eyes this time. "You usually do. If I am about and something goes wrong, you always look to me first."

She was absolutely right. Tarquin winced at the recent memory of barking at her over the fallen painting in front of most of his guests. That memory was quickly replaced by one of himself some dozen years earlier, bumping down the same set of stairs near which the painting had fallen. He had made the descent on his back, rather than his head, for which he supposed he should be grateful.

He had been in a hurry; a first edition Spenser had just arrived from York. He'd rounded the first landing at a lope, and done the rest of the stairs in a jarring slide, courtesy of a greased bannister. Sibyl had bent over him as he lay gasping at the bottom of the steps, graciously explaining that she had been practicing her sidesaddle bannister-riding.

Tarquin caught himself smiling at the memory and turned the chuckle into a harsh cough. "You know, Sibyl, as much blame as I am willing to take for my behavior toward you, you must admit that I have had ample reason for anger on more than one occasion."

"I always accept responsibility for my actions."

"Yes." It occurred to him that Sibyl had spent a good deal of her life taking responsibility for a great many things. "Yes, you do. I . . . Sibyl . . ."

"What are you going to do to Julius?"

"I beg your pardon?"

"For taking your clothing. What are you going to do?"

He had not thought much on the matter. He'd been too concerned with the possible consequences should he be caught running about naked in the vicinity of his potential bride. Whichever one she was. "Nothing, I suppose. Unless I catch him in a midnight swim."

Approval warmed Sibyl's remarkable eyes. It was, he decided, quite a lovely sight. "Good," she said gently. "Very good." She hugged her knees more tightly and grinned. "So, how was it, swimming in the moonlight?"

"It was . . ." *Frigid? A ridiculous thing for a grown man to do?* "It was absolutely marvelous."

And it had been. He could not recall having felt quite so

121

relaxed—nor so invigorated—in a very long time. The moon had seemed brighter, the air fresher, the wonder of his great good fortune in possessing the pond and castle and estates clearer. Then, too, he had been completely, blessedly itchless for the first time in days.

Some things simply did not last. As if on command, the skin beneath his arm prickled. Stifling a curse, he reached under the blanket and scratched at the spot. Then he started as Sibyl slapped her palm against the arm of her chair.

"I forgot!" she announced, springing to her feet. He followed, fumbling with the blanket in an effort to be polite and remain covered at the same time. Sibyl bounded over to the dressing table, scrabbled among the collection of objects there, and lifted a small glass jar with a triumphant nod.

She returned and thrust the thing at Tarquin. He nearly lost his grip on the slippery surface. It reminded him disconcertingly of the bannister incident. He peered through the glass. Whatever was inside was faintly green and jiggled sluggishly when he tilted the jar. "What is it?"

"It is a balm for your itching. I made it especially for you this afternoon."

He sniffed at the lid. It smelled like the remains of supper. "What on earth is in it?"

"Marigold, golden seal, cucumber, and leek." She beamed at him. "Try it on the itchy spots. I assure you, it works beautifully. Great-aunt Ophelia discovered it while trying to create a poison one could cook into a meal. It quite cleared up a nasty nettle rash she had on her hands."

Tarquin winced. "I am meant to put this . . . on my skin?" He unscrewed the lid and glanced dubiously at the slippery concoction. Appreciation for the gesture waned at the prospect of actually dipping his finger into the stuff. "Thank you, Sibyl. I shall try it later, in my own chamber."

"Why wait?" she demanded.

"It would . . . er . . . hardly be . . . proper . . ."

"Oh, don't be ridiculous. You are already dressed for the occasion. And the itching will stop immediately. I promise." When he made no move to comply, she huffed, "I will turn my back, of course."

She did. Tarquin was tempted to scoop a portion of the ointment into the gap between the chair frame and cushion. He
couldn't. He had far too much respect for the condition of his
furniture. So, grimacing, he dipped the tip of his index finger
into the jar and dabbed a small amount of the salve onto his
lowest rib. He did not rub it in.

"More," Sibyl commanded.

He jerked his gaze up, but she was standing exactly as she
had been, back to him and face firmly averted. He gingerly
spread a bit more over his skin. Perhaps it was nothing more
than the force of Sibyl's formidable will and his own desire to
get out of the situation, but the stuff seemed to be working. He
dabbed some under his arm. Then, leaning forward, got as
much of his back as he could reach.

"Are you finished?"

"Yes." He still did not like the smell, highly potent now that
he had the ointment spread over a fair amount of skin, but he
had to admit the covered areas were not itching. The middle of
his back was. He flexed his shoulder blades.

"Here. I'll help."

Tarquin almost upset the chair when he stumbled backward.
"You will do no such thing! For God's sake, Sibyl!"

"For God's sake. For God's sake. You keep saying that, and
what goes on here has nothing whatsoever to do with God. You
have a rash in spots you cannot reach. I have two perfectly
capable hands. Now turn around."

"Sibyl, I absolutely will not have you touching me. It would
be indefensible, indecent, unconscionable—"

"Oh, for God's sake, Tarquin, cork it!"

She plucked the jar from his fingers and slipped behind him.
She tugged at the top of the blanket; he tugged back. In any
other circumstance, he would have won in an instant. As it was,
he realized a few more back-and-forth tugs and the blanket
would end up around his ankles.

Whoever insisted that women were the weaker sex, he
decided, had never envisioned Sibyl Cameron against a naked
man. The outrageousness of that thought was swamped moments
later when her hands slid over his back.

He nearly groaned with the sensation. The touch stroked

from shoulder to shoulder, then in a downward sweep over his spine. He could feel heat emanating from where her skin met his. As she stroked downward once more, his knees sagged. And other parts rose.

"Good God," he groaned, and staggered forward.

"Lovely, isn't it?" He heard Sibyl say softly from behind him. "All done."

He waited for the count of ten before turning around. At present, he was convinced the tentlike blanket was the best raiment he'd ever worn. As an added bonus, Sibyl was facing away from him, cleaning her hands on a square of cloth.

"I predict you will feel ever so much better tonight." She gave him a slightly lopsided smile over her shoulder. He readjusted the blanket. "I make even better predictions than salves, you know."

Curiosity was not an emotion Tarquin was used to feeling around Sibyl. Overwhelming curiosity was not an emotion he was used to feeling at all. "Tell me," he commanded gruffly. "Tell me what you predicted. On the lawn."

"You truly wish to know?"

"Yes."

"Well." She crossed the room and pulled her sketch book from beneath a pile of novels. Tarquin thought he saw Ann Radcliffe's and Walter Scott's names among the others. Sibyl, it seemed, prefered tales of Adventure and Romance. He should not have been surprised. "Are you quite certain?"

"Hmm? Oh. Yes."

"Very well." She withdrew a sheet of paper from inside the cardboard cover. Tarquin noted the tidily torn edge. "The price is the same."

"I beg your pardon?"

"The Montefiore, Tarquin. Goodness, you gentlemen have appalling memories. I will trade you the remaining predictions for the Montefiore."

The last vestiges of tingling warmth vanished. "You still demand the Montefiore."

She rolled her eyes. "At least your hearing is unimpaired."

"You tore off a third of whatever nonsense you originally wrote," he snapped, "yet want the same reward for what remains."

"Precisely."

"Ridiculous!" Past annoyance now, he reached for the paper. "Give me that."

She darted out of his reach. "Do I get the book?"

"You must be jesting!"

"I shall take that as a no. So be it." She gave a dramatic sigh. As before, she neatly tore the paper, this time in half. "I hope you will not regret your choice, my lord." She tossed the strip into the fire. "Now, I daresay it is safe for you to go to your chamber."

"For God's—"

"Ah!" She held up her hand, silencing him. Then she strode to the door, opened it partway, and peered out. "Quite safe," she whispered, pulling the door wide. "Good night, my lord. Don't forget to take the ointment with you. I am certain your valet will serve you just as well as I."

Tarquin mutely collected the jar and wandered into the empty hall. He turned back to bid Sibyl a good night—or something to that effect—but she closed the door smartly in his face.

Head spinning, legs not quite as steady as usual, he made his way to his chamber. As he dropped the blanket on the floor and climbed wearily into bed, he could not get past one thought: If his valet had anything close to the effect on him that Sibyl just had, the future of the Hythe earldom would be in dire trouble.

11

Sibyl stood at the gallery bannister the following after-noon and silently willed the large Flemish tapestry to fall on Caroline Reynolds. Unlike the El Greco, however, this piece had been hung with attention to the maths. It was not going to fall on anyone.

"My great-great-grandmother commissioned the series in 1706." Tarquin gestured around the Great Hall. It was raining again and, as best Sibyl could tell, Miss Reynolds was getting the grand tour and a discreet evaluation. "Her husband, the second earl, had fought with the Duke of Marlborough at Blenheim, and she did not want to be outdone by the Duchess Sarah's decorations in Blenheim Palace."

Caroline did a graceful twirl, giving the six massive tapestries a cursory glance. "I have been invited to Blenheim Palace on two occasions," she announced complacently. "The duke was most attentive."

The duke, Sibyl knew, was seventy-five years old and as attentive to his dogs as to people.

"I do believe they have tapestries just like these," Caroline continued. "I remember being forced to stand near the windows of one of the salons through a terribly long evening. I had the most exquisite pink dress, and it would have been quite spoiled had I stood beneath that red." She pointed to a dramatic battlefield scene. "The Marlborough tapestries are all pictures of war, too. Dismal, if you ask me."

"Blenheim was a decisive victory against the French," Tarquin said mildly. "Ultimately it saved Vienna from invasion."

Caroline tilted her blond head and pursed rosebud lips. Sibyl sighed. Even from a distance, she could see just how lovely the girl was. "Well, that's curious."

"Curious?"

"That we fought the French at Blenheim. I thought the last French invasion of England was in 1066."

"Well, as a matter of fact—" Tarquin began.

"And isn't it marvelous how a victory in Oxfordshire can reach as far as Vienna? Oh, I do love being English. We are so very clever."

Sibyl saw Tarquin look quickly—twice—at Caroline before clearing his throat and fixing his attention on the tapestry. It was a heartening sight. Sibyl was delighted to know that he did recognize abject stupidity, regardless of how beautiful the idiot was.

Miss Reynolds had no excuse. No matter how pretty a girl was, nor how accomplished or sought-after, she should know that while Blenheim Palace was in Oxfordshire, its name-sake was in Holland. Next, ignorant twits would be placing Waterloo in Hyde Park on the banks of the Serpentine.

Sibyl's smug contentment was short-lived.

"What a perfectly stunning figure!"

Caroline had reached an alcove and was admiring the statue within. It was Greek, Sibyl knew, probably fourth century B.C. The woman was slender, delicate, and the object in her hands, now worn down so as to be unidentifiable to an uneducated eye, would have once been a sunflower.

"Is it Aphrodite, my lord?"

Tarquin had snapped back to attention. He joined his companion at the alcove, nodding his approval at her appreciation of the piece. He proudly stroked one finger down the stone cheek. "Clytie."

"I have never heard of her. Was she a great goddess or a little one?"

"She was a mortal."

"Oh." Caroline was clearly disappointed. "Why does she have a statue?"

"Clytie was beloved by Apollo," Tarquin explained. "When he deserted her, she turned into a sunflower, tilting her head to follow the passage of the sun across the sky."

"That sounds rather dull."

"It is, I believe," Tarquin remarked, "meant to sound rather romantic and tragic."

Caroline giggled. "Yes, well, I suppose she could have found herself a mortal man and borne a passel of Greek children."

"She is the symbol of love and unwavering devotion."

"Oh. Well. I daresay Apollo was a dashing fellow after all."

"So rumor has it" was Tarquin's dry response.

"He certainly cut a swathe through the unfortunate ladies of Greece," a voice murmured into Sibyl's ear.

She started and spun to face Lord MacGregor. "You move like a cat," she accused him, keeping her voice to a whisper.

"Thank you, my dear. I am far more used to being told I act like a wolf."

"Somehow I doubt that bothers you overmuch."

"On the contrary. I am a soft, harmless creature. It wounds me to be seen as anything else."

"What a clanker," Sibyl shot back, amused. Then, "Hush. I don't wish to be seen."

"Spying, are we?" He rested his forearms companionably on the railing beside her. "Anything interesting to be seen?"

There was no use in trying to come up with an explanation for her presence there. She'd been caught, red-faced if not red-handed. "Lord Hythe has been giving a tour of the Hall. Miss Reynolds has been demonstrating her knowledge of history."

"Ah. Has she recited the rhyme of Henry VIII's wives yet?"

"The rhyme . . . ?"

"'Divorced, beheaded, died. Divorced, beheaded, survived.' I thought that was the mainstay of an English girl's history education."

"Handy," Sibyl commented, "but it isn't much of a rhyme. And I grew up in Scotland, you know."

"Oh, aye. So ye did." MacGregor flashed the familiar grin and jerked his bold, very Scottish chin at the figures below. "I say we take the claymore tae the lot o' them, *Sasunnach*. Ye wi' me, lass?"

"The possibility has occurred to me."

Caroline was giggling again, and clinging to Tarquin's arm as he flexed the elbow of one of the suits of armor. When he took the thing's hand and pumped it with an astonishingly frivolous flair, the girl laughed merrily. Sibyl's shoulders slumped. It just wasn't fair. Caroline Reynolds did not deserve to see him like this.

"Yes, I imagine the possibility has indeed occurred to you." MacGregor reached out to tug at a loose curl beside her cheek. "He's a pinheaded fellow at times, our Hythe."

Perhaps it should have surprised her, finding such perceptiveness and sympathy in Lord MacGregor. Somehow, it did not. For all his bold carelessness, Sibyl suspected he was a very good man at heart. It really was a pity that Tarquin had an unbreakable hold on her heart. The handsome Scot would make a perfectly splendid husband. If he managed to marry for love, of course.

"I don't think he is so much pinheaded as pragmatic," she said sadly. "It is a very good plan, really, bringing the potential wives to the home over which they would preside. Quite an ingenious plan, when one thinks on it."

MacGregor grunted. "It is a bloody ridiculous plan."

Sibyl managed a smile. "Well, the best-laid schemes o' mice an' men gang aft a-gley."

"Ah, Burns. The man knew what he was saying and he said it damned well." MacGregor waved over the bannister. "So, what shall we do about our man an' mousie?"

"Must we do something?"

"That, lass, is a daft question. We cannae have our boy marrying that creature."

"Why not?"

"Other than the fact that she's dim as a Tuscan cave?"

Sibyl muffled a laugh. "I suppose that is reason enough."

"It ought to be. But beyond that, I rather like my open invitation to Rome Castle. It saves me the great expense and substantial bother of entertaining myself when I am in England."

"You think Miss Reynolds would forbid you to visit?"

"Not at all. Miss Reynolds thinks me a splendid fellow. For the present, anyway. No, I am concerned that were I forced to listen to her prattling and tittering for more than the occasional quarter hour, I would feel compelled to drink myself into a stupor. I have been known to howl at the moon when drunk."

He levered himself away from the railing. "Then I usually cast up my accounts on the nearest person's feet. Most unpleasant for all involved, I assure you. Now, Miss Cameron, will you allow me to escort you downstairs?"

He gallantly extended an arm. Grinning, Sibyl took it. "Thank you, Lord MacGregor. I should be delighted."

The other pair was examining a massive Cordovan leather chair when she and MacGregor reached the bottom of the stairs. ". . . gift from Queen Elizabeth," Sibyl heard Tarquin announce.

"Daughter of the unfortunate Anne Boleyn," MacGregor said cheerfully. "She had six fingers, you know, our Annie did."

"Six fingers?" Caroline's smooth brow furrowed. "Goodness. Was that three on each hand?"

"Five," Sibyl declared, stifling a laugh when Caroline's eyes went blank and her ten fingers shifted against her skirts. Apparently beauty did not guarantee any proficiency at maths. "I have heard she was fond of wearing eight rings at a time."

"But five added to five . . . and you said six, not eight . . ."

Tarquin cleared his throat. "What Lord MacGregor and Miss Cameron meant is that Anne Boleyn had a sixth finger on one hand. Eleven in all."

Caroline gave a delicate shudder. "How horrid."

"Ah, but she was incomparable at the harp," Sibyl improvised.

"Tremendously fond of Mozart," MacGregor added.

"Oh, for heaven's sake," Tarquin muttered.

Caroline brightened. "I positively *adore* Mozart. I wonder which pieces the queen favored."

"The *Messiah*," MacGregor suggested.

"Surely not," Sibyl insisted. "I am certain she preferred Pachelbel's *Canon*."

"Dear Miss Cameron, that is not Mozart." Caroline patted Sibyl's hand consolingly. " 'Tis Haydn."

Tarquin closed his eyes wearily. He was tired. It had never occurred to him that the simple act of spending a half hour with a potential bride would be so draining. The constant effort of trying to entertain Miss Reynolds, while waiting tensely for her next harebrained comment, had left him ready to creep back to bed for the remainder of the party.

130

He had no energy with which to halt the little game Sibyl and MacGregor were playing. He didn't have much desire, either. It was no doubt an example of a serious flaw in his character, but dammit, he was only human. And, God help him, he was finding the whole exchange somewhat amusing.

"Now, she was the fourth wife, was she not?" he heard Sibyl asking.

MacGregor hummed thoughtfully. "No, I do believe she was the third. Or was it second? Well, damn, I used to know this sort of thing. Divorced, died, beheaded . . . no, divorced . . . Bother it. Miss Reynolds? Do help me out here."

"Well, I . . . I really do not . . ."

"Come now," MacGregor urged. "Don't tell me you've no interest in the history of this fair land. And here you are in Rome Castle, historical gem of Kent. I daresay there hasn't been a monarch in three hundred years who didn't walk through that portal at some point. You had the king here a few years back, didn't you, Hythe?"

Tarquin nodded. It had been an interesting experience. While His Majesty had seemed quite himself during most of his brief stay, he had passed the last evening in an animated conversation with the pair of gargoyles outside his bedchamber window. They, he'd insisted, were the Archangels Gabriel and Walter.

Julius still saluted Old Walt whenever he passed beneath that window.

"One cannot step into this place without imagining the clash of swords, the sweet song of minstrels, the screech of ladies with bats caught in their towering white wigs." MacGregor propped a hip on the edge of the massive mahogany table beside him. "Did I not hear once, Hythe, that this is the very table where King John signed the Magna Carta?"

"My grandfather enjoyed telling that tale. But it is most certainly not true."

"Pity. Did you know, Miss Reynolds," the Scot demanded soberly, "that King John was *not* a good king? His brother was the rum'n in the family. But then, I am certain you know all about him. Splendid lad, world traveler."

Caroline was in obvious distress now. "I . . . I had an audience with the king once. He was . . . most attentive."

"Was he now? Well, that's quite a feat you've accomplished, seeing as how he has been dead some . . . oh, help me out, Miss Cameron. Six hundred years?"

"I believe so."

Tarquin glanced at Sibyl. Her eyes, alight with mischief only moments before, were serious now. He wondered at the change. No one would fault her for having a bit of sport at Miss Reynolds's expense, save perhaps Miss Reynolds.

"I should very much like to hear the story," MacGregor continued. "Quite attentive, you say. Are you certain we are speaking of the same monarch?"

It was time to step in, Tarquin decided. The confused flush in Caroline's face had drained away, to be replaced by dismayed pallor. He suddenly felt heartily sorry for her. He knew from experience that there was nothing quite so humbling as being smacked in the face with one's own ignorance.

"Perhaps," he began, "we ought to—"

He broke off when Sibyl stepped forward and shook her head at MacGregor. "For shame, my lord, the two of us jesting so. Miss Reynolds knows perfectly well that King Richard is long dead. I am certain she knows, too, that King John was not a good king and that both you and I have a perfectly dismal sense of humor. She is simply far too polite to take us to task for it."

She turned to Miss Reynolds then. "Do forgive me. I ought not to have imposed on your generous character and you have been more than kind to tolerate my poor jests."

Caroline's pretty mouth opened and closed soundlessly. After a long moment, she managed a faint, "Yes."

Sibyl nodded as if she had just been graced with a divine blessing. "Marvelous. We are all friends again. Now, I am certain Lord Hythe intended to show you the painting of his mother done by Reynolds. Was he a relation of yours? Ah, no matter. Lady Hythe was an Incomparable, of course, a great beauty. And you know, now that I think on it, I believe there is a similarity between you. . . ."

She guided a clearly bemused but smiling Miss Reynolds

back toward the stairs. Tarquin decided he had best go along, but not before he'd had a word with his old friend.

MacGregor had removed a tiny pocketknife from his coat and was starting to clean beneath a thumbnail. "That was not very well done of you," Tarquin informed him with far less censure than perhaps was due.

"No? But very well done of Sibyl, I'd say."

"Yes, it was. I am finding myself continually impressed with Sibyl. The fact remains, however . . ." Tarquin regarded his friend through narrowed eyes. "Well, damn. I suppose you think yourself terribly clever."

MacGregor moved to another nail. "Clever? Not at all. As Sibyl said, I displayed a rather poor sense of humor. It happens on occasion."

"You made Miss Reynolds look exceptionally bad—"

"Did I? I don't think she needed any assistance there."

"—and Sibyl look very good."

MacGregor looked up at last, eyes sharp. "She, too, did that completely on her own. In fact, I believe both ladies were very much what they always are, in all ways."

"I am beginning to suspect you have a very poor opinion of my brain, MacGregor."

"On the contrary. I have full faith in your brain. I have even envied it on occasion. It is the connection between your brain and other parts of you which concerns me."

Tarquin scowled. "Don't be crude."

MacGregor surveyed his fingertips, then closed the knife with a snap and returned it to his pocket. "Don't be daft. I was referring to your eyes and your heart. Now, I suggest you go after the ladies. They will appreciate your company. Forgive me, old man, but I trust our years of friendship will count for something when I say that I am finding you rather tedious."

Tarquin did not have the requisite energy to take offense. "You sound just like my mother."

"I have often thought your mother the most intelligent woman of my acquaintance. In fact, I believe I will seek her out now. She promised me a game of Commerce. High stakes, no less. Julius and Lady Leverham expressed an interest in joining us."

With that, he pushed himself away from the chair and, with

a jaunty salute, strode off toward the drawing room. His boots, Tarquin noted as they clicked along the marble floor, were worn down at both heels. Nonetheless, he managed to look like a conquering monarch as he went, arrogant satisfaction trailing in his wake.

Tedious, was he? As far as Tarquin was concerned, he was by far the most diverting person present. Not that he intended to be anything of the sort. It seemed, however, that fate was determined to make him the fool of the piece. For all of his careful planning, he was coming out of each situation looking rather inept, if not outright ridiculous.

He studied Sibyl's departing back. Yes, she looked very good indeed, next to the blonde—*Miss Reynolds,* he amended. And he most certainly did not need MacGregor to point out Sibyl's appeal. He had always liked her. Well, perhaps not always, but often enough.

Deciding that her company was preferable to any other presently in the house, he plodded after her. And the blonde—*Miss Reynolds.*

Sibyl turned to find him striding briskly across the floor. In delightful contrast to the scowl he had been wearing minutes before, he was now smiling. Her heart did its customary little flip at the sight. He had clearly run a hand through his hair recently and his cravat was slightly off center. In truth, he did not look quite like himself somehow, and he looked unspeakably wonderful.

"Ladies, I believe you were on your way to view Sir Joshua Reynolds's portrait of my mother." Sibyl's pleasure faded a bit when he turned his smile onto Caroline. "Did we ascertain that he was a relation?"

The girl promptly scooted away from Sibyl's side and attached herself to Tarquin's sleeve. "He was a very talented painter, was he not?"

"Very. Unequaled, some say."

"Yes, well, I have thought on the matter and, yes, I do believe he was a cousin of my father's."

"A fortunate connection," Tarquin remarked, gesturing toward the stairs.

"To be sure. Why, I am certain I remember my grandmother speaking often of dear Sir Joseph."

"Joshua," Sibyl muttered under her breath.

"God bless you," Caroline said absently. Then, as she urged her host up the first step, "I am most eager to see the portrait. Family, of course. And I am certain your mother was absolutely lovely in her youth. . . ."

Sibyl was ready to slip off, unnoticed. She stopped at the base of the stairs. Tarquin stopped several steps up, pulling the chattering Miss Reynolds to a halt. "Are you not joining us, Sibyl?"

She tapped her toes against the riser. "I thought I might . . . seek out my aunt. She does tend to get a bit blue-deviled when it rains."

The truth of the matter was that she had no desire to spend another minute watching Tarquin smiling at Miss Reynolds. Beyond that, Aunt Alfie tended to get cheerfully adventuresome in the rain, rather than dispirited. Over the years, she had ferreted out two secret passageways and a family Bible in Cameron House. The Bible had been missing for eighty years. The current family had a very good idea why it had turned up in an unmarked hidey-hole in the west wing. Apparently, late Cousin Theodoric, Member of Parliament and eventual baronet, had been born on the wrong side of the blanket. The Bible had turned up in the room he had inhabited during his residency.

The kindest word for what Alfonsine did on rainy days was *exploring*. Sibyl did not want to take any chances that her aunt might take apart a precious cabinet or poke a hole in some plaster surface while she explored Rome Castle. "If you will excuse me . . ."

"Lady Leverham, I believe, is soon to be engaged in a game of high stakes Commerce," Tarquin informed her. "So, please, join us."

To attempt another excuse would be rude, and transparent. "Thank you," Sibyl muttered, and prepared to be invisible for the next half hour or so.

As expected, Caroline ignored her. Oddly enough, Tarquin did not. When they reached the gallery landing, where Sibyl and MacGregor had been standing earlier, he smiled and motioned to a large portrait. "Does this bring anything to mind, Miss Cameron?"

It did. The picture was of Tarquin himself at the age of seventeen, proud and serious, his hand resting on the bust of Plato that presided over the library. Sibyl and her parents had been guests of Lady Hythe during the week in which it was painted. In her eagerness to watch the proceedings, ten-year-old Sibyl had made rather a nuisance of herself and had soon been banished from the room.

Undeterred, she had climbed down the ivy from the chamber above to the library window and observed the session from an unimpeded, if uncomfortable, upside-down position. All had gone perfectly well until the painter had decided to take a rest. He and Tarquin had quitted the room. Sibyl, deciding to have a rest herself, had attempted to get back up to the window. After a brief struggle, which left her firmly caught in the vegetation and a bit woozy in the head, she had been forced to call for help.

Tarquin had been the first to reach her. In perfect Romantic hero fashion, he had climbed up, disentangled her, and handed her safely down to a waiting footman. Unfortunately, the ivy was not quite up to supporting his weight for long. He had landed rather hard, though thankfully not on his head, and only been required to wear a sling on his arm for a fortnight.

The portrait was completed some weeks after the Camerons' departure. On her next visit to the Castle, Sibyl had been delighted to see it in all its solemn splendor. She had been somewhat dejected, however, to see that all of the picturesque ivy had been stripped from the outer walls.

Now, gazing into the grave face of the younger Tarquin, she smiled sadly. "Oh, yes. I remember."

It had been during that visit that she had realized, with certainty born of great prophetic skill, she would never love anyone but the Sixth Earl of Hythe.

"I have always thought I looked a bit pained there," Tarquin remarked thoughtfully. "As if someone were twisting my drawers from behind."

Startled, Sibyl gave a choked laugh. The ever proper Lord

Hythe *never* mentioned anything so wonderfully improper as twisted drawers. Miss Reynolds made a faint gasping sound.

"Now that I think on it," he continued, "I have a very good idea what was ailing me."

"My presence?" Sibyl offered resignedly.

"Not at all. No, I have just recalled that Mr. Copley used to like to eat while he worked. He had the most distressing penchant for raw onions."

This time, Sibyl laughed aloud. After a moment, Tarquin joined her. It was such a novel sound, his laughter, and he looked so unfamiliar with his eyes crinkled and mouth wide open that she went into a new fit. In the end, she was forced to bend over and grasp her knees while she struggled for air.

It wasn't so very funny, she insisted to herself as she wheezed. Not so funny at all. Then she glanced up. Tarquin was leaning forward, one hand braced against the wall, head down and shoulders shaking. He turned his head, their eyes met, and it all started again.

Only when she began to see spots did Sibyl make a concerted effort to stop. She managed to draw a deep breath and, after a few more helpless giggles, regained control of herself. Tarquin was still hooting away but he, too, chuckled his way to a shaky stop after a minute.

"My God, that felt marvelous!" he declared, groping in his pocket for a handkerchief. Not finding one, he wiped his tearing eyes with his shirt cuff. "Now, where were we. Miss . . . er . . . Reynolds?"

Caroline was standing very still next to the somber portrait, eyes wide and hands clasped tightly at her waist. She looked as if she had seen a ghost or, Sibyl thought, a raving lunatic.

"I fear I must return downstairs, my lord," she said tremulously.

"Ah, but you wished to see the Reynolds portrait. It is but a few feet down."

"I . . . another time, perhaps. I believe I . . . er . . . heard my mother calling."

Sibyl and Tarquin glanced down into the vast, empty Great Hall. Then they looked at each other. His lips twitched. She

137

stifled a giggle. Caroline edged her way toward the stairs. Sibyl obligingly stepped out of the way.

All three started when the banging came at the front door. Deafening and insistent, it echoed off the vaulted ceiling. Caroline took advantage of the distraction to scuttle down the steps. She nearly collided with Gareth when he stalked from the back hall.

The racket continued. Whoever was at the door had abandoned the massive brass knocker and was pounding away at the door with something hard and, from the sound of it, the size of a Scottish caber.

Caroline disappeared through the drawing room doorway just as several people came out. Lord Broadford was holding a game book; Lady Hythe had her hands full of playing cards. Behind them, the lovely faces of Lady Theresa and Miss Vaer peered out. Gareth, his own craggy face set in customarily irritable lines, reached the door and hauled it open.

Sibyl could just see the top of a grizzled gray head over the butler's shoulder. "I want to see the earl!" a reedy voice declared. Gareth's reply was inaudible. "Don't you be telling me to wait, you hairy behemoth! I will see him, I tell you, and directly!"

Sibyl heard Tarquin sigh from behind her. A moment later, he was on his way down the stairs. Curious, she followed. They reached the bottom just in time to hear Gareth grunt and see him hop backwards, one hand gripping the shin of his uplifted leg. A diminutive figure immediately scooted around him and into the Hall. Snapping eyes beneath hoary brows swept the area before locating Tarquin.

"There you are, you damned scurvy thief!" The little man raised a hefty, knobbed walking stick in a threatening arc. "You've robbed me of my life's blood, you devil," he bellowed, "and I'm here to see you pay!"

Nearly every member of the party was gathered outside the drawing room now, eyes swinging between Tarquin and the new arrival. No one moved.

"Blackguard!" the man shouted, brandishing his stick. "Spineless, soulless spawn of the devil!"

Sibyl saw him start to topple forward with the weight of the stick. Apparently Tarquin saw it, too. Together, they rushed forward and caught the still cursing fellow before he hit the floor. "Robbed me of my life's blood, you did!" he managed once more before collapsing into a fit of wheezing coughs.

Tarquin sighed again. "Do try to understand, sir," he said dryly. "I was under the impression that you were dead."

12

"DEAD, YOU SAY? I'll show you dead!" The little man tried to raise his stick again. It was a futile move, as he was leaning with his face no more than two feet from the floor with Tarquin holding one of his arms and Sibyl the other. He did manage to poke Tarquin in the stomach. It was a weak thrust, but still induced a grunt. "I'll see you gutted, I will, and dragged behind wild horses all the way to Aberdeen!"

Sibyl clucked her tongue as she helped Tarquin raise the old fellow to his feet. "Now, Uncle Percy, you will do nothing of the sort."

"Uncle Percy?" Tarquin demanded over the grizzled head. Sibyl nodded, then grasped the stick before it could connect with his jaw. "The honorary uncle of rare book fame?"

"The same. Now, Uncle, will you promise not to brain Lord Hythe if I release your cane?"

"Won't promise a thing." Sir Perceval Fraser tugged ineffectually against her grip. "And I'll thank you not to defend the knave. Remember your heritage, girl!" Relatively steady on his feet now, though still held by his erstwhile rescuers, he peered owlishly at Sibyl. "Just what are you doing here, Sibby?"

"I am Lord Hythe's guest. He is hosting a house party. What are *you* doing here?"

"Seeing to justice" was Fraser's muttered retort. He jerked his arm out of Tarquin's grasp and would have gone down again, backwards this time, had he not leaned right into Sibyl. "Party, eh? Dancing with the devil, I say. Damned blackguard stole from me."

"Yes, so you've been telling us all. Forgive me, Uncle, but I find that hard to believe. His lordship is not the sort to steal anything from anyone."

"Thank you, Sibyl," Tarquin said blandly. "I appreciate your faith in me."

"Show you faith, I will," Fraser promised grimly. "May the hand of God come down and smite you where you stand."

"Perhaps you ought to move out of the way, then," Tarquin suggested. "We wouldn't want you to be smitten as well. Or is it smote?" he asked Sibyl. "When one is discussing acts of divine retribution, one wants to get the conjugations correct."

This time, the cane whistled past his nose. "Do be quiet, Tarquin," Sibyl admonished as she grabbed once more for the wood. "You are making matters worse."

Tarquin's gaze drifted from his sputtering bibliophile rival to the crowd gathered a few yards away. As far as he could tell, not a guest was missing. "You are assuming matters could get worse. I tell you, my dear, I am not at all certain that is true."

"Who are you calling your *dear*?" Sir Perceval thundered. "Insolent pup! I'll call you out, I will, for insulting my Sibyl! Let go of me, dammit, girl, so I can smack the scoundrel right and proper for besmirching your honor."

"Oh, Uncle Percy, *really*. My honor is quite unsmirched. Unbesmirched. Whichever. Now, shall we go somewhere comfortable and sit down? I am certain Lord Hythe's staff could have some tea prepared quickly. Or something stronger," she added, giving Tarquin a pointed look.

"I'll see to it, Tarquin." His mother appeared suddenly at his elbow. "Would some Skye whiskey suit you, Sir Perceval?"

Fraser's hoary head snapped around. Tarquin saw the sharp eyes go from enraged to appreciative. "Well, if it isn't little Lizzie Hathaway. Haven't seen you in years. Damn, Lizzie, you haven't changed a bit. Still the prettiest girl in the land."

"Thank you, Sir Perceval. You have not changed, either. Allow me to welcome you to Rome Castle. Shall I send for that whiskey?" Tarquin watched, astonished, as his mother took Fraser's arm and guided him, docile as a kitten, toward the drawing room. "You must tell me where you have been keeping yourself all these years."

"Oh, here and there. Here and there. Skye, you say? Aye, a

drop would be welcome. 'Twas a miserable drive, you know, all the way from Glasgow. Took me near a sennight, it did. Neither my coach nor I are as young as we used to be."

"None of us are, sir." The countess patted the man's gnarled hand. "But here you are and I am certain you will be comfortable in my home."

Fraser scanned the elegant walls. "So you married Hythe, did you? Always did have the devil's luck, old Charlie."

"You are too kind."

"Not a bit of it." He tottered to a halt just outside the drawing room. "I hate to say this, Lizzie, but your son is a scurvy knave."

"Is he really? How fascinating."

"And a base thief."

"My goodness."

Fraser glared at Tarquin over his shoulder. "I haven't finished with you, young man! You filched my book, and I'll have it back!"

Tarquin gave a terse bow. "I will be happy to discuss the matter with you, sir."

"Discuss, my ars . . . er . . . elbow! Beg pardon, Lizzie. You'll return what's mine, Hythe, and no bloody discussion about it!"

Tarquin ran a weary hand through his hair, then tugged at his cravat. "Gareth," he said to the glowering butler, who had released his cane-smacked shin but was still listing somewhat to starboard, "see if we have any Skye whiskey about. Sir Perceval would like a glass. And I," he added grimly, "will take the rest of the bottle."

The gathered onlookers had scattered to let his mother and Fraser through. Now they turned as a unit and stared at Tarquin. The Vaers and Reynoldses, he noted, were wearing similar expressions of horror. The Broadfords merely looked confused. And the three daughters were wide-eyed and open-mouthed. Tarquin found himself thinking of a trio of very pretty, pastel-scaled trout.

From the back of the group came Lady Leverham's unmistakeable soprano. "A bit of marauding is all well and good for a knight, dear boy," she trilled, "but one mustn't let the maraudee into one's house after. Very careless. Soon something of yours will go missing, then something else, and it all becomes a matter of retribution. Sooner or later, someone ends up with a mace in the posterior, and all because of a book."

"Thank you, madam. I shall take that under advisement. Now, if everyone would be so kind as to return to the drawing room, I believe it is teatime."

One by one, the party filed back into the room. Tarquin had a feeling that some persons were not so certain about taking tea with a thief, but none were about to miss the event.

Sibyl gently touched his elbow once they were alone. "Did he poke you very hard? I have a marvelous tisane for an upset stomach."

Tarquin rubbed absently at his gut. It was churning, but Sir Perceval's stick had nothing to do with it. "Thank you, but no. I shall be quite fine."

"Well, good. Then perhaps you would care to explain why Uncle Percy is so intent on hastening you into the hereafter."

"I expect it has something to do with the Montefiore."

"Yes, I rather thought it might. Do forgive me for asking, Tarquin, but how did you come to be in possession of the book?"

He gave her a humorless smile. "Having some doubts about my honesty now, are you?"

"Certainly not!" she shot back, eyes sparking. "I am quite certain you did not steal it. It appears, however, that someone did. Uncle Percy is most careful of which books he chooses to sell."

"I am aware of that." Tarquin sighed. "I purchased the Montefiore from a perfectly reputable dealer of antiquarian books."

"Perfectly reputable?"

"Well, I thought so. I suppose it is possible that Wilkins was not so careful this time in his source. It does happen occasionally."

Sibyl crossed her arms and fixed him with a stern gaze. "How occasionally?"

"Oh, stop scowling at me, Sibyl. I never purchase stolen manuscripts. Or rather," he amended grimly, "I never knowingly purchase them. But I have heard the dismal tales from other collectors."

"Hmm. I believe you, of course. I daresay everyone else will, too, as soon as you explain the situation to them."

Tarquin grunted.

Gareth reappeared through the rear door, bearing a silver tray. On it rested two bottles and two glasses. Behind him, several maids carried the tea service. Tarquin ignored the glass, accepted the bottle, poured a glass for his guest, then watched in awe as the dour butler bowed to Sibyl, his face cracking into a beatific smile.

"Worked again, did it, Gareth?" she asked.

"Like a charm, Miss Cameron."

"Oh, I am so glad." She beamed. Gareth beamed back. Then he bowed once more and, maids in tow, tromped into the drawing room.

Tarquin closed his slack jaw with a click. "Considering the fact that I have yet to have a drink, I suppose I must believe what I just saw."

"What? Oh. It is quite simple, really. When I was making your salve in the kitchens, Cook informed me that Gareth suffers from aching joints whenever it rains. I made him some of the ointment that worked so well for Grandfather Cameron's rheumatism."

"I take it his joints stopped aching."

"Immediately," Sibyl declared, nodding in satisfaction. "It seems he tried it on his shin. The stuff works marvelously on bruises, too."

Tarquin shook his head, awed. "Sibyl, you amaze me sometimes."

"Yes, well, you frequently surprise me, too. Now, what are you going to do about Uncle Percy and the Montefiore?"

"For the moment," he announced, "I am going to stand right here and see how much of Scotland's finest I can consume in a swallow. After that, I have absolutely no idea."

Ignoring the fact that Sibyl was standing not two feet in front of him, he tilted the whiskey back. It flowed, warm and velvet-edged, down his throat. Some ten years had passed since the last time he had consumed a drink in this manner. He'd been rather good at it during his early days at university, however, and had not completely lost the skill. He managed to put away a third of the bottle's contents before having to come up for air.

He closed his eyes and felt the liquor spreading comfortably from his gut to his fingertips. Sighing with pleasure, he waited until he could feel it all the way to his toes. He opened his eyes. Just in time to see Galahad, perched firmly atop a beagle, go streaking across the floor and up the stairs. They disappeared at the first landing.

He looked at the bottle in his hand, then at Sibyl. She was gazing in the opposite direction, eyes vague and one hand rubbing thoughtfully at her jaw. "Ah, Sibyl . . ."

"Hmm?" She blinked at him. "Yes?"

"I . . . er . . . Never mind." He pointed the neck of the bottle toward the drawing room. "Do I have to go in there?"

"Yes, I am rather afraid you do."

He groaned quietly. "God help me."

The smile she gave him was quick, lovely, and almost completely sympathetic. "According to Uncle Percy, God is on his side here. Will I do instead?"

For a fleeting moment, Tarquin saw a bit of the humor in the situation. He chuckled and held out the bottle. "Care for some fortification?"

Sibyl tilted her head and appeared to contemplate the offer. "No, thank you," she said after a moment, "I think not, but should I change my mind, I shall certainly let you know."

"Don't wait too long," he warned, "or there might be none left."

"I'll keep that in mind."

"Well, then." He squared his shoulders and offered her his arm. "Shall we?"

Several hours later, dressed for supper and ready for battle, Sibyl prepared to quit her chamber. Tea had not been so bad, really. Uncle Percy had muttered into his whiskey; Tarquin had smiled vaguely into his. Lady Hythe had maintained a cheerful stream of conversation, more or less with Aunt Alfie alone. The rest of the party had been unusually sedate.

Apparently the possibility that one of their daughters might or might not soon find herself betrothed to an earl who might

145

or might not be a thief of some sort had stilled collective parental tongues.

Elspeth, it seemed, was still recovering from her encounter with the worms—or perhaps Tarquin—in the garden. Caroline, brow furrowed again, appeared to be debating the weight of madness against larceny as it applied to a husband. Sibyl had silently admitted that the two girls were quite as likely to be planning their trousseaux as contemplating escape from Rome Castle. Their expressions, however, said otherwise. They had both looked supremely inconvenienced.

Lady Theresa had simply looked bored. In fact, when, by some tacit agreement, Tarquin and Sir Perceval had quitted the room, she had not even watched them go. The rest of the party had perked up immediately. In fact, Lady Reynolds had twisted so far around in her seat to watch the pair depart that she'd nearly fallen off.

Sibyl was curious about what was transpiring between the men, of course. They had still been closeted in the library when the rest of the party had dispersed to dress for supper and, as far as she knew, might still be there. She was far more interested, however, in the other girls' lack of visible emotion.

In truth, she was impressed. Everyone knew it was Tess's turn next. She would have her solitary time with the earl, her opportunity to prove what an exceptional countess she would make. Everyone was also aware, without knowing the specifics, that things had not gone well for Elspeth and Caroline.

There was every possibility that Tarquin might still settle on either of them. Men, after all, could frequently be counted upon to make the absolutely wrong choice. But Sibyl couldn't help feeling that her own happiness, at least for the foreseeable future, depended on Lady Theresa Wardour.

The question, therefore, was whether Tess's impressively cool demeanor was based on confidence or disinterest.

With that in mind, Sibyl had dressed for dinner with special care. The sky-blue dress was a season old, but still stylish. It was by far the most daring item in her wardrobe, the overskirt of gossamer net and the bodice showing far more pale skin than usual. Of course, she had far less to show than Lady

146

Theresa, but there wasn't much she could do to rectify that situation.

She'd tried. Unfortunately, rolled-up stockings when tucked into a dress bodice looked like . . . well, rolled-up stockings.

Sibyl knew she was no match for the gorgeous redhead as far as looks were concerned. She also knew that she was an appealing enough young woman in her own right. She had no intention of trying to outdazzle Tess in Tarquin's eyes. She simply wanted to make him look at her long enough for him to realize how perfectly suited they were on the inside.

With a final, stiff-lipped look into the cheval glass, she scooped up her silver-threaded shawl and left her chamber. A click caught her attention just as she rounded the turn to the stairs. She peered back and saw her aunt trundling down the hallway in the opposite direction. "Aunt Alfie?"

Alfonsine started and spun about, one plump hand clasping a small parcel to her bosom. "My goodness, Sibby, you startled me! Why are you not downstairs?"

"I took a bit of extra time to prepare. And you?"

Her aunt squinted at her. "You do look very well, my dear. Very well. Me? Oh, I am just dawdling about. You go on down. I shall be there directly."

"Shall I wait?"

"Oh, no. No, thank you, dearest. I must stop in my chamber first."

"Very well." Sibyl smiled and continued on her way. She was nearly at the bottom of the stairs when the thought hit her. If Aunt Alfie needed to go *to* her chamber, where had she been coming *from*? "Oh, dear," she muttered, and hurried back up the steps.

It was still raining. If her aunt had been poking about in search of secret passageways, Sibyl wanted to know. When not in one's own home, she firmly believed, one must be very careful of what interesting items one brought to light. There was no telling what would be best left undiscovered. Beyond that, she wanted to be certain Alfonsine had not dismantled anything fragile.

She quickened her steps—and nearly collided with Lord MacGregor when she once again rounded the bend in the hallway. She skidded to a halt, and he reached out to steady her with one hand to her elbow. The other slipped into his coat pocket.

"If the house is on fire, my dear, you are going the wrong way."

She returned his smile. "No fire, but I really must go to my aunt."

"Is she unwell?"

"Oh, no. No . . ." Sibyl peered around his shoulder. The hall was empty, all the doors closed. "I simply must speak to her before supper."

MacGregor released her and tugged at the cuff of his dinner jacket. It was, Sibyl noted, slightly frayed at the edges. "Ah. I was just heading down, myself. Shall I wait and escort you?"

"Thank you, no. I am not certain how long we will be."

"Well, then, I shall see you when I do." He gave her a smart bow and strode off in the way she had just come. "Keep in mind, the last one to the drawing room always gets the farthest seat from the fire."

Sibyl chuckled as she made her way toward her aunt's room. No doubt everyone else was already gathered and comfortable, if not precisely cheery. There was an advantage to being the last present, even if it meant a more distant chair. She would be forced to spend slightly less time in the company of the Graces and their families. And each minute was a blessing.

Alfonsine was closing her jewel box when Sibyl entered. "Oh, Sibby, dear, I told you not to wait. Now you will be late as well."

"I don't mind, Aunt. We can walk down together and you can tell me how you have been occupying yourself this evening."

"I am very much afraid you would find that dull fare indeed, dearest. I have done little more than read and chat with Galahad." She fastened the little catch on the case and shook a beringed finger at the monkey. "Now, you will not open this while I am gone. Is that clear? He swallowed one of my pendants this morning," she explained to Sibyl. "I was looking forward to wearing it."

They left the monkey staring speculatively at the jewel case and returned to the hall. Julius was just pulling a door shut

148

behind him. "Well, good evening, ladies," he greeted them, clasping his hands behind his back and bowing. "I assume you are on your way down to supper."

"We are," Alfonsine agreed, adjusting her silk turban. "We have been primping. Does not Sibyl look exceedingly well?"

Julius nodded emphatically. "She does indeed, madam. You do indeed, Sibyl. Exceedingly well. That color suits you. Always has."

Pleased with the compliment, even if Julius was the master of gallant charm, Sibyl smoothed her azure skirts. "Thank you, Julius. You look quite dashing, as usual."

He grinned and shrugged inside his smart uniform coat. "Saves me the trouble of choosing among my wardrobe." He tucked one hand briefly inside his lapel, then offered one arm to each lady. "May I escort you downstairs?"

"You may." Alfonsine pinched his cheek before taking his arm. "Hythe might have the knightly bearing, young man, but you have chivalry down to an art."

"Thank you, madam," Julius replied seriously. "I do try."

Tarquin was standing in front of the faux Magna Carta table, adjusting his cravat in the mirror above. He glanced over his shoulder. "Good evening, ladies, Julius. I do believe it is supper time."

"So says the clock, old trout." Julius studied his brother carefully for a moment. "Ah, Tarquin."

"Yes, Julius?"

"If you don't mind me pointing it out, you have just tied your collar point into your cravat."

Tarquin leaned over the table and pushed his face as close as he could to the mirror. "Why, I do believe you are right." He tugged at the linen. "Thank you."

"Ah, Tarquin."

"Yes, Julius?"

"Where is Sir Perceval?"

Having freed his now-wilted collar, Tarquin stepped back from the table. And bent down to peer under it. "Well, he is not here."

Sibyl blinked. By all appearances, and his appearance was

decidedly messy, Lord Hythe was sotted. He was also now on his knees, halfway beneath the table. "My lord?"

"Yes, Sibyl?"

"Do you have any idea where we might find Uncle Percy?"

"He is not here."

"No, I believe we ascertained that." She turned to Julius. He shrugged, eyes wide. It was, Sibyl decided, the first time she had seen him look completely serious in years. "Aunt Alfie."

"Yes, dearest." Alfonsine stepped forward. "My goodness, I do believe Lord Hythe is whistling."

True enough. Mozart was vaguely recognizable in the wheezing sounds coming from the floor. Tarquin had never cared for Mozart.

"Aunt, perhaps you could go to the library and see if Uncle Percy is there."

"Certainly, my dear. And what shall I do if I find him? I pride myself on my fortitude, but I have my doubts about whether I could carry him up two flights of stairs." As always, Alfonsine's sensible streaks appeared when they were least expected. "Perhaps Julius can check for Percy in the library while I go fetch Elizabeth."

"What a marvelous idea." Julius was already bouncing on the balls of his feet. "Sibyl, will you be all right here?"

Tarquin was coming out from under the table. He was still whistling, but it sounded suspiciously like a regimental ditty. He paused long enough to announce, "Try the library. For old Percy, I mean. I daresay Mother is elsewhere. She does not care for the library. Stuffy, she calls it. Fancy that." Then he was back to his tune.

Sibyl grasped her aunt's wrist before she could scuttle off. "I think the best option would be to inform Lady Hythe that his lordship is . . . unwell. She can make his excuses."

"And you, dear?"

"Best say that I . . . er . . . I . . . I shall join you as soon as I can. Oh, make something up."

Alfonsine giggled. "That will be my pleasure. Now, off with you, Julius. Percy is too old to be sleeping on the floor somewhere."

As soon as they had gone off in their respective directions,

Sibyl got a grip on Tarquin's arm and helped him get to his feet, which were covered with a pair of embroidered slippers. They went quite well with his brocade waistcoat but, she thought, were not quite appropriate for supper. It was becoming clear that the only place he would be going was to bed.

It was more than clear that she would have to get him there.

"Do you think you can manage the stairs?" she asked.

He squinted at them. "Certainly. Can you?"

"Oh, I will give it my best effort."

"Yes, you always were a sporting little minx."

"Thank you, Tarquin. Now, if you would loop your arm over my shoulder . . . Very good."

She staggered a bit under his weight. By the time they reached the stairs, the novelty of the experience was wearing off. When sober and upright, Tarquin was an impressive figure. Drunk and leaning, he was a formidable challenge. To his credit, he did try to help, but he kept missing steps. He nearly went down several times before they reached the first landing, taking Sibyl with him.

"Not a bad fellow, old Fraser," he announced when she paused for breath, one hand tangled in his waistcoat to keep him from going back down, tip over tail. "Not bad at all."

"I am glad you think so. Now, lift your feet, please, Tarquin. No, no, we are heading *up*."

By the time they reached the top, she was breathing like a winded horse and he had lost a slipper. "Y'know, Sibyl," he mumbled as she guided him toward his bedchamber, "you smell quite nice." He poked his nose into her hair, loosening her careful topknot and sending it sliding down over her ear. "Look splendid, too. Meant to tell you that earlier. Blue suits you."

She fumbled with his door, got it open. The chamber was dark; the servants had not yet been in to stoke the fire for the night.

"Moonlight suits you, too," Tarquin murmured.

Sibyl felt a sweet tug at her heart. It was still raining outside, with no visible moon whatsoever. "You are a daft man," she said softly, stepping out from under his arm.

"Not at all. Merely a bit tipsy." He turned and went down

like a felled tree, landing on his back across the bed. "Should you be in here, Sibyl?"

"No, I shouldn't." She left the second slipper on his foot, but leaned over him to remove the mauled cravat. "In fact, I am leaving now—"

Her breath went out in a soft gasp as he tangled a hand in her hair. "Sweet Sibyl," he whispered. "I wonder what I'll do without you."

His fingers curved around the nape of her neck. Slowly, gently, he pulled her face toward his until their lips met. For a fleeting instant, there was an insistence in his touch, a barely suppressed power that thrilled and terrified her at the same time. Then he let her go, his hand sliding from her neck to drop against the mattress. Sibyl stayed where she was, her lips pressed tenderly to his for several heartbeats before she realized he was asleep.

Shaky, her pulse hammering in her ears, she pulled back. She dragged the counterpane over him with trembling hands, then made her wobbly way out of the room. "Oh, my love." She sighed as she pulled the door shut behind her. "I don't know what you will do without me, either."

13

SIBYL HAD THE breakfast room to herself for a few minutes the following morning. Sleep had been evasive, and filled with disturbing dreams when it came. Sipping gratefully at steaming hot tea, she decided the one with Tarquin and Lady Tess at the altar had been the worst. It had seemed so terribly real. In comparison, those minutes in his chamber, which had been very real, seemed like a dream.

In all the times she had dreamed of her first kiss, Sibyl had always imagined Tarquin being the one. She had never imagined that it would happen in his bedchamber, however, on his bed, nor that he would be drunk as a bishop on alms day at the time.

No matter how much she wished to the contrary, she did not think he would remember kissing her. And she had a strong feeling that he wouldn't be terribly happy to be reminded of it. He was on the verge of offering for another woman—within the next two days, most likely. A moment's drunken indiscretion might not upset Tarquin's careful plans, but Sibyl knew it would upset Tarquin.

She had not felt nearly so miserable since— No. She had not felt nearly so miserable, ever.

She was at the sideboard, pretending a good serving of smoked kippers would fill the hollow feeling in her stomach, when Julius stumbled in. He was rumpled and unshaven, and there was a noticeable green tinge to his unusually pale skin. It appeared Tarquin had not been the only one to overindulge the night before. Julius looked as if he felt every bit as badly as she did.

"Good morning, Julius," she greeted him with brittle cheer. "Would you care for some breakfast?"

"Urgh," he replied, and slumped into a chair.

"Coffee, I think, and perhaps some toast. You will feel better for it."

He regarded her through bloodshot eyes. "This is partially your fault, you know."

Taking pity on him, Sibyl carried her loaded plate to the far end of the table before fetching him a cup of coffee and some dry toast. "Is it indeed?"

Julius averted his eyes from the food. "If you hadn't sent me after Sir Perceval before supper, he wouldn't have commandeered me after."

Uncle Percy had missed the meal, snoring contentedly on the library sofa. He had appeared in the drawing room several hours later, however, fit and cheerful and ready to play. He had settled on Julius to accompany him to the billiards room. They had been well into their third game and second bottle when the rest of the party had retired.

Now Julius gingerly propped his elbows on the table and lowered his face into his cupped hands. "Kept me up till three. Bloody miserable luck, too, that Mother put him in the chamber next to mine. He woke me up an hour ago, thumping and banging around his room."

"Yes, he is an early riser. Now, you really ought to eat something, Julius. It will settle your stomach."

"Urgh," he said again.

Gareth poked his head into the room. Sibyl beckoned and announced, "I think Mister Rome could do with some of the tisane I had Cook ready for his lordship."

The butler took one look at the prostrate figure and nodded. "I'll have it sent in immediately."

"That would be grand, Gareth, thank you."

The craggy face split into a warm smile. "Of course, Miss Cameron." To Julius, he declared, "We'll have you feeling better in no time, sir."

"Bleagh," said Julius.

True to promise, a steaming mug appeared several minutes later. Julius showed his first spark of interest of the day when Gareth placed it in front of him. His eyes opened wide and he shot upright in his chair. "Good God, what is that?" he demanded, then clapped his hands over his own ears as if the sound of his own voice caused him terrible pain.

"Nothing poisonous," Sibyl replied. She knew the smell was bad enough to suggest some rather unspeakable possibilities. "Just drink it."

"I think not." He pushed the mug away. Gareth promptly pushed it back. "Smells like something crawled in there to die."

"I know it does, but it really will help. Great-uncle Machulus swore by it."

Julius eyed the concoction dubiously. "He did?"

"Absolutely. And all of Scotland knew how fond Machulus Cameron was of his whiskey."

"I trust you will forgive me for mentioning this, Sibby, but the man *died*."

She laughed. Julius winced. "He was ninety-six and passed on with a smile on his face."

"Splendid man, Machulus Cameron!" Sir Perceval thumped his stick for emphasis and tottered through the door. "Didn't know a book from the end of a haggis, but damned if he wasn't a fine fellow when it came to sharing a bottle."

"Good morning, Uncle Percy." Sibyl noticed that he looked far better than Julius that morning and felt a new surge of pity for the young man. There was no more dangerous drinking companion, she knew, than an old and well-seasoned Scot. "Did you sleep well?"

"Fair to middling, girl. Beds here are godawful squashy things." He rattled a few lids at the sideboard. Julius slid lower in his seat. "Can't complain much, though. Had a good run at the billiards table last night. Didn't I, lad?"

Julius gave a jerky nod, followed by a soft moan. "You did, sir. Trounced me soundly." Gareth, who had been standing impassively by, nudged the tisane a bit closer. Julius went so far as to wrap his fingers around the mug.

"I'll take that twenty pounds whenever you care to hand it over."

Sibyl frowned. "Uncle Percy, you didn't wager on the games!"

"'Course we did, girl. A crown a ball. And young Rome took a few from me."

"Four, I believe," Julius said weakly. He lifted the mug a few inches off the table. "Or perhaps five."

"Five." Sibyl rolled her eyes. "Well, I suppose it is far too late to warn you." She turned back to the older man, who was busily heaping coddled eggs onto a plate. "Did you and Lord Hythe get matters sorted out, Uncle Percy?"

"Hmm? Oh, aye."

"And . . . ?"

He plodded over to the table and plunked his plate down in the place next to Julius's. "And that's all I'm going to say on the matter, Sibyl, so you may refrain from hounding me on it. Good God, man, what *is* that stuff? Smells like old brogans."

"Cheers," Julius muttered, saluting, then tipped back the mug. Sir Perceval helpfully thumped him on the back when he began to cough and sputter. "Taste as bad as it smells?"

Julius gasped and wiped streaming eyes. "Worse."

"Must be good stuff, then. Don't you even think of tossing it up." When Julius shoved the mug out of the way and rested his brow on the table, the older man patted the top of his head absently. To Sibyl, he said, "Quite a racket going on upstairs. Some female shrieking and throwing things about."

"Have you any idea who or why?"

"None at all. Just thought you'd like to know."

Deciding she had better go see what was happening just in case her aunt was involved, Sibyl rose to her feet. Julius was very still, and she gave him a worried glance. Uncle Percy waved her away. "I'll see to the lad. You go deal with the squawking. People are trying to sleep up there."

Images of Tarquin filling her mind, Sibyl hurried from the room.

At first, he thought the screeching was coming from inside his own head. It certainly felt as if someone were scraping away at the inside of his skull. Tarquin opened his eyes, squinted painfully into hazy sunlight, and groaned. Someone had pounded his skull while he slept, pummeled his stomach, and rinsed his mouth with lamp oil.

It took him a moment to identify the ceiling of his bed-chamber. Had he not recognized the moldings, he would have thought himself in hell. As it was, he was convinced that hell had somehow relocated itself to Kent.

Another screech pierced his ears, followed by a loud thump. Cursing, moving as slowly as possible in deference to his stomach, he slid to the edge of the high mattress and groped about with his toes for the floor. As much as he would have liked to turn over and smother himself in the sheets, he knew he had to determine what ill was befalling his house.

He got himself into a seated position and managed to maintain it for a moment before sheer agony had him leaning forward to drop his head between his knees. He noticed that he was wearing one slipper. The other was nowhere in sight. He was also, he discerned, wearing the clothing he had donned for supper. He recalled dressing. Everything after that was a shadowy blur.

Well, he had clearly gotten himself to bed, a good sign. Whatever else he'd done in his unfortunate state, he hadn't crawled under any furniture to sleep. More than once, during his early Oxford days, he had woken beneath the narrow bed which had occupied his student rooms. He'd never been quite sure how he had ended up there.

Whimpering quietly now, and clenching his teeth, Tarquin struggled to his feet. He leaned against the bedpost to gather strength, then staggered to the washstand. He was convinced that nothing in life had ever felt so good as the water he splashed over his face. Well, there had been one positively spectacular night with the now-abandoned demirep. . . .

Feeling capable of facing whatever lay beyond his chamber door, he dried himself off and flipped over his shaving mirror. He took one look at the glass and promptly backed away from the red-eyed, wild-haired creature in horror. Then he bent tensely over the wash basin for a long minute, waiting for his gut to settle. "God," he moaned, and groped for his comb, "kill me now."

Nothing happened. Resigned to at least a few more hours of life, he dragged the comb through his hair, wincing as each strand protested, then stumbled into the hall.

As seemed abysmally common of late, half of the house's occupants were gathered in a tight knot. Tarquin scanned the group for Sibyl, but did not see her. He did locate his mother, however. She was comforting a clearly hysterical Lady Broadford. It was an incongruous sight, as the marchioness stood nearly a head taller and outweighed her by a good three stone.

"Now, are you certain you brought it with you, Regina?" his mother was asking. "Is it possible that your maid left it behind?"

"No, no," Lady Broadford moaned. "I specifically recall seeing it yesterday morning when I chose my earrings for the day. It was in my jewel case then, I am certain."

Lady Theresa appeared in the doorway. At the countess's inquiring look, she shook her head.

Tarquin cleared his throat to announce his presence. A lumpy frog seemed to have lodged itself there in the past few minutes, so he did it again.

"Ah, Tarquin." His mother looked far more pleased to see him than she had since the party began. "We have a bit of a situation here."

"Situation!" Lord Broadford bellowed. Tarquin winced. "What we have is a thief in our midst." The marquess glared at his host. "A thief with an eye for heirloom objects."

"The bracelet is from the Broadford family jewels," his wife wailed, clutching at the countess's slender arm. Tarquin winced. His mother winced. "The emeralds are perfectly matched, my favorite piece. Priceless."

Tarquin remembered seeing her wearing the bracelet several nights earlier. Priceless it might well be, but his first adjective would have been *garish*. He did not think Lady Broadford would appreciate his opinion, however, so he said instead, "I am certain there is a reasonable explanation, madam—"

"Seems there is, young man," Lord Reynolds declared, stepping into the melee. "Someone stealthily entered this chamber and scarpered with the piece."

At least eight pairs of eyes were now fixed on Tarquin's face. His mother, he saw, was staring at his feet. He looked down and sighed. He was still wearing one slipper. Wordlessly, she handed the trembling Lady Broadford into Lady Tess's capable hands and squeezed through the knot of guests to a small, marble-topped table. When she approached her son moments later, she was holding out the second slipper.

"We would not want to see you ill-attired," she said dryly.

He accepted the slipper and dropped it to the floor. It took a bit of shuffling, but he managed to get it on. He didn't want to risk bending over. "Are we certain the bracelet is gone?" he demanded quietly.

"Quite. Regina was very thorough in her search." From her pinched expression, Tarquin decided he had just been informed of the origin of the thumping. "And Tess looked again."

"I see. Well." He turned back to his guests. "I am confident the piece will reappear," he announced. "Should it not, Lady Broadford, rest assured that I will compensate you for its loss."

Her snuffling stopped abruptly. Lord Broadford's scowl vanished. Even Lord Reynolds, who was not really involved in the situation at all, suddenly looked mollified. There was nothing, Tarquin mused with resignation and some annoyance, quite like hinting at one's vast wealth to solve any problem that appeared.

For the moment at least, all thoughts of theft—and those of the Earl of Hythe as a possible culprit—would be set aside. Tarquin could see nine faces, six parental and three Incomparable, calculating shillings and pounds.

"Now, unless there is another matter for me to attend, I believe I will go down for breakfast."

No one stopped him as he turned and tromped down the hall in his slippers, evening coattails flapping. He had no intention of eating anything for the next decade or so, but he did not want to go back to his chamber. Once there, he was certain he would crawl back under the covers and refuse to move till winter. Besides that, he had a very good idea that he would find Sibyl downstairs. With luck, she would be able to fill in some of the gaps in his spotty memory.

He ran a weary hand over his jaw as he descended the stairs, cringing at the stubble there. He could not remember the last time he had quitted his chamber in the morning without shaving. On the same vein, he pulled his shirt away from his chest and sniffed. He detected the distinct aroma of Scotch and something slightly riper. He couldn't recall the last time he had left his chamber in the morning without bathing, either.

At least he was not itchy. So what if he were a bit smelly, decidedly rumpled, and resembled a plague victim? He was in his own home, dammit, and perhaps it was high time that he collected the reputation of being something of an eccentric. So much less was expected of a man when he was known to possess a few quirks in his character.

Coffee, he decided, sounded like a very good idea. With a dash of lemon in it. He had always wanted to try that particular combination, but decorum had prevented it. Now he would drink whatever he bloody well chose.

The aroma of grilled kidneys reached his nose as he approached the breakfast room. The coffee was momentarily forgotten as he debated making a dash for the privy. By breathing through his mouth, he was able to control the roiling of his stomach and enter the room. To his disappointment, Sibyl was not present. Only his brother was seated at the table.

Julius looked a bit rough around the edges. He was contentedly sipping at a cup of coffee, however, and had a newspaper and plate of toast in front of him. He raised slightly bleary eyes as Tarquin groped his way into a chair.

"Good heavens. Do I look as bad as you do?"

"No," Tarquin replied shortly, and lowered himself into a chair.

Julius ignored the snarl and gestured to a hovering footman. The man scuttled off. Gareth appeared almost immediately, bearing a large mug of steaming liquid. He took one look at the inert form of his employer and plunked the thing in front of him.

Tarquin felt his eyes beginning to water. "What is this?" he demanded, pushing it as far away as he could.

"Sibyl cooked it up," his brother answered blithely, and leaned over to push the mug back. "It's not so bad, really. I feel considerably better than I did when I awoke."

Too miserable to protest, Tarquin took a tentative sip. His

eyes shot wide open. "Bloody hell!" he sputtered. "The witch is trying to poison me!"

"Now, my lord," Gareth coaxed, "if you would just—"

"Where is she? Let her come and drink this vile rot."

Julius smiled indulgently over a triangle of toast. "Really, old man, it wasn't Sibyl who overindulged last night. She is simply being helpful, as always."

"Sibyl's idea of being helpful," Tarquin muttered, "usually ends with me flat on my back, gasping for air, or wearing a bandage."

"That's hardly accurate, Tarquin."

"True. She has rendered me unconscious once or twice, as well. Poison would be the natural next step." He then found himself recalling a slippery salve and two very soft hands. "You honestly feel improved?"

"Vastly."

"Well, then." The second sip was every bit as bad as the first. The third merely tasted like mud. By the time he was halfway through the stuff, Tarquin decided it had destroyed most of his senses. "Now what?"

"Now you wait to see if you turn into a toad," Sibyl said tartly from the doorway. "Sometimes I get the measures wrong and the transformation happens piecemeal."

Tarquin suddenly felt better. A bit off-center, perhaps, but greatly improved. He spread his hands in front of him and examined them carefully. "No warts," he said, adding ruefully, "My eyes feel as though they are bulging a bit, however."

Sibyl crossed the room to where he was sitting and, catching his jaw in her hand, leaned in to have a look. "Red," she commented, "but otherwise fine. I must have confused my recipes again. Do you, by chance, have any desire to chase mice?"

The desires he was having at the moment had absolutely nothing to do with mice. Sibyl was wearing blue this morning, a smoky color that made her skin glow. Funny, he had never noticed how very well she looked in blue.

His gaze drifted as if by its own will to her mouth. He had never really contemplated Sibyl's mouth before. It was full, soft, the color of damask rose petals. Tarquin found himself wondering how it would taste. . . .

"Have an apple, my lord." She released his chin. "They are very good for the stomach, especially for one that has been as abused as yours."

She crossed to the sideboard and ran her fingers over the selection in the fruit bowl. She turned, her choice in hand, and nearly dropped it onto her feet. Tarquin was lounged back in his seat, one arm draped over the back of the neighboring chair. With his open shirt collar and day's growth of beard shadowing his lean cheeks, he looked like a brooding corsair. He was breathtaking.

Sibyl returned to the table on shaky legs. The idea of climbing across the linen-draped expanse and into his lap seemed perfectly sensible. She chose the chair nearest to hand, and farthest from him. "I . . . I have just been seeing Uncle Percy off."

"Oh?" Julius peered over his newspaper. "Pity. He certainly livened things up."

"Yes, he can always be counted upon to . . . er . . ." She watched as Tarquin, having moved on to coffee, lifted the cup to his lips. ". . . to be . . ."

"Dangerous," Julius supplied. "But a splendid fellow for all that."

"Dangerous. Yes, absolutely."

Desperate suddenly for something to do, Sibyl picked up a knife and prepared to peel the apple. She set the blade down after a moment. Trying to maneuver a sharp object didn't seem wise just then.

"I don't suppose you would care to tell us just what sort of deal you struck with him, Tarquin," Julius said hopefully.

"No" was his brother's terse reply. He was still staring at her, eyes hooded and expression unreadable.

"You can't fool me, old trout. For all the whiskey you put away, I daresay you might have signed over all your worldly possessions. You won't tell because you don't remember."

"Wrong." The corner of Tarquin's mouth twitched. "Simply because I imbibed more than is my custom, it does not mean I forgot what transpired. I have a very good memory."

Sibyl busied herself with aligning the silver at her place. She was frightened that if she met Tarquin's eyes now, she would burst into tears. Or go scrambling across the table and into his lap after all. He *had* forgotten. And she couldn't think of a way to remind him without one of them being thoroughly humiliated.

All things considered, one more humiliation shouldn't matter to her. She had experienced plenty through the years. This time, though, she wasn't sure she could stand it.

"So, Tarquin," Julius said, "since you refuse to entertain me with the tale of your encounter with Sir Perceval—and, I feel compelled to state, I would be more than happy to tell you all about mine—perhaps you will be so kind as to give me twenty pounds."

"Whatever for?"

"To replace that which I had to hand over to the fellow. After you became unavailable, he deprived me of twenty pounds at the billiards table. Since you were the one responsible, I think it only fair that you pay up."

Tarquin's brows rose. "I fail to see how I am responsible for your poor showing at billiards."

"It's really very simple, brother mine. Had you not been so charmingly sotted that Sibyl had to mop you off the flagstones, I would not have been forced to represent you on the felt field of honor."

"Sibyl mopped . . ."

She kept her eyes fixed on a spoon.

"She did indeed. So, will you hand over the blunt?"

"Yes, yes. You will have the twenty pounds. But Sibyl . . ."

"Splendid." Julius buried himself in the newspaper again. A moment later, he was whistling a very familiar tune.

Sibyl glanced up to see Tarquin's gaze swinging from her to his brother and back again. His brow was furrowed, as if in concentration. Sibyl held her breath. Perhaps if he thought hard enough, he would remember.

"The name was *Clydea*, Elspeth," Caroline Reynolds's voice carried through the open door, "or something like that. She is the goddess of enduring love and devotion. Or something like that. It is a terribly tragic and romantic tale."

Tarquin blinked, then got to his feet to greet the arrivals.

Feeling rather like the ill-fated Clytie, Sibyl turned her face to watch him as he moved. Tragedy she understood. It seemed that Romance was still determinedly eluding her.

14

SIBYL'S TISANE HAD done much to relieve Tarquin's discom-
fort. A bath, shave, and change of clothes had helped as
well. He felt very nearly human as he guided his team down
the rough lane. Beside him in the tilbury, Lady Theresa sat
calmly, hands clasped in her lap. She was a picture indeed, her
red hair bringing to mind the rich change that would transform
the distant maples, her rippling muslin skirts sharing the soft
color of the waving grass.

A man could not ask for a more attractive driving companion on a beautiful late-summer day.

Tarquin was rather proud of himself for having come up
with the idea of taking the party on a tour of the estate. The
decision had been threefold: He would have an opportunity to
see how much, if any, damage the rain had caused; his guests
would be released from the wearing confines of the house for
an hour or two; and he would have a bit of time with Lady
Theresa.

She had readily accepted his suggestion that she ride with
him in the two-person tilbury. The rest of the group had
climbed into various vehicles and were following behind. Tarquin gave her a contented smile, then turned his attention back
to the reins and the road.

The avenue of towering elms soon opened into rolling
fields. Stone tenant cottages dotted the landscape, lush fields
filled with fodder grass and vegetables stretching between
them. Men paused in their work to tip their hats at the passing
carriages. Tarquin noticed that Peter Brown was off his crutches
and back among his potatoes. His small son was skipping
behind, shooting pebbles at invisible rodents in the plants. The

boy would be in the estate school soon, but for now, he seemed happy to be helping his father.

Tarquin smiled to himself, wondering if little Peter would grumble and balk at the necessity of spending his days inside, learning his letters. He remembered staring wistfully out the schoolroom window as a young boy, wishing he could be among his father's tenants in the sun and hay. He had never spent much time contemplating whether those same people would eagerly trade their lives for his. Later, he had known better than to ask. A quirk of Fate had put him in the castle, his tenants in their cottages. Pride was fierce among the simple, practical Kent people. He hadn't wanted to offend them by asking what they thought of blithe, arbitrary Fate.

Surveying the rich fields, Tarquin felt the same surge of satisfaction that he always did. This was Hythe land, on loan from the earth itself to his family for as long as they could hold it. He would pass it on to his son, and that son to his. With luck, there would be an Earl of Hythe on this little patch of England for centuries to come.

With that in mind, he turned his attention to his companion. She was studying the scenery from beneath the brim of a fetching, green-silk-and-straw hat. Sensing his gaze, she turned to face him. Her quick smile was stunning and a bit mischievous. "What a lovely kingdom you have, Your Majesty."

"It is hardly a kingdom," he replied easily. "Simply a little demesne."

She laughed. "How very feudal. Lands, serfs, castle. All you require is a moat."

"Oh, I am not much for moats." He resisted the urge to turn around in his seat and look for Sibyl. When he had driven off, she had been cheerfully moderating an argument between MacGregor and Julius over whom she would accompany. "I . . . ah . . . Kent is very different from Yorkshire. I imagine you find it rather dull."

Theresa shrugged. "I seem to spend most of my time either in Town or traveling between house parties. I daresay I have seen all of England since my debut. Kent is as pretty a place as any."

"Where will you go from here?"

"I would say that depends a great deal on you."

Tarquin blinked in surprise. "I beg your pardon?"

"Come now, my lord. I am not unintelligent. Nor are my parents, contrary to appearances. We all know precisely why I am here. So, should you decide I suit you, or even that I might, I imagine my mother will drag me back to London so she can gloat to whoever is still in Town and start badgering modistes about a trousseau. After that, there would be a string of visits to unsuspecting persons who have retired to the country. For more gloating, of course.

"Should you decide, however, that I am not to your liking, I expect we will travel to Yorkshire posthaste so Mama can gnash her teeth in private. Then she will sort among the invitations for harvest and winter parties and we shall be off again."

Tarquin raised his slack jaw. "I must say, my lady, that was—"

"Impertinent? Brazen? I have often been called both."

"I was going to say 'forthright,' actually. Do you always express yourself so candidly?"

"No," she replied, smiling, "I do not. Only with persons I either like a great deal or abhor absolutely. Otherwise, I am as demure and dull as every good girl is supposed to be."

Tarquin gave a choked laugh. "I am almost afraid to ask into which category I fall."

"Oh, I like you, Lord Hythe. Or at least I think I do. You are not an easy man to get to know. Just when I am becoming fully convinced that you are priggish as my maiden Aunt Ermintrude, you do something to completely change my opinion. It is most frustrating, my lord, being proven wrong time and again."

There was something blithe and self-deprecating in her voice. Tarquin smiled and wryly shook his head. He had never set out to be a complicated man. On the contrary, he had always wanted his life to be as simple as possible. As it happened, though, he had recently arrived at the conviction that the only people who really knew him at all were the woman who had given him life and the one who had always seemed intent on upsetting it.

"I hardly know what to say, my lady."

"Tess," she corrected. "I have never been able to shake the

feeling that people who call me 'my lady' are either being unctuously polite or have forgotten my name."

"Tess," he repeated. "Very . . . pretty."

She laughed again, a charming sound. "Thank you. And you needn't be concerned that I shall call you Tarquin. Hythe, perhaps. As pleasant as you are today, you still do not encourage informality."

He tried to remember when Sibyl had started using his Christian name. He couldn't recall the exact moment, but knew it had sounded rather nice. "So . . . Tess, tell me this. Does it offend you, knowing why I orchestrated this party?"

She studied him thoughtfully with stunning, smoky blue eyes. Tarquin was struck yet again by how very beautiful this young woman was. He was also impressed by her clear intelligence. "I would not say I am offended, my lord. A bit amused, perhaps, and somewhat flattered. Definitely wearied."

"Wearied? By . . ."

"By the constant pressure to behave, entertain, and look well, of course, though not necessarily in that order. And by the conviction that all of that is more or less wasted."

"Good heavens. Why?"

"Because I am neither behaving nor looking well to please myself," she said tartly. "A man who chooses me for those things will ultimately be disappointed. I will eventually get spots and wrinkles like every other woman. Probably sooner than most," she added, without bitterness. "Redheads tend not to age well. Beyond that, I do not always care to behave decorously or reasonably, and cannot be expected or bothered to do so."

"Well." Tarquin was torn between admiration and exasperation. "It appears I have just been warned off."

To his surprise, Tess gave him a gentle smile and reached out to cover one of his hands with hers. "Not at all. I should like to do my own choosing, but if you ultimately decide that we would suit, I will be more than happy to discuss it. No," she said when he opened his mouth to reply, "no need to respond now. We are not planning to depart until the day after tomorrow. There is ample time for discourse and debate."

Tarquin realized he had nothing to say. He wasn't about to tender an offer of marriage—not yet, at least. There was indeed ample time for that. A whole, entire, complete day, in fact, if he were to keep to his plan. His plan had been to be betrothed by the end of the sennight. It had seemed like a very good plan. Even now, it made a great deal of sense.

Unfortunately, sense no longer seemed to be everything, or enough.

They were approaching the estate's original mill. Abandoned nearly two centuries earlier, it was a scenic spot. Nature had reclaimed the land, sending trees and deep grass up among the stones, while the Little Stour River ran unchanged through it. Tarquin had always enjoyed this corner of his property and had settled upon it earlier as a perfect place to stop.

He guided the team to the side of the road and pulled them to a halt. Fixing the reins to the board, he climbed down and held out a hand for Tess. She ignored it, grinning, and jumped lightly to the ground. "If we did not have such a large audience," she said saucily, "I would think you'd brought me here to propose, Hythe." Then she skipped off to examine a massive millstone that was almost lost in the grass.

One by one, the other vehicles rolled up behind his. Misses Vaer and Reynolds spilled out of the first as soon as it came to a halt and rushed to join their comrade. Desperate to hear if they'd been routed, Tarquin thought wryly. He watched as they bracketed Tess like pretty bookends, faces composed but eyes fierce. He wondered if Tess would keep them in suspense and decided she just might.

"Well, they are unquestionably a stunning picture, dear."

Tarquin glanced down. His mother was beside him, neatly buttoning her gloves while she gave the trio an impassive perusal. "They are indeed, madam. Pity we are not in Arabia, is it not, where I could marry all three and alternate them to suit my mood."

"The thought certainly gives one pause" was her bland reply. "I never fancied you the sort to maintain a harem, dearest, but you do surprise me on occasion."

"Funny, Sibyl said much the same to me yesterday."

"That is what I like about Sibyl."

"What is?"

169

His mother gave him a tight little smile. "She reminds me of me."

With that, she wandered off to join Lady Leverham, who was inspecting the mill's sixteenth century foundations with great interest. Tarquin watched the last of the party arrive. Apparently MacGregor had won the dispute, for he was the one assisting Sibyl from the gig. A slightly beleaguered-looking Julius rolled up moments later in a carriage that also contained the Ladies Broadford and Vaer, and George Reynolds. The remaining group disembarked from the last two vehicles.

Tarquin started in Sibyl's direction. He stopped after a few yards when it became clear that she was content in Mac-Gregor's company. The pair, laughing and chattering, headed away from the rest of the group, choosing the path down to the river.

Feeling inexplicably irritable all of a sudden, Tarquin considered his options. The three young ladies were pulling flowers from among the fallen stone walls. He was certain they would welcome his presence readily enough. He, however, wasn't certain he wanted to be in theirs just now. Lady Leverham and his mother were, for some reason, climbing the picturesque rubble that had once been the miller's house. He considered wandering over and advising them to be careful, but could easily imagine what the response would be.

His brother had disappeared, no doubt to lounge in the sun somewhere and have a brief nap. The rest of the gentlemen were beating at the shrubbery with their sticks, probably thinking about shooting small furred or feathered creatures.

Tarquin plodded after MacGregor and Sibyl.

He spied them at the edge of the river. Both were leaning over the water, paying rapt attention to something there. Trout, perhaps. He had come here as a boy with his father and brother to fish on countless sunny afternoons. Most of their catch had gone right back into the river. Some had reached the supper table. Several had ended up mounted on the library wall. The old earl had been tremendously proud of his sons' catches.

Tarquin had removed them when his father died. At the time, he'd told himself it was because they did not suit his idea of proper decor. Now he realized they had been a vivid reminder of lighthearted days now irretrievably lost.

He decided to go have a look. At the trout. Sibyl and Mac-Gregor had simply chosen the best spot from which to fish-watch. That was no surprise, really. The Scot had been on several of those long-past expeditions.

Tarquin was just picking his way over a collection of slippery, knee-high rocks when he heard the call. Turning, he spied Elspeth Vaer coming down the bank toward him. He was certain she did not intend to look so silly doing it, but in trying to keep both her hands and skirts free of the mud left in the wake of the rain, she was descending with a particularly amusing, duck-footed gait. He stifled his smile and went to assist her.

Perhaps had he moved more quickly, disaster would not have struck. But he was in no particular hurry, and certainly did not expect her to lose her footing. As it was, he was still several yards away when, arms flailing, she began to slide down the bank.

He jumped forward, one arm extended. She just missed it. His last view of her before she landed on her bottom and slid right over the path, out of his view, was of wide, vividly emerald eyes and a wide open, audibly shrieking mouth. There was a loud splash, and the screaming abruptly ceased.

Tarquin scrambled quickly off the path and down to the river's edge. Elspeth had come to a stop a mere foot or two out. The recent deluge had lifted the water level, unfortunately, and rather than sitting on visible rocks, she was submerged up to her waist.

Heedless of his boots, Tarquin plunged in after her. Above, he could hear the shouts of the rest of the party and, from the corner of his eyes, he could see MacGregor scrambling along the river's edge. Elspeth was no longer shrieking. Instead, she had taken up a low, rhythmic wailing that raised the fine hairs at his nape.

"Hold on," he called gently, "I will be right there." It was an inane statement, he realized even as he was speaking it. She wasn't going anywhere, and his presence was more a matter of politeness than necessity. She was perfectly capable of getting to her feet and wading through the three feet of water to the bank. By all rights she should be done with the feat already.

In his admittedly resentful musings, he stopped paying attention to his footing. His toes skidded on the downward slope of a slippery rock. Before he could do more than curse and windmill his arms, he was falling forward. He landed on his belly, sending up a spray of water and bumping his still-sore chin on Elspeth's knee.

Blinking to clear his eyes, coughing a good pint of the river from his lungs, he looked up. Elspeth had been wet before, from the waist down, and spattered above. Now she was drenched. Her hair hung limply in her eyes; water dripped from her lashes. And she was screaming again.

"Oh. Oh, my poor girl!" Lady Vaer's strident voice carried from the bank. "What in God's name did he do to you?"

"He . . . he . . ." Elspeth began, but broke into racking sobs.

Tarquin spat the last of the water from his mouth and sighed. His plans always seemed so clear, so *flawless* when he made them.

Dinner that night was an uncommonly tense experience. Sibyl picked at Cook's beautiful apple tart and studied the rest of the table. Elspeth was sniffling, the tip of her pert nose a pretty shade of deep pink. The girl's parents, along with those of Caroline and Tess, were maintaining a dramatic silence. Even Aunt Alfie, who could usually be counted upon to chatter her way through a meal, was gazing vaguely into her wine.

Tarquin, who appeared no worse for his second cold swim of the week, had eaten little, but had worked his way through several glasses of bordeaux. He was lounging in his chair at the head of the table now, tapping a slow rhythm with his fingertips on the linen cloth.

As for the rest of the party, there was an even mix of boredom and smugness. Lady Theresa exemplified the former, Caroline the latter. Sibyl found she envied them both. She was miserable. Tarquin had not so much as looked at her all afternoon. True, he had spent the last several hours closeted in his chamber, but there had been no communication either before or after.

She was beginning to think it a very good thing that she and her aunt were planning to depart the following afternoon. She had never before wanted to leave Rome Castle; in fact, she had always dragged her feet through the last day. This time, she was more than ready to go. They would pass several nights with Viscount and Lady Tarrant in East Sussex, then they would begin the journey home to Scotland. There would be ample time on the road in which to ponder all that had gone wrong during the visit. There always was.

She had no idea when the others would be departing. That, she thought, depended a great deal on Tarquin and whatever decision he made. The victorious young lady and her family would no doubt remain at Rome Castle for a time. The others would probably huff off to London or their country house to sulk and comment on how a connection to the Earl of Hythe simply was not what it used to be.

Sibyl would return to Tarbet, on the shores of Loch Lomond, and try not to mourn for too long. She would attend the wedding, if invited. After that, she had no idea when she would see Tarquin again. It was unlikely that she would spend much time in England as the London Season held no appeal for her. And Tarquin had little reason to come to Scotland. Perhaps he and his countess would travel north occasionally to visit the Duke and Duchess of Conovar, but almost certainly would do so at the Conovars' estate in Northumberland rather than their house in Tarbet.

Unspeakably depressed now, Sibyl was relieved when Lady Hythe indicated that supper was over. As they had done during each of the past nights, the ladies trooped obediently into the drawing room, leaving the men to their port and conversation. Assuming, of course, that there would be conversation.

In the drawing room, Caroline went straight to the pianoforte, Tess to the window seat and Walter Scott. Elspeth sniffled her way to the seat closest to the fire. The mothers sat as far apart from each other as they possibly could.

"Fascinating, isn't it?" Lady Hythe murmured as she and Sibyl settled themselves on a brocade sofa. "They cannot seem to decide where to aim their disapproval. Poor Tarquin. Or not."

"My lady?"

"If he chooses to marry one of these girls," the countess declared quietly, "he deserves the parents."

Of course, Sibyl agreed wholeheartedly, but held her tongue.

"Tea, anyone?" Lady Hythe lifted the ornate pot. No one responded. "Hemlock?" she added under her breath.

It appeared they were going to have a particularly tedious wait for the gentlemen to join them. After that, Sibyl mused, it could be an equally tedious wait for bedtime. She had just resigned herself to the longest hour of the visit when there was a shout in the hallway. It was followed by a chorus of barking and a familiar simian shriek. In a moment, all of the ladies had scuttled from their seats and into the doorway.

Apparently the gentlemen had tired of their own company sooner than usual. Obviously they had been interrupted on their way to the drawing room. Julius was struggling to restrain two howling dogs who were trying to go in opposite directions. He was laughing hard enough to redden his cheeks. Several feet away, Tarquin was cursing fluently and doing a jerky dance over the marble floor.

"Get off, you flea-bitten little cretin!" he shouted, and spun in a tight circle, one hand thrust under his coat.

Sibyl gaped at his back. There was a significant hump there, and it was moving. "Oh, Galahad!" she groaned, and went to help.

A beagle got there first. It shook off Julius's tentative grip on its tail and made a flying leap at Tarquin's back. Not having gotten much of a launch, the dog bounced off Tarquin's hip. He staggered, the hump shrieked and heaved to the side. Galahad's mustachioed face appeared briefly at Tarquin's waist.

"Get off!" Tarquin swiped a fist at his own midsection and struck empty air.

The monkey dropped to the floor and scampered toward the stairs. He coiled and hurled himself at the banister. Apparently everyone's aim was off that night. He missed and went flat up against the paneling before hitting the floor with a squawk. He might have stayed there indefinitely, shaking his furry head, had not the second beagle broken free. In an instant, monkey and dog were streaking up the stairs and out of sight.

"Oh, oh, my darling!" Alfonsine was right behind, a dog on her heels, too.

For a long moment, the only sound was Julius's laughter. Then MacGregor joined in. Sibyl felt her own lips twitching, but she didn't dare laugh. Tarquin was standing in the middle of the hallway, one button hanging from the placket of his coat, his stormy eyes daring anyone to comment.

Lady Hythe stepped forward and, with admirable solemnity considering the fact that her shoulders were shaking, announced, "Shall we all have a nice cup of hemlock . . . er . . . tea?"

MacGregor had to lean against a wall. Julius sat down in the middle of the floor. Both were holding their sides. Tarquin gave each a glare that nearly stripped the lacquer from the wood paneling, then stalked regally into the drawing room. The Graces and their mothers scurried out of his way.

He waited in icy silence for the ladies to be seated. Then he lowered himself into the chair beside Sibyl. "Tea?" she asked, knowing more than a single word would have her giggling helplessly.

He gave a single jerk of his chin. Taking it as an affirmative, Sibyl accepted the cup his mother poured and passed it toward him. When he lifted his hand to take it, a sparkle at his waist caught her eye. She blinked.

He followed her gaze. "Oh, bloody hell."

The emerald bracelet was hanging halfway out of his waist-coat pocket. He removed it with the tips of his thumb and forefinger and held it away from his person as if it were a worm. No, Sibyl corrected. He didn't mind worms.

"Madam," he said to a slack-jawed Lady Broadford, "I believe this is yours."

Not knowing what else to do, Sibyl stretched out her free hand and clasped his. She gave it a quick squeeze. He closed his eyes and sighed. Then he jerked his hand away. Sibyl was stung by the rejection—until he reached inside his coat and began to scratch.

15

RAIN WAS ONCE again pattering loudly against the windows. Tarquin had overslept, and woke with clear eyes and a clearer head. He knew exactly what he had to do, what he needed to say, and to whom he needed to say it. He bounded out of bed and rang for his valet. The room was cold, the water in the wash basin colder when he splashed it on his face. Ordinarily, he would have been vastly annoyed that a servant had not come in to stoke the fire and bring fresh water. Now he was in too much of a hurry to waste time on piddling issues.

He paced the room, dressing gown flapping around his legs, while he waited for Barton. He wasn't certain how best to get on with the matter at hand and wanted very much to get it right. He supposed he could gather the entire party in the drawing room and make the announcement.

No, he decided, too public. If there were to be any scenes, better to have them in private.

He could settle himself behind his desk in the library and have the relevant parties come to him one at a time. That way, anyone who wished to rail, rant, cry, or faint could do so without disturbing the rest of the party.

No, he thought with a faint smile, too schoolmasterish. He was bound to ruffle some feathers as it was. There was no sense in compounding the situation through arrogance. Besides, he really did not care to be railed and ranted at, nor cried or fainted upon—especially not in the haven of his library.

There was a tap at the door. "Enter," he commanded, silently adding, *about bloody time*. The doorknob rattled. "Dammit, man, come in already!"

His valet's voice came through the panels. "I beg your pardon, my lord, but you will have to unlock the door."

Grumbling, Tarquin stalked across the room. He did not recall locking anything. When he reached the door, he stared at it in confusion. There was no key in the lock. He seized the knob and turned it. The door remained shut tight. "Barton," he said through clenched teeth, "Where is the key?"

"It is always on the inside, my lord."

"Well, it isn't here now."

There was an ominous silence on the other side of the door. Then, "I will go fetch Gareth, my lord."

"You do that. And bring hot water when you return!"

He went back to the bed and sat down heavily on the edge of the mattress. His gaze fell on the door connecting his room to the next. Scrambling to his feet, he rushed to try it. It was no great surprise to find it locked. *Sibyl,* he thought, eyes narrowing. She had been placed in the chamber next to his. For whatever blasted reason she might have . . .

His shoulders slumped. Sibyl had been placed in the chamber on the other side of his. This room, the room his countess would eventually occupy, was empty.

Anyone at all could have entered and locked the door.

He heard voices in the hall. "My lord?"

"Open the door, Gareth."

"I . . . er . . . if I but could, my lord."

"Tarquin, dearest?"

He scowled. "Yes, Mother?"

"I am very much afraid there is something stuck in the lock."

"Well, get it out!" he snapped.

He heard a chorus of whispers, then, "Dearest, Gareth thinks it might be bread dough."

"Dough?"

"He is not certain, of course, though I must agree the color and texture seem right. Whatever it is is quite deep in the lock and quite hard."

"Dough." Tarquin dropped his forehead to the wood with a thump. "Have you checked the connecting door to the next chamber?"

"Why, no, but that is a very good thought, dear."

Moments later, the second door rattled. "Dough?" he demanded.

"Not that I can see, my lord," Gareth replied. "I believe it is merely locked."

"Unlock it!"

The butler cleared his throat audibly. "I am afraid I cannot do that, my lord. I do not have the key."

Tarquin's bellow nearly rattled the windows.

"Now you mustn't shout at Gareth, Tarquin," his mother admonished. "The butler never has a key to that door. Only the countess has a key."

"Fine. You are the countess."

"Yes, dear, but I am the Dowager Countess. You know I have not occupied that chamber in a good many years."

This time, he thumped his head against the door twice.

"Wait a moment, dearest. Sibyl might have a solution." There was more muffled discussion, a long pause, then, "We have it. The door opens out from your chamber. Gareth can remove the hinges on this side. What a clever girl Sibyl is!"

"Marvelous," Tarquin muttered. "Grand. Brilliant. Get on with it!"

In the next several minutes, there was a great deal of scuffling, a few thuds at the connecting door, and the clear shift of the group's voices from the hallway to the Countess's Chamber. "We shall have you out in no time, my lord," Gareth announced. Then he gave a lurid curse.

"Gareth?" Tarquin growled.

"I beg your pardon, my lord. The hinges are somewhat stiff."

"Oh, you poor man!" Tarquin heard his mother cry. "Your knuckle is bleeding. Put that down at once! Take yourself downstairs this instant and have someone see to your hand."

Tarquin slapped his palm against the door. His forehead was already sore. *"Mother!"*

"Be patient, dearest. Gareth will send James Footman up. He can remove the hinges."

Resigned to more waiting, Tarquin collected his clothing and, ignoring the fact that there were people grouped just outside both doors and that the water in the basin seemed to have dropped in temperature, he had a makeshift bath. Then he quickly dressed. He had the matter of his marriage to deal with, and he didn't want to waste any time once the door was opened.

Of secondary importance was determining just who was going out of his way to make him look the fool—or worse. Oh, there had been some unplanned mishaps, he knew. No one had pushed the brunette . . . *Miss* . . . *Vaer* into the river. He didn't think his own nosefirst tumble onto the drawing-room rug had been orchestrated, either. But Lady Leverham in the broom closet, his missing clothing, Lady Broadford's bracelet, all had been deliberate acts.

He couldn't fathom why anyone would want to lock him in his chamber. But then, he could think of no good reason for any of it. Nor could he decide if the motivation was mischievous or positively malicious. He intended to find out. Once he was released from his own bedchamber, of course.

"James is here, dearest," his mother called.

"Marvelous," he muttered to himself. "I should be out by Michaelmas."

"Have you out in a lick, m'lord."

James, if Tarquin had the right footman in mind, was built like an ox and was probably of the same intelligence. No doubt the fellow could rip the door off its hinges if he so desired. The question was whether he could negotiate removing a pin from a hinge.

Minutes ticked by. He heard countless grunts, the pinging of metal against metal, and some quiet suggestions from his mother. The door remained closed. Cursing to himself, he paced the chamber again. When a man made crucial decisions, he wanted to get on with them, dammit.

"Sibyl?" he called, having a feeling she would be lurking somewhere near the action.

"Yes, my lord?" Her voice came from behind the hall door. Tarquin tromped across the room to stand in front of it.

"Who else is with you there?"

"No one at the moment. Aunt Alfie is apparently in the process of discovering a secret passageway in the back pantry and nearly everyone has gone to watch. Forgive me for saying so, but it is far more interesting than waiting for you to be liberated."

"No doubt." He quashed his concern for his downstairs walls and asked, "Why are you not among the audience?"

There was a notable pause before she replied, "I thought I might be of some use here."

He couldn't imagine what, but did acknowledge her contribution thus far. "It was very clever of you to think of the hinges."

"Not so very, really. Someone else would have thought of it eventually."

It occurred to Tarquin that he had never before spoken to Sibyl without seeing her. He rarely spoke to anyone without seeing them—there was the occasional order to a servant, of course—but somehow this struck him as fascinating. And rather nice.

"Have you been standing out there all this time?" he asked.

"Not all, no. I went and had a look at the hinges."

"Of course." He had never noticed what a lovely voice she had: soft, slightly husky, and tinged with the faintest of Scots lilts. He reminded himself that the Camerons were Scottish as Highland heather, and twice as deep-rooted. "Well, don't feel you must stay."

He couldn't prevent the pleased smile when she replied, "I don't mind. I'm hardly likely to be wanted downstairs. I'll be happy to stay . . . if you wish it."

He did. For all the years he had wished her anywhere but in his presence, he wanted her there now. He pictured her, standing in the hall, speaking to him through a blocked keyhole. Her hair would be escaping its pins, no doubt; her eyes would be calm and lovely in her engaging face. He tried to complete the picture, to envision her dress. An image of soft, floaty blue fabric and an expanse of creamy skin flashed into his mind. He blinked and it was gone. Not Sibyl. He had never seen Sibyl in any such state.

But for that instant it had seemed so real—and so very appealing. He thought of her again in the hall. Oh, he was tempted, but it would hardly be appropriate to ask her to describe what she was wearing. To describe it in that gentle, Skye whiskey voice . . .

He cleared his throat and shifted his stance, trying to recall the last thing she actually had said. "I, ah, I don't think James is much for conversation," he remarked, lowering his voice and hoping she would still be able to hear him. "Tell me something, if you would."

"Certainly." Her voice, too, was quieter.

"Do you think me a fanciful person?"

Her laugh was immediate, clear, and cut off abruptly. "No, Tarquin, I do not."

"Right," he said, and wondered why he was so offended by the exact reply he had desired. "Naturally suspicious?"

"Only of me."

That had him gaping at the panels. "What on earth is that supposed to mean?"

"Oh, honestly, Tarquin! Whenever anything goes awry, I am the first to fall under your stern eye."

She was absolutely right. "You are frequently responsible . . ." he began, then, "Forgive me. That isn't fair. You have changed rather remarkably, Sibyl."

"Have I?" She sounded pleased. "I am glad you noticed."

"Well, of course I . . . Bother it." He wanted to sit down. It seemed too much trouble to drag over a chair, however, so he simply lowered himself to the floor and rested his elbows on his bent knees. "What do you want from life, Sibyl?"

"Goodness, what a question to ask."

"I am sorry. I didn't mean to be intrusive."

"No, it's quite all right. I am just not accustomed to discussing serious matters through an oak door." She didn't speak for several moments. Tarquin heard a very faint sliding noise and wondered if she, too, was now sitting on the floor. "I suppose I want what everyone does. Comfort, some joy, the occasional flash of excitement. And you?"

His jaw went a bit slack before he realized she had been returning his question, not adding him to her list. "I . . . You would probably think me addled—or jesting—if I were to tell you."

"You might be surprised."

181

"Yes, well, I am beginning to think myself addled." He leaned his head back against the wall and sighed. "Do you still want the Montefiore?"

"*What?*"

"Do you?"

There was a quiet thunk. "I . . . I suppose . . ."

"It's yours. I promised Fraser I would see it into truly appreciative and deserving hands. I imagine he meant a museum, but it seems to me that there is no one who will value it as much as you. You've always been the wildly romantic, adventurous spirit. Comes with being a Cameron, I suppose. Who better to appreciate an infamous collection of the world's most mythic tales?"

"I . . . Tarquin, I have no idea what to say. This is incredibly generous of you."

He was glad she could not see his wry grin. "Not nearly so generous as you might think. But you may say 'Thank you,' then go fetch those remaining predictions."

"Thank you, Tarquin." He heard a scuffling. "I shall be right back."

Less than a minute later, a piece of paper came sliding under the door. He recognized the torn edge. Feeling inexplicably nervous, he started to unfold the sheet.

"I've got it!" The bellow came from the adjoining room. As Tarquin watched, the door teetered, leaned outward, and was steadied by a pair of ham-sized hands.

His mother's face appeared in the opening. "Well, good morning, dearest. Whatever are you doing on the floor?"

"Tempting Fate," he muttered, and, tucking the paper into his coat pocket, shoved himself to his feet. "Now, I have an announcement to make downstairs."

As he stalked toward the doorway, he spied Barton hovering behind his mother, large basin in hand. Gareth was there, too, wearing a large bandage on one hand and the customary scowl on his face. Sibyl appeared on the other side of the valet. She was wearing pink.

The entire group, including the door-wielding James, tightened and stepped back in unison as Tarquin approached. "Come along," he snapped at no one in particular. "It is time—"

The rest of the phrase was lost to a cascade of tepid water as his valet suddenly stumbled forward.

Tarquin stood, dripping from nose to knee, gaping into four pairs of wide eyes. "I . . . I am so terribly sorry, my lord!" Barton stammered. "I do not . . . I cannot . . ." He raised the empty basin in a helpless gesture.

Closing his eyes, Tarquin counted ten. "Barton," he said through clenched teeth, "Get me some dry clothing. Now!"

Sibyl sat tensely in the drawing room with the rest of the party, save Aunt Alfie, who was still poking at the pantry floor and refused to be interrupted. When Tarquin had stormed back into his chamber to re-dress, his mother had scooted the others downstairs. Lady Hythe was now seated calmly on the brocade chair next to Sibyl's, examining a square of embroidery. Her brow furrowed occasionally, but cleared as soon as she corrected a faulty stitch.

Everyone else appeared to be in various states of nervous anticipation. Lord Broadford was muttering at a china dog on the mantelpiece; his wife was fanning herself furiously in her seat. Lords Vaer and Reynolds were pacing opposite sides of the room, their wives twitching on opposite sides of a settee.

Elspeth Vaer stood stock-still between two windows, staring, if Sibyl was following her line of vision correctly, in rapt interest at the opposite baseboard. Caroline Reynolds sat at the piano, repeatedly striking the highest keys. It was an increasingly annoying sound and might have gone on indefinitely had not Lady Theresa strode across the room and closed the instrument's lid with a snap. Caroline had pulled her hands back in a hurry, blinked at Tess, then had proceeded to tap her nails against the polished wood. A fierce glare from above soon stilled that activity.

According to servant gossip, which Cook had gleefully passed on to Sibyl that morning, the money was still on Lady Theresa. But over her breakfast chocolate, Aunt Alfie had whispered that she'd heard Reynolds sweetening the pot with an added two thousand pounds to Caroline's dowry. Then, too, Lord Vaer possessed an unequalled collection of old, sharp objects. All of Society knew that the Earl of Hythe appreciated pretty arms. His own swords were unrivaled.

Tarquin was not a shallow man. Sibyl knew that with complete certainty. She also knew he was a practical one. For him, much as her heart ached at the very concept, marriage was a matter of business, duty, and honor. Love would only be a messy inconvenience.

Now the entire party was waiting for him to arrive and announce his cool, careful, sensible decision. Only Sibyl did not think it sensible at all. Whichever of the three Graces he chose, it was the wrong one. Even Lady Tess, with her staggering beauty and decent character, did not deserve him. Tarquin Theodore Fitzmorris Rome, the Sixth Earl of Hythe, needed a wife who truly appreciated him. Who saw beyond the fortune and title to the person.

More importantly, he needed a wife who saw behind the rigid, proper facade. Who saw him stripped of his perfect control to the vastly appealing, humorous man beneath.

The image of the rigid, proper, stark-naked earl bouncing across her chamber to dive behind the bed flashed into Sibyl's mind. She stifled a giggle. She could do nothing to prevent the tingle and warm flush that followed.

Well, she told herself firmly, she would simply have to get over it. Get over him. There had been no impediment to her adoring him through the years—except his own aversion, of course. Aversion had always seemed a surmountable obstacle. A wife did not.

Not that the existence of a new Countess of Hythe, or lack thereof, signified overmuch. Sibyl knew maths, and physics, and many of the certainties of nature. She knew the earth would stop turning, the seas would run dry, and the square root of five hundred twenty-nine would become seventeen before she stopped loving Tarquin. Like the Cumaean Sibyl and Clytie—both of whom, she attempted to comfort herself, would be found in *her* Montefiore—she would watch him go into the arms of another woman and not be able to do anything about it.

It seemed that at last she would attain the grand, slightly scandalous Cameron Dash. She would pass the remainder of her life wholly, unrepentantly, and passionately in love with a married man.

"Appalling, isn't it?"

She turned to face her hostess, jaw slack. "I beg your pardon, madam?"

"The pattern." Lady Hythe held up her embroidery. "I never much cared for it. Now I know why. It is dreadful."

Slightly dizzy and vastly relieved, Sibyl examined the square. Pale lilies tangled with vivid roses. "It appears . . . perfectly attractive to me."

"Rubbish. It is ugly as sin and well you know it." The countess tempered her words with an impish smile. "The chairs I am re-covering are hideous, too, so I suppose it is only fitting. I believe I will move them here and take the parlor set to the Dower House."

There was an audible shuffling around the room at the mention of the Dower House. Even Julius and MacGregor, who had been engaged in a sluggish game of cassino, came to attention.

Sibyl ignored them. "Surely there is no reason for you to leave your home."

"I believe my son is soon to be married," Lady Hythe replied mildly.

"But countless mothers-in-law remain in the household."

"Mmm. Yes, many do. I, however, fancy I will not be one of them."

Sibyl leaned forward to grasp one of the woman's hands. "I cannot believe it possible that any woman would wish you gone. It would be utter stupidity!"

"Thank you, Sibyl, dear. I am touched." The countess returned the embroidery to her lap in order to pat Sibyl's hand. "But you misunderstand me. I am not in the least concerned with the new countess's opinion of me, nor her wishes on the matter. I am merely thinking of my own." With that, she gave Sibyl a cheerful wink, the room a sunny smile, and queried, "Shall I ring for tea?"

There was a heavy silence. Then, with a muffled chuckle, MacGregor announced, "I would very much like some tea, Lady Hythe."

"By all means, Mother," Julius agreed. "Let us all have tea. Splendid idea."

"Thank you, dearest. Of course, we could have sherry, as well. It is a bit early in the day, but considering the . . . weather, I cannot see the harm in it. Anyone?"

"No harm," Lord Vaer offered readily. "None at all."

"Sherry," came Lady Reynolds's shaky contribution, "would be very nice indeed."

"That is settled, then. Tea for some, sherry for others." The countess rose and reached for the bellpull.

Heels rang across the marble floor outside the room. Gareth appeared briefly in the doorway, then pulled back. Tarquin took his place. He had replaced his wet, soft-brown jacket with a severe black one. His collar points were sharp, his cravat crisp, intricate, and neat as a pin. To Sibyl's eyes, he looked cool, collected, and austerely, breathtakingly beautiful.

She still found herself missing the rumpled, hooded-eyed corsair.

"I apologize most sincerely for my absence," he said briskly. "I was unavoidably detained. I trust you have not been terribly inconvenienced."

"Oh, not in the least, my lord," Miss Vaer cooed from her place. "We have been enjoying the pleasant time in this delightful room."

"And your mother's gracious hospitality" was Miss Reynolds's fluttery addition.

"We mustn't forget the warmth and camaraderie of our fellow guests," Lady Theresa announced.

To Sibyl's ears, she sounded slightly wicked. And typically bored. Yes, the money should well be on Tess. How very vexing, Sibyl thought sadly, that the woman who would soon be responsible for ruining her life, should be such an admirable creature. Lady Theresa still did not deserve Tarquin, but it would take a far meaner spirit than Sibyl possessed to deny her great appeal.

Tarquin smiled blandly. "Good." He strode several yards into the room and cast a magisterial glance over the gathering. "Now, I had meant to do this in a more private setting, but since we are all gathered—"

"You will not believe what I have found!" Aunt Alfonsine's voice echoed through the Great Hall, accompanied by a loud rattling of metal. "In the passageway, of course. Well, the keys. The clothing was in a cunning little hidden cupboard. It appears to be quite fine . . . Oh!"

The keys appeared first, a good twenty of them on a massive ring, flying into the room. As everyone watched, they crested a low arc—and smacked directly into Tarquin's forehead. He stood, a stunned look on his face, then slowly sank to his knees on the plush carpet.

Alfonsine, gripping a collection of men's clothing against her chest with one arm, skidded to a halt in the doorway. "Oh. Oh, heavens. I was swinging them—quite a lovely sound—and they simply flew from my fingers. Oh, goodness." She tilted her head and sighed. "It appears they were not needed after all. Uther, why did you tell me the dear boy was trapped in his chamber? Everyone can see he is right here!"

For a long moment, no one moved. Then Sibyl jumped from her seat, hurried across the room, then dropped to her knees beside Tarquin. He was staring blankly at the carpet, one palm pressed to his forehead. "Here, let me look," she commanded, gently coaxing his hand away from his head. "I don't see any blood. Are you seeing spots, my lord? Are you seeing *any-thing*? Tarquin?"

He looked up then, and blinked owlishly at her. "Sibyl. I just wanted to make a simple marriage proposal," he said hazily.

"Yes, we know." She held up three fingers and waved them in front of his nose. "How many?"

"Two."

"Oh, dear. Tarquin—"

"Just two bloody words, dammit," he groaned. *"Marry . . . me."*

Then he toppled facedown into her lap.

16

"TARQUIN. TARQUIN, LOVE, can you hear me?"

He blinked, groaned, and remembered. "Sibyl?"

"Oh, dear. Perhaps you ought to fetch Mr. Simmons after all, Julius. I fear the bump was worse than we thought."

At the mention of the man who had poked, prodded, and dosed him with countless vile remedies over the years, Tarquin came fully awake. "Not Mr. Simmons!" He struggled to sit up. "I am fine. Truly."

Above him, his mother's face broke into a brilliant smile. "Never mind, Julius. He seems quite coherent now." To Tarquin, she said, "You look better, too. You have been terribly pale for the past several minutes. How is your head?"

He levered himself upright on the sofa, wondered which fortunate person had had to get him there, and gingerly touched his forehead. "It hurts like the devil."

"Yes, well, that is only to be expected. The old butler's ring is quite heavy, and Alfonsine is a good deal stronger than she looks."

Alfonsine, Tarquin decided fuzzily, could single-handedly fell Napoleon's entire army. He glanced around the room. Everyone appeared to still be present—except that lady and Sibyl. "Where is she?"

"Here I am, dear boy." A turbaned head popped into view from behind MacGregor's formidable bulk. "I really am so terribly sorry about the keys. I did not mean to—"

He waved away her apology. "No, I meant Sibyl. Where is Sibyl?"

"She is in the kitchens, preparing something for your head."

His already nervous stomach lurched at the thought of consuming another of Sibyl's potions. "God help me." He moaned. Then, "So be it."

His mother shoved a firm hand into his shoulder when he started to rise. "Where do you think you are going?" she demanded.

"To fetch her, of course."

"No, you are not. She will be back soon enough. You need to be still for a while yet."

"Nonsense." His scowl had no effect on his mother's own resolute frown. It never did. "I am perfectly well, madam."

"The goose-egg on your head says otherwise. Now, you will behave, or I will have Julius and Adam come sit on you. It is your choice."

A quick glance at his brother and MacGregor had him leaning back sulkily. Both men looked more than ready to comply. "Fine. Someone else can go retrieve her."

"Why?" his mother asked quietly.

"Because I intend to finish what I started before I . . . er . . . before the key incident. And I damn well cannot do it without her here."

"Don't you think perhaps you ought to wait until later? You took a nasty knock on the head, you know."

"Believe me, Mother, I am aware of just how hard a knock I took."

"Oh, Hythe, I cannot tell you how badly I feel." Alfonsine bounced into view again. "I truly did not mean to hit you nearly so—"

"Yes, yes, Lady Leverham. I know. You did not mean to smack me in the head with ten pounds of hard metal. It is quite all right."

"Thank you, dear boy. Most chivalrous of you, but I feel I must explain."

"Later," he said tersely. "Julius, go get Sibyl. She must be here."

"Why, for God's sake?" Lord Broadford pushed his paunch into the center of things. "Just get on with what you were saying . . . er . . . before. The chit will hear of it soon enough."

"Yes, do continue, my lord," Lady Vaer urged. "We

are simply dying of curiosity about . . . whatever you were saying . . . ah . . ."

"Before," MacGregor offered helpfully.

Tarquin glared at him. "Thank you, Brutus."

"Not at all. But for what it's worth, I, too, believe Sibyl needs to be present."

"Rubbish!" Lady Reynolds snapped. She did have the grace to flush when Tarquin, MacGregor, and Lady Leverham all turned to glare at her.

"Suppose you tell us why Sibyl's presence is so important, dearest," his mother suggested.

Irked beyond the limits of patience, Tarquin pounded his fist against the sofa's arm. "I need her here because I am going to marry her, dammit, and it would help matters considerably if she were present to accept the bloody proposal!"

There was a crash of crockery against marble. "Oh. Oh, goodness."

Tarquin was out of his seat in a shot, pounding head be damned. He reached the doorway and caught Sibyl just as her knees gave way. She was soft in his arms, trembling, smelling sweetly of . . . vinegar? Glass crunched under his heel. He glanced down at the small puddle on the floor.

"For your head," she said weakly. "I knew it would hurt."

"What was in this concoction?"

"You probably don't want to know."

"You're probably correct." He stared into her lovely, upturned face and pulled her closer. "Remind me not to ask in the future."

"The . . . future?"

"Of course. I daresay you will try to pour a great many different brews down my throat over the next fifty or so years. I shall have to remember not to ask what is in them."

"Oh, Tarquin."

"Ah, but I am getting ahead of myself here. It is entirely likely that you will not want to marry a rigid, dull, stuffy creature like me." He gazed at her hopefully, ready to argue for the next millennium or so if she refused. "Would you?"

"Why?" she breathed. "Why me?"

"Why? What a silly question, my dear. You bewitch me."

She frowned. "What rubbish."

"Not at all. Simply looking at you makes me weak in the knees. But there is more. You have known me for many years and still manage to like me. You do like me, don't you?"

That coaxed a smile. "I do like you."

"You understand my humor, such as it is, seem fond of my family and home, such as they are, have a heart of pure gold, and," he added vehemently, "a mind that makes me nearly as dizzy as your delectable person."

"What nonsense," she retorted, but without much force.

He grinned, sensing victory. "You have seen me at my most . . . er . . . vulnerable and did not run screaming. Sibyl, my darling, you have no idea how much that meant."

Her cheeks pinkened delightfully. "I have something of an idea, Tarquin. But it still is not enough to justify marriage."

"No? What of this, then?"

He took his time with the kiss, waiting until she parted her lips with a soft moan to deepen it to his desire. Her arms, which had been hanging limp at her sides, reached up to twine around his neck, and suddenly she was kissing him back with a sweet fierceness that nearly had his knees buckling. In the end, he was forced to pull back. Otherwise, they would have ended up in a molten heap on the floor, and he felt they had both spent ample time there already that day.

Sibyl was certain her limbs had melted. Even now that Tarquin's lips were inches away, hers tingled. Her vision was hazy, there was an ocean roaring in her ears, and parts of herself that she did not often contemplate were humming like a plucked harp string.

"You do remember," she breathed, bringing a shaky hand to her trembling mouth.

"What? You mean we've done this before?"

At her stricken look, he grinned. "I remember, sweetheart, and can only apologize with all my heart—and feel heartily sorry for myself for the lost time—that it took a knock on the head for me to do so. Sweet Sibyl," he said softly, and leaned down to kiss her again.

This time, she pressed her shaky hand to his lips, halting

their descent. "Was it my predictions? That changed your mind, I mean?"

"Changed my mind? About what?"

"About me. And"—she felt herself flushing anew as she gestured to their forgotten audience—"your other choice."

"My . . . Ah. There was no other choice. You see, I created a very clever scheme, bringing you here for a sennight. *You* made up my mind."

Sibyl heard Lady Hythe cough, but the lady made no move to inform her son that he had not been the one to bring Sibyl into the party. Aunt Alfie was surprisingly silent, too. She was merely smiling complacently.

Not surprisingly, the Graces and their parents were not smiling. Lady Theresa did not appear overly put out, but the rest all looked as if—to use Tarquin's phrase of some days before—someone was twisting their drawers from behind. Lady Reynolds's face was an unattractive and rather alarming shade of red.

"Perhaps you ought to let me go," Sibyl whispered.

"No," Tarquin shot back. But he did haul her up so she was standing straight by his side. "Not during this lifetime." His eyes narrowed then. "You still haven't answered, Sibyl."

"Answered what?"

"My proposal. I have asked twice and declared once."

She tried to coax her still-spinning mind into submission. "I recall the declaration, but only one request."

"Not listening, were you? The first time was just before I keeled over—"

"*That* was a proposal?"

He rolled his eyes. "I said 'marry me', didn't I? I did manage to stay conscious until I got the important words out."

"Oh, Tarquin." Heart near to bursting, she threw her arms around his waist and clung to him with all her strength. "I do love you!"

"Do you?" He sounded inordinately pleased. "I wasn't certain."

"You great, daft man! I have been in love with you since the day we met. How could you not have known?"

"You never told me," he said simply.

She waited for him to repeat the words. And waited. Apparently others were waiting, too, for an exasperated Julius finally snapped, "For God's sake, old man, get on with it!"

Tarquin stiffened slightly. "Julius. I have meant to have a few words with *you* in private. But since we're already having a beautiful public moment, I shall include you. Would you care to tell me now why you enacted all those godawful stunts? Taking my clothing while I was in the lake I comprehend. I would have done much the same . . . fifteen years ago."

"Clothing?" Julius repeated. "I have no idea what you're talking about."

Sibyl had been watching the exchange. Julius looked genuinely puzzled. She instantly and completely believed he'd had nothing to do with the theft of Tarquin's clothes. Apparently Tarquin believed him as well. "If you didn't . . ."

"I did it." Lady Hythe stepped forward, not appearing in the least repentant. "Oh, don't look so shocked, Tarquin! I am your mother. It was certainly not the first time I saw your bare bottom."

There were several muffled chuckles. Sibyl glanced up to see that Tarquin was indeed blushing. "Why on earth did you do it, Mother?"

"Honestly? I rather hoped other members of the party would see you scooting about unclothed in the middle of the night."

"Good God. *Why?*"

"Because," she said tartly, "it appeared you were on your way to making a very bad mistake. I thought our esteemed guests might take exception to your nighttime antics and take the choice away from you."

Sibyl felt her jaw dropping. "You screamed. You woke everyone just as Tarquin was coming in."

Lady Hythe winced. "Most unladylike, I am afraid. But it worked."

"It certainly did," Tarquin said. "I suppose you locked Lady Leverham in the broom closet for the same reason: to make me look the monster to my guests."

"I did nothing of the sort!"

"Actually . . ." Julius cleared his throat. "That was me. So

193

sorry, Lady Leverham. It was most unfair of me to take advantage of the situation as I did."

Alfonsine cheerily waved off the apology. "Think nothing of it, dear boy. I thoroughly enjoyed the adventure."

"You are too gracious, madam. And as for making you look the monster, Tarquin, I was merely doing the same as Mother. Neither of us wanted to see you tied to an unsuitable woman."

This earned him a loudly resentful snort from Elspeth Vaer. The other two Graces and their parents simply looked shocked.

"So you were in league in this?" Tarquin demanded. "My own family. Bloody hell. So which of you locked me in my chamber?"

Julius and his mother glanced at each other blankly. "We were not in league, dearest," his mother replied. "And neither of us had anything to do with your locks."

"I . . . er . . ." Lord MacGregor hesitantly raised one hand. "I couldn't have you rushing down here this morning to toss your life away, Hythe. I had no idea it was Sibyl to whom you intended to propose."

"Bread dough," Tarquin muttered.

MacGregor shrugged. "It was all that was handy at dawn."

Sibyl felt a giggle welling up in her throat. She tamped it down. By her side, Tarquin was taut as a bow. He clearly was not finding the situation half as delightful as she.

"Fine," he grumbled. "Splendid. Have you anything else to admit? Hmm? Did you jostle Barton's arm this morning, Mother? He has never thrown water on me before."

"I . . . ahem. I beg your pardon, my lord." Gareth drew himself to his full, impressive height. "I am responsible for that incident."

"Didn't want me proposing to anyone, either, Gareth?"

"Not precisely, my lord. Had I known that Miss Cameron was your intended, I would never have interfered. I will resign now if you wish it."

Tarquin closed his eyes for a weary moment. "I do not wish it. Perhaps you would be so kind as to explain matters to Barton. He has not been himself since the incident."

"Of course, my lord. Immediately."

Once the butler had departed, Tarquin glanced around the

room. His gaze fell on Lady Leverham. She was beaming at him like an aged cherub. "Don't tell me you have something to confess as well, madam?"

"Why, I already did. I tried to explain and apologize several times, but you would not listen. No matter. Men in love rarely do."

His memory clicked. "Yes, of course. You did not mean to hit me . . . so hard." She nodded approvingly. "Well, my lady, allow me to commend you on both your strength and your aim. Few persons could launch a ring of keys with such accuracy and force."

"It was not easy, dear boy, I assure you. But I simply could not wait and take a chance that you would propose to one of those creatures."

This raised an indignant huff from the young ladies and their parents.

Tarquin ignored them. "And the bracelet? Was that your doing as well?"

"You know, dearest," she replied solemnly, "I have been giving that some thought. I do believe Galahad is responsible for the bracelet."

It certainly made sense, at least it did if one didn't think too hard on the matter. "Allow me to speculate," Tarquin said dryly. "He wanted me to marry Sibyl, too."

"Oh, no. Well, yes, I am certain he did, but in this instance, I think he was simply being a monkey."

"Heaven help us." Tarquin racked his brain for any other relevant incidents. "The painting!"

"Now, Tarquin—"

"Oh, *Sibyl!*"

"Don't you dare look at me like that," she said sternly. "I told you at the time that it was not my fault. I also told you that the maths were wrong."

"The maths," he repeated dully.

"Indeed. The chain should have been shortened by a third—"

"And the hook increased by half. Yes, I remember. Ah, Sibyl." He gave her a weak smile and pulled her more firmly against him. "I do love you."

"Do you?" She looked immensely pleased. "I am so glad. I thought so, after you proposed, but wasn't certain."

"Are you blind, woman? Deaf?"

"You never told me," she remarked mildly.

"Well, I just did . . ."

"And you never told me if my predictions made a difference."

He blinked at her. "Good Lord. I forgot all about them. They are still in my coat pocket upstairs. The wet coat," he added, wincing.

She smiled. "It doesn't matter. I got the Montefiore."

"You gave Sibyl that old book?" his mother demanded, astonished.

"Which old book?" Julius asked.

"What predictions?" was MacGregor's intrigued query.

"I told you I was not being wholly generous this morning," Tarquin said quietly. "I was hoping neither the book nor you would leave this house. Of course, you could have refused me. Well, bloody hell. You still haven't *answered* me!"

Sibyl grinned up at him, love glowing in her extraordinary eyes. "Yes, I will marry you, Tarquin. On one condition."

"Anything."

"The next time the urge hits you to have a midnight swim . . ."

"Curb it?"

"Not at all." Her eyes sparkled now. "Take me with you."

His entire body went to flame. "God help me," he muttered, ruthlessly curbing the urge to grab her by the hand and run for the pond at once. "Oh, Sibyl."

Postscript

8. *If you marry* [illegible due to water damage], *her parents will have you in Bedlam within a fortnight.*

9. *You will find your only true happiness with* [illegible due to water damage].

10. *The best laid schemes will always go awry.*

Celebrate the publication of Patricia Rice's fabulous
new contemporary romance, *BLUE CLOUDS*!

A DOZEN GOOD REASONS
TO TREAT YOURSELF
TO *BLUE CLOUDS*
BY PATRICIA RICE.

*Enter our drawing and win one of these twelve
truly romantic gift baskets!**

1. Satisfy your sweet tooth with a fabulous feast of
   chocolate chip and other cookie favorites.

2. Slip into something more comfortable with a
   selection of luxuries for the bath.

3. Awaken your senses with a collection of aromatherapy
   preparations to ease your mind and soothe your soul.

4. Spend an evening at the movies without leaving
   home—popcorn, candy, and video versions of three
   romantic movies.

5. Spoil your inner child—with teddy bears and fudge.

6. Enjoy sweet dreams with a selection of calming
   aromatherapy products and relaxation tapes.

7. Spice up dinner with authentic Italian sauces, pastas,
   sun-dried tomatoes, and imported cheeses.

8. Savor sensual desserts to die for!

9. Surrender to everything chocolate—from buttercreams to mints to sumptuous truffles.

10. Indulge in tea for two with exotic teas and trimmings.

11. Make your garden grow with tools, gloves, bulbs, and a gardening book for inspiration.

12. Arouse your taste buds with rich, mellow coffees from around the world—and beautiful mugs to go with them.

*Each basket will have a retail value of approximately $250.00 and will also contain a copy of Patricia Rice's first wonderful contemporary novel, *Garden of Dreams*.

Mail this entry form, to be received by
September 30, 1998, to:
BLUE CLOUDS SWEEPSTAKES
PMI Station, P. O. Box 3581
Southbury, CT 06488-3581

Name_____

Address_____

City/State/Zip_____

Phone (day)_____

Phone (night)_____

See next page for official rules.

THE BALLANTINE PUBLISHING GROUP
"A DOZEN GOOD REASONS TO TREAT YOURSELF TO *BLUE CLOUDS*" SWEEPSTAKES

OFFICIAL RULES

1. ELIGIBILITY: NO PURCHASE NECESSARY TO ENTER OR CLAIM PRIZE. Open to legal residents of the United States and Canada (excluding Quebec) who are 18 years of age and older. Employees of Random House, Inc., its subsidiaries, affiliates, advertising and promotion agencies, and members of the immediate families and persons living in the same household of such employees are not eligible. Void in Quebec and where prohibited by law. All federal, provincial, state, and local laws and regulations apply.

2. TO ENTER: Complete an official entry form or hand print your name, complete address, daytime and evening telephone numbers, and the words "BLUE CLOUDS" on a postcard. Mail your entry, to be received by September 30, 1998, to: Blue Clouds Sweepstakes, PMI Station, P.O. Box 3581, Southbury, CT 06488-3581. Limit one entry per person. No mechanical reproductions permitted.

3. PRIZES: On or about October 15, 1998, a random drawing will be conducted from among all eligible entries received by Promotion Mechanics, Inc., an independent judging organization, to award (12) prizes of a romantically themed gift basket. Contents of each basket will be different and will be valued at approximately $250. Winners will be notified by mail. 1,500,000 entry forms will be distributed, but odds of winning depend on the number of eligible entries received. Canadian residents, in order to win, must first correctly answer a mathematical skill testing question administered by mail.

4. GENERAL: All taxes on prizes are the sole responsibility of winners. By participating, entrants agree to (a) these rules and decisions of judges that shall be final in all respects and (b) release sponsor from any liability, loss, or damage of any kind resulting from their participation in the sweepstakes or their acceptance or use of a prize. By accepting a prize, winners agree to the use of their name and/or photograph for advertising, publicity, and promotional purposes without compensation (unless prohibited by law). Sponsor is not responsible for late, lost, misdirected, or illegible entries or mail. All entries become the property of sponsor. No prize transfer. No prize substitution except by sponsor due to unavailability. Return of any prize/prize notification as undeliverable will result in disqualification, and an alternate winner will be selected. Limit one prize per household.

5. WINNERS' LIST: For a list of winners, send a self-addressed stamped envelope, to be received by October 15, 1998, to: Blue Clouds Winners, PMI Station, P. O. Box 750, Southbury, CT 06488-0750. List will be available after January 1, 1999.

Sponsor: The Ballantine Publishing Group, 201 East 50th Street, New York, NY 10022.